PRAISE FOR

"I loved the human drama that pulses through this story. Atkinson's unique social fluency allows for a captivating delve into America's troubled class. With Pere and his young ward Tammy as guides, this book travels among a carnival of lost souls painted with perfect resonance and vitality. This unlikely duo's warmth and growing affection buoy them from turbulent lives, and make them indelible among the world of gambling ships, charter boats, and the shadow of correctional facilities rendered so shimmering yet gritty by this superb writer."

- Devin Murphy, author of *The Boat Runner* and *Tiny Americans*

"As a lifelong fan of stories about found families and unlikely alliances, I love everything about *Tiki Man*, an unflinching look at life on the edges of society. Atkinson shows us there is hope in the smallest of hearts and love in the roughest of gestures."

- Catherine Ryan Hyde, author of forty published and upcoming books including *Pay It Forward*

Tiki Man

Thomas M. Atkinson

Regal House Publishing

Published by
Regal House Publishing, LLC
Raleigh, NC 27587
All rights reserved

ISBN -13 (paperback): 9781646030835
ISBN -13 (epub): 9781646031085
Library of Congress Control Number: 2020951948

All efforts were made to determine the copyright holders and obtain their permissions in any circumstance where copyrighted material was used. The publisher apologizes if any errors were made during this process, or if any omissions occurred. If noted, please contact the publisher and all efforts will be made to incorporate permissions in future editions.

Interior and cover design by Lafayette & Greene
Cover design © by C.B. Royal

Regal House Publishing, LLC
https://regalhousepublishing.com

The following is a work of fiction created by the author. All names, individuals, characters, places, items, brands, events, etc. were either the product of the author or were used fictitiously. Any name, place, event, person, brand, or item, current or past, is entirely coincidental.

Printed in the United States of America

for Tracey
and our boys
Miller & Walker
Tougher than the Rest

1

THE HAITIANS

A few months back, when Tammy first came down here to Florida, I had a hard time figuring out what to do with her when I went to work. Before he disappeared, her dad stuck her on a bus up in Ohio without bothering to find out how Missy's sentencing went. He's a Franklin, from the meth 'n incest part of that state, and I never heard Missy say his last name without adding "trash" to it, like Franklin-Trash might actually be his name. Maybe he thought the judge would take her condition into account. No such luck. She's doing a two year bit up at Lowell Correctional in Ocala. Three hots and a cot and free dental, which is better than us most days. I'm stuck here, squatting in the condo me and Missy shared, trying to take care of her daughter from a marriage gone bad years before we met.

I left Tammy alone at first, let her sleep late and came home a little early. But she didn't like that, being home alone all day. She wouldn't leave the house, not even to play in the driveway, and even a ten-year-old can only watch *Tom and Jerry* cartoons for so long. Clyde's wife, Vera, watched her some, but I didn't want to impose. They're our neighbors across the street and he's the unofficial mayor because they've lived here forever, and Vera, she never comes out of the house but still knows everybody else's business. He told me that since they threw these condos up twenty-two years ago, they've been the only Black family, and that's saying something since half the street swaps out every night.

Then I took Tammy to work with me a few times, but you can get killed a hundred different ways in a boatyard even if you know what to watch out for. She'd hang out some in the Ship's

Store and make the rounds talking to the charter captains, but I think all my boss could see was a little barefoot lawsuit.

One time I let her stay at my buddy Barry's because his neighbors have two girls, and I thought it'd be nice if she got to spend some time with kids her own age. Barry's the Neil Diamond impersonator on the gambling boat and he's scared to death of his emcee, Bertrand. Bertrand wears mirrored aviator sunglasses and was in the Tonton Macoute death squads down in Haiti. Barry doesn't care much for the neighbor girls either, because one time when he was airing out his blue-sequined shirt, they dressed their dog in it before it got loose. They're from Kentucky and there's a deflated UK basketball on top of a birdbath pedestal in the little yard. The dad calls himself Wildcat and has ".38 Special" tattooed across his shoulders. The wife doesn't own a bra and the smell of caustic chemicals and fried food hangs around their trailer like wet laundry. They cut the dog's vocal cords and keep it staked out in the yard, and it doesn't seem to like anyone but Tammy.

But on the way home that day, the day I left her there, she didn't have much to say at first. And everything I asked her—like if she had fun, and if she liked those girls, and if she wanted to go back—she just shrugged and wouldn't look at me. Then I asked her if Barry made her Kool-Aid, because Barry's enough of a friend to keep Kool-Aid around if we happen to come by and visit.

And then it all came out at once, like when they open the locks up at Port Canaveral where you can go watch the manatees. She said, "Sometimes I call Barry Neil 'cause I forget he's just Neil on that boat. Those two girls that live across from him, they dress like some sluts on MTV and they both got bedbug bites all over. You must've told him I like horses 'cause he put on the horse races on the TV, which really isn't the same thing as liking horses. I mean, watching some little monkey man up beating the holy hell out of a big, beautiful horse just isn't the same thing. If I had a horse like that I'd curry comb him every day and he'd eat carrots out of my hand and know I had a sugar cube stashed in my pocket."

She sighed and squinted into the sun. "But he tried real hard. He knows which horses are good racers and which ones like muddy tracks and which ones are probably getting doped and he let me pick my own flavor of Kool-Aid. It was store brand and I picked orange and it tasted just the same. After a while there wasn't much left to say about those race horses and the girls in the next trailer came out and started throwing those big magnolia seed pods up on his roof so I went out to play with them, not that I wanted to, 'cause I didn't, but I could tell he'd had a lot of those magnolia pods throwed up on his roof."

She took a breath and I was still trying to remember which ones were the magnolia pods. She said, "One's a year older than me named Scarlett and the other one named Ashley is a year younger and they said it's 'cause their mom likes this old movie about ladies in the Civil War. I *told* them it was *Gone With The Wind*, 'cause Grandma loved it and I've seen it about a million times on a two cassette VCR Deluxe Special Edition—seen it so many times that I knew when to get up to put the second tape in. I don't know what happened to it. I told them Ashley was a man in the movie and the Ashley girl didn't believe me and Scarlett just laughed mean that her sister'd been named after a man. If I had a sister, or a brother, I wouldn't laugh mean at him. I thought to tell them he was really pretty but I didn't think that was going to change much.

"They wanted to play a game called 'Bitches,' which wasn't much more than smoking candy cigarettes and walking around shaking their fat butts and pretending to talk to their drug-dealing, rapper boyfriends on broken cell phones."

She took an old clamshell cell phone out of her pocket. "They gave me this one," she said. "It doesn't work or anything. Not really." She held it up to her ear for a moment like she was just checking to make sure, then she folded it shut and said, "It's been so long since I had one of those candy cigarettes and I'd forgot they taste like sweet chalk."

"I always liked those candy cigarettes," I said. "The ones with the red tips."

She shook her head and said, "These didn't have red tips,"

like it was the saddest thing in the world. "Their dad came out and said we could play inside and they call him 'Wildcat.' What kind of a man has his own kids call him Wildcat? I mean, either he's *not* their dad or he *is* their dad and he's trying to pretend he's not. Or maybe he's trying to pretend he doesn't have kids so he can still be lead dog. Probably, with that stupid dyed hair spiked up like that."

I wasn't even sure she was talking to me anymore, or if she was talking about Barry or Wildcat, because Barry spends a lot of time and some serious money on that Neil Diamond 'do.

She wrinkled her nose up. "It smelled worse than Grandma pickling in there and burned the back of your throat. He said we should play hide-and-seek, and I was alone in that back bedroom, piled up with so many dirty clothes you could see the stink, like wavy lines on a cartoon." She stopped and kicked one grubby flip-flop at the sidewalk, and then she said, "He had his thing out. In his hand. He told me to touch it."

It took me a minute. It took a minute for that to sink in. Then I said, "Barry told you to touch his thing?"

She shook her head hard and said, "No. Not Barry. Barry would never do that. Wildcat. Smiling creepy with his old rotten teeth like it was something special. He told me to touch it and I shook my head, and when he started to close the door one of those girls started bawling down the hall. He winked at me and I pushed by him to get the hell out of there. I heard him laugh and yell, 'I'll find you next time!' I waited at Barry's till you come back to get me."

"Wildcat?" I said.

She glanced at me for a second and said, "I didn't say anything to Barry. Who knows what he'd a done? Call the cops, and a bunch of questions I can't answer."

And I asked, "Questions?"

"Yeah, questions. Like where's my mom and dad? And who might you be? And where's the piece of paper from Ohio saying I'm supposed to be here?"

She knew more about that stuff than I did, because I didn't

know anything. But I knew somebody's shit was about to get jumped in with both feet, and just knowing that brought back that pure adrenaline rush from the bad old days, like somebody'd shot fat lines of uncut coke way back in my sinuses with a blast from an oxygen tank.

She shook her head, like she had water stuck in one ear, and started walking again. She said, "What is it with you guys and your wieners?" But not like she really wanted an answer because I'd have been hard-pressed to explain that to anyone, especially my girlfriend's ten-year-old daughter that I didn't hardly know. She said, "I've seen two for real ones. Well, three now, I guess. I saw dad's when he passed out drunk in a towel on Grandma's couch. He dumped his truck load of rendered animal fat on an interchange outside of Cincinnati. *That* was a long day, let me tell you what. Even after he run out the hot water and rinsed off in Brut, he still smelt like roadkill and cheap bourbon. Grandma made him go sleep in his truck and sprayed the couch with Lysol and whatever Dollar General sells they pretend is Febreze. And at lunch one day at school, the Christian Athletes Club got ahold of a short-bus kid named Jimmy Belcher and pulled his pants down in the middle of the cafegymtorium. He screamed like a tornado siren, like it was high noon on the first Wednesday of the month, and squeezed that little thing so hard it turned purple like a grape about to pop."

She laughed, but not like she thought it was funny.

I dropped her off at Clyde and Vera's and told them I had to run back up to the marina for a quick minute. I know she didn't believe me, but she was kind enough to pretend she did.

᠊ᕦ᠊

Barry was off at work, singing "Girl, You'll Be A Woman Soon" to blue-haired old ladies tethered to nickel slots, and the old Monte Carlo with Kentucky plates was gone. I could see Wildcat passing back and forth behind the greasy kitchen window. There were three steps up to the little front porch and I stood on the bottom one and leaned forward to knock down low on the screen door. The sound of rattling glass stopped and after a long moment of quiet, he yelled, "Yeah?"

I tried to sound casual, like I knew him, like I was supposed to be there. I laughed and yelled, "C'mon, Wildcat! Open up the goddamn door!"

I heard him turn the lock, then he pushed open the screen door and stepped out just far enough to rest one shoulder against the trailer while the screen tried to close against the other. He had one hand behind his back, like maybe it was resting on the butt of a pistol tucked down the waistband of his jeans.

He smiled and his teeth were all corroded with decay along the gumline. "I know you. How's your little…"

I'm not sure what he was going to say next. In boxing they always tell you to use your legs. I gave him an uppercut so hard in the nuts that he lifted up on his toes, and I jammed my wrist on those low bones in his pelvis. He crumpled down, and when his elbow went through the screen it made a sound just like a zipper. He'd just been pretending he had a gun. The dog started snapping and rasping and jerking against his chain.

"Guess you shouldn't have cut his cords," I said.

When I pushed him back inside the trailer, he sprawled across vinyl tiles snowed over with empty blister packs of store-brand cold medicine and tore up matchbooks. The first thing that came to hand was an old cordless phone, as big as a WWII walkie-talkie, and when he tried to get up, I hit him across the face with it. It broke apart and the battery pack flew down the hall. It opened a cut over his left eye, and for the briefest moment, I could see a pink crescent of skull before it filled up with blood like an overflowing toilet. The next thing that came to hand was an old fan belt hanging on the back of a dinette chair. I whipped him with it, and kept on whipping him until the grease marks faded from black to light grey, and all he managed to get out between blows was "why" and "what the." But I think he knew why.

If he'd ever had any fight in him, it was gone. He'd curled up on his side, covering his head with one hand and his balls with the other. I think he was playing possum, just hoping I'd go away. I dropped the fan belt and took a look around. He was bleeding like a bitch, like head wounds always do, and his blood was the brightest thing in the whole trailer. The countertop and dinette were covered with Pyrex pots and glassware, cans of camp stove fuel and wide-mouthed bottles of lye, nail polish remover, plastic jugs of iodine for horse hooves and concrete etcher. I hooked a jug of iodine and squatted on my heels beside him. I unscrewed the top and knelt across his throat.

"Better get something on that cut," I said, wiping the blood out of his eye. "Seven percent?" I tapped the label on the jug. "This might sting." It stained his face a yellow-red and my knee made his keening scream sound like something far away.

When he finally quieted down, I said, "If you ever even look at her again, I'll field-dress your dog. I'll have your skanky bitch back blowing bikers in Daytona Beach before the sun goes down." I leaned in close and whispered, "I'll sell your little girls to the Haitians."

I stood up and took the open can of camp fuel off the counter. I poured it around him, like chalk around a dead man and said, "Then I'll chain you to the stove, fill your mouth with lye, and burn this fucking trailer to cinders and ash and a handful of teeth."

On the way home, I'd wondered if all that meth Missy jacked up was cooked in Wildcat's dirty kitchen. She had to buy it somewhere. Maybe that's what he was going to say through a smile rotted just like hers, "How's your little woman?" I knocked on Clyde and Vera's patio door and waved Tammy home, then we sat at the table as quiet as mice. Every time a car passed by, she turned her head slowly, following the sound. I think we were both listening for sirens. I know I was. The sun started fading and we still didn't put any lights on.

She started tearing up and touched the swollen knuckles on my right hand. She picked gently at the spots dried black and whispered, "When CPS comes, who'll take care of me?"

"I will," I said.

She shook her head and said, "But Pere, you got no standing. If CPS comes, you got no standing."

"I'll take care of you," I told her. "And when your momma comes home, we both will. Nothing's going to change that."

She thought about that, like she was trying to believe it, and then she said, "Let me get that shirt in some ice water. Go get cleaned up."

When I padded back down the carpeted stairs, showered and almost born-again in a clean pair of old fatigue shorts, I could hear her talking low in the kitchen. I peeked around the corner and she was on the broken cell phone, holding it up to her ear with a skinny shoulder, scrubbing the shirt against itself, pink ice cubes rattling in the stainless kitchen sink.

"You wouldn't believe all the blood…no, you wouldn't. I think he must've about torn it out by the root…Jimmy! Yeah!… Dad came home covered in blood too, but it was always his own… He's forever picking fights and getting his ass handed to him. You know, the only fight he ever won was when he beat my mom up, and that didn't happen but once 'cause Grandma found out and told him she'd park one in his ear."

I didn't know if pretend phone calls were too old or too young for a ten-year-old girl, and I didn't even know who she was pretending to talk to. The last time I kept company with any ten-year-old girls is when I was ten myself, and I didn't understand anymore about them back then than I do now. But I knew something about picking fights and getting your ass handed to you. I used to be pretty good at it myself, but I learned early on that if getting drunk makes you want to fight, you best get as good as you can. I'm not saying that didn't take a while, because it did, and it can change from night to night, depending on how drunk you are and who, exactly, you decide to fight.

She whispered, "I think he's coming. Gotta go," and clapped the phone shut.

I walked around the corner like I hadn't heard a thing and

she said, "You should get some ice on that wrist." Then she pointed to the iodine stain down my calf.

"That's not coming off anytime soon," I said.

She wrung out the shirt and snapped it just like her mom, like she'd been doing it her whole life. She said, "That little one, Ashley? She said, 'Go on. It feels funny!'"

That was the last day I worked regular.

2

FRENCH CLOWNS

Tammy looked up at me and shouted, "It's LY."

She and I were sharing an orange, watching our neighbor cut down what was left of the last coconut palm on our street. This morning, or maybe yesterday by now. The whole top fell off a couple weeks back, tore the gutter off their garage, and ploughed a trough through the sun-warped siding. Now, the palm looked just like a phone pole. Duane was standing in the back of his shitbox Chevy pickup with a running chainsaw, one flip-flop up on the edge of the rusted bed. His wife, Pearl, was on the little concrete stoop with her arms crossed.

Pearl yelled, "You be careful now, Duane."

And Duane yelled back, "Ya think, Pearl? Jesus H. Christ."

I yelled over, "Is the show about to start?"

Pearl lifted her chin at me and yelled, "Hey, Pere. You got a ladder?"

I pointed across to Clyde's condo. He worked in maintenance over at NASA for thirty years and has things like ladders and leaf blowers and phone service that the short-timers don't. His oldest boy married a Seminole girl last summer and they live down in Pahokee.

Pearl yelled at Duane, "I *told* you to wait till Clyde gets home. When Clyde gets home you can use his ladder."

"She's right," I told Tammy. "He ought to wait for the mayor. He prob'ly went fishing."

Tammy asked, "Why do you call him that?"

Duane stepped up on the edge of the bed, and after a moment of wild maneuvering, held a nervous balance. He smiled down at his feet and screamed, "Clyde can kiss my ass!"

I palmed Tammy's blonde head and turned it slowly from side to side. "Don't ever try that. Not even sober."

She kept shaking her head and said, with a conviction I don't remember having at ten, "I'm not ever going to drink."

Duane gunned the chainsaw a few times, the blue exhaust hanging around his head in the humid air, and then lunged at the tree. He got in the better part of an inch before the chain caught in the wet wood, jerking him off the truck and bouncing him off the palm trunk. He landed with his arms folded over his head, the stalled chainsaw stabbing into the sand beside him.

I turned to Tammy and said, "Funny as a French clown."

Pearl disappeared into their condo and slammed the door.

"Is he okay?" Tammy asked.

I shrugged. "You okay there, big guy?"

Duane found his other flip-flop, then pulled the chainsaw out of the sand like a sword from a stone, and threw it against the garage. One of the vinyl sliders opened upstairs and Pearl yelled out, "You're going to look pretty funny with my chainsaw book-marking your ass crack."

Tammy scrunched up her nose and whispered, "Miss Poopy Mouth."

Duane looked like he might be thinking of going inside, then got in his Chevy.

"And don't go tear-assing off either," Pearl yelled. "This is a residential neighborhood street and if you had any goddamn lead in your pencil, our kids'd be playing on it."

Duane drove off like a senior citizen with Michigan plates. He's a 'local,' which down here in this part of Florida is a rare thing, and Pearl calls herself a "Buck Owens 'billy from Bakersfield," but she looks Mexican to me.

Tammy's little pencil-thin fingers tugged at the fold of loose skin over my elbow. It's what she does to get my attention, usually when my mind has wandered off. I think because my elbow is right at her eye level. "It's LY," she said.

"What's LY?"

"LY. Lethal Yellowing," she said. "It's what's killing all the palm trees."

I looked up and down the street, and then said, "Christ, that's the last one? Besides Logan's ficus? And you can't kill those goddamn things with an electric drill and a funnel full of gas. And it's not like I ain't tried."

"Mom said you should try and watch your language," Tammy said. "Remember when all the coconuts fell off?"

If you remembered every time a coconut fell off a tree in Florida, you wouldn't have time for much else. But it seemed important to her so I said, "Yeah, I guess."

"And they looked wet? They all fell off and they looked wet? Right after I got here?"

"Yeah, sure. June?"

"End of May," she said. "It's the first symptom. Of Lethal Yellowing. All of the coconuts fall off at once. They call it 'shelling.' Once they drop, three to six months tops."

I frowned at her. "They teach you that up in Ohio, do they? They teach plant diseases in fourth grade up in O-hi-o?"

She gave me that sympathetic smile she has, usually when I say something stupid, and said, "Fifth grade. But, no, I looked it up on the internet. Doris helped."

"Doris. Now there's a nice lady. Want to head over there?"

She scrubbed the sole of her foot on the concrete for a moment and then said, "It's Thursday."

"Is it?"

She smiled. "Yeah, it is."

I looked at her feet and said, "Remember when you got here? You were a tenderfoot. Soft as a baby's—"

"She doesn't come in until noon."

"When did you meet Doris?"

Her eyes went wide in disbelief. "On that first day," she said. "That first day I got off the bus. Remember?"

"I took you over to the library on that very first day? No kidding?"

She shook her head. "You don't remember? It was only three months ago."

"I thought we went to the beach. So you could see the ocean."

"We *did* go to the beach, 'cause I'd never seen the ocean," she said. "But then you took me up to see Mom. I'd never seen the ocean, and Mom promised we'd see it together just as soon as I got down. When you and Clyde picked me up in Titusville, I thought the Indian River was the ocean, 'cause it doesn't look like any river I ever seen in my life. Clyde says you can walk from one side to the other without getting your shirt wet, even where it's miles from one side to the other."

And I shrugged my shoulders and said, "Well, your shirt might get wet when you hit the channel."

"And it's not all catfish stink and coal dust like the Ohio," she said. "After a day and a half on that bus with the toilet that clogged in north Georgia, I was just happy to be breathing air that didn't smell like everybody else's air-conditioned poop. But Mom wasn't there. Just some bald guy with army shorts and a sleeveless T-shirt worn to holes."

She smiled up at me, and I said, "Me?"

"Yeah, you. And Clyde. Clyde's the biggest old Black guy I ever seen. Most people shrink up when they get old, but Clyde's still big as a house, just with some grey hair and one of his eye teeth gone. You asked me if I was Tammy. I knew it was you, and if you was to ask me now how I knew, I don't know that I could tell you."

"How'd you know it was me?" I asked.

She giggled. "Mom never said much on the phone, except that she was 'in love.' But you weren't all tattoos and attitude like most of the losers she thinks she's in love with. And you're not like all those short-time buddies Dad brought around, that talk to you like you're a little kid but look at you like you're not."

I knew exactly the short-time buddies she was talking about. It's not like I didn't have a bunch of them back in the day. I don't know what I would have done if she hadn't believed me, because there wasn't much of a backup plan for either of us.

And like she read my mind, she said, "I can't believe I got in the car with you and Clyde, just like all those fakey videos they showed us in school said not to. What else was I going to do?

Maybe it was your eyes. Mom says that a lot. She says you look like somebody that might slit your throat and laugh at you for dying, but not if you look in your eyes."

Missy always liked my eyes. And I liked hers, back before they started looking glassy and fake as a stuffed shark hanging over a restaurant bar.

I said, "I swear we went to see the ocean."

"We *did* go see the ocean, *then* you took me up to see Mom. It's the biggest thing I've ever seen, and it stole my shoes right off, right from where you said I could leave them 'cause the tide came in."

"That's right. I forgot the tide was making and not going out."

She nodded. "We watched ships disappear over the horizon, over the very curve of the whole earth. And I didn't know it tasted just like tears. It really does."

"That's right. Then I took you up to see your mom and Doris showed you how."

"Well, Doris is real nice and all," she said, "but I already knew how."

⤚

On that first day, after we'd walked out to the beach so she could see the ocean, we walked down to the library, nine blocks south along the water, then three blocks over, almost to the A1A. I'd only just found it, when the A/C at the condo finally crapped out. It has free air conditioning, until eight p.m. on Tuesdays and Thursdays, when the sun is finally thinking about getting down, and all you have to do is pretend to read a book or a magazine. We'd stood blinking in the cool for a moment, waiting for our eyes to adjust, and then I'd led her over to the computers. I was tapping on some keys, trying to make something happen, when Doris got up from behind her desk with a clipboard, saying, "Excuse me? Excuse me?"

She's slim and pretty, and pretty in that plain way that doesn't need much make-up or jewelry in funny places or a skunky hairdo. Or maybe she's just that much prettier than you expect an assistant librarian at a low-rent local library to be. And even though she's stoop-shouldered and her hips are a little too wide for the rest of her, you'd think about her in the morning when you woke up in grubby sheets next to Skunky Hairdo in smeared make-up scratching at her infected jewelry.

Doris handed me the clipboard and said, "You have to get on the sign-up sheet before you can use the computer."

I looked around. Besides the three of us, there was an old man filling out a racing form and some South-of-the-Border woman with her head down on a table. All four computers were empty and the sign-up sheet on the clipboard was empty too.

"It's the girl," I said. "She wants to, you know, do the inter-web thing."

Doris took the clipboard gently from my hand and gave it to Tammy. She said, "Honey, print your name right here and we can get started." Then she reached behind her head and pulled a yellow pencil from a twist of sandy brown hair. She looked at me and said, "That last chair is, by all accounts, the most comfortable. Magazines are right there, and I'm betting *Bass Masters*, *Hot Rod*, and *Sports Illustrated*, but not necessarily in that order, which you will find on the top, middle, and bottom shelves. In that order."

She took the clipboard and read it as she gently led Tammy by the shoulder to the first computer. "Tammy!" she said. "I love that name! You hardly ever hear it anymore and I don't know why. Now, there's supposed to be a half-hour time limit on the computer, but if there's not anyone waiting, I can certainly forget to tell time."

And just like that, I was standing there in the middle of the floor all by myself. I sat down close enough to listen and pretended to look through the classifieds in yesterday's *Florida Today*.

Doris asked, "Where, exactly, do you want to go, Tammy?"

And Tammy smoothed out a small slip of paper she'd probably been holding all morning, since Clyde drove me up to Titusville to meet her bus.

"You know what to do?" Doris asked.

Tammy nodded and Doris passed her upturned palm over the keys and said, "Then have at it."

Tammy swirled the mouse around and then typed slowly from the slip of paper. And there, on the screen, was a picture of Missy, on the Florida Department of Corrections website, in her prison issue. And next to the picture, her DC number, name (Misty), race (white), sex, hair color (brown, but blonde like Tammy's when she was little), eye color (green, with little flecks of yellow around her pupils), height (5'03"), weight (gaining), birth date, initial receipt date (not so long ago), current facility (Lowell C.I.), current custody (minimum), and current release date (two years, give or take). Medical grade 9. Possession of a Controlled Substance/Other.

Tammy said, "Hi, Mom."

Doris sat back in her chair and covered her mouth with her hand, then she glanced at me over her shoulder with a question in her eyes, like I might be able to explain the whole goddamn mess with no words at all, with just a look. It's not bad, as jailhouse photos go. Her color was still good back then, and the prison blues set off her eyes.

Tammy whispered, "Pere."

But I pretended to read the paper since I was pretty sure I didn't want to see whatever she wanted to show me, or hear whatever she wanted to ask.

After a couple of more whispers, she finally shouted, "Pere!"

The Hispanic woman moaned in her sleep, and Doris smiled and said, "Shhh."

Tammy waved me over. I stood behind their chairs as Tammy pointed to the screen, at the little box marked "Scars, Marks, and Tattoos." Under "type" it said "tattoo," and under "location" it said "back," and under "description" it said "Tammy Angel Heart."

"That's me!" she said. "That little angel she has on her shoulder, holding the heart?"

And I said, "And the heart says, 'Tammy'?"

"Yeah. That's me. And it's on the internet. Anybody in the world can look at this."

"That makes you kind of famous, doesn't it?" Doris said.

Tammy smiled and said, "Does it?"

Doris looked up at me but said to Tammy, "Who knows how many hits a site like this gets?"

"'Missy' is an *alias*?" Tammy asked.

"That just means what other people might call her," I said.

"Then why isn't 'Mom' there?"

Doris asked, "What's medical grade 9?".

"Look! Look," Tammy cried, "it's counting down her sentence. See, it's already down to zero days."

"No," I said, "that's just her jail sentence. Her sentence was two years, six months. They just didn't have anything to put in that last box."

She frowned. "So it's not counting down? So if we come back next week it won't say…two years, five months and…"

"If we come back in two years, it'll say the same thing."

It came out sounding mean, even though I didn't mean it to. Or maybe it just sounded that way because sometimes the truth hurts. It almost always does.

"Two *years*?" Tammy said.

Doris pointed at the screen and said, "She's very pretty, you look just like her." Then she looked up at me and said, "But I think you got your father's eyes."

Tammy held her hand lightly over the mouse for a moment, then made Missy disappear. As she pushed her chair back, she turned to Doris and said, "Maybe I did, but *he's* not my father."

❧

Pearl's chainsaw was weeping bar oil into the sand, and Tammy was saying, "And you should call her Misty."

"What?"

"You should call her Misty," she said again.

"I do call her Misty, but she's your mom."

She punched my forearm and said, "You call her Missy. I hear you kissy kissing on Clyde's phone." Then she looked across the street at Clyde's old johnboat, bottom up in a fringe of weeds. Holding something there just behind the wetness of her eyes, she said, "Well, not last night."

No, not last night.

I tried to smile. "And that's not Clyde's phone. That's Vera's phone."

She looked up the street and said, "They're not supposed to be this far north. Not really."

"Who?"

"Coconut palms," she said.

3

FLEUR DE MERDE

I looked at the scar on the palm trunk and said, "Looks like the show's over for a while."

"Good thing," Tammy said.

"And Doris doesn't come in till noon."

"We need to go to Publix," she said.

"Didn't we just go to Publix? What do we need at Publix?"

"Stuff," she said.

"Like what?"

She looked at me and squinted one eye shut.

"What?"

And she looked away and whispered, "Toilet paper."

"Toilet paper?"

She sighed. "Pere, those McDonald's napkins are making my you-know-what sore."

I didn't know what to say to that because I wasn't sure which you-know-what she was talking about, not that I guess it mattered.

"We're about out of everything," she said.

"Yeah, but if we wait till later on that that grocery store A/C will feel better."

Tammy smiled. "Yeah, down the freezer aisle."

"Want to go up to the pier and watch the gambling ship go out?"

She shrugged her skinny shoulders almost up to her ears. "I guess. Will we make it?"

I looked up at the sun and held my palm to the sky, the edge of my thumb on the horizon. "We got time," I said. "Clyde's prob'ly up there fishing."

While we were waiting to cross the street, Tammy said,

"Look at that." She pointed to a small access lid next to the sidewalk, maybe ten inches across, probably for a water line. It was spray-painted pink and baby blue. She smiled. "I had a unicorn just those colors. Back home. Named Buddy."

"Buddy the unicorn?" I asked.

She nodded and said, "I did. But I don't remember why."

I didn't know if she meant she didn't know why she had a unicorn, or that she didn't know why she named him Buddy, or if she didn't know why she still didn't have a unicorn named Buddy.

And while I was thinking that, she said, "That wasn't there yesterday. Why would someone do that? It's like art."

I knew it was just the city water works marking it for repair or something, but it seemed a small thing not to say so.

I stepped to the low curb. "Wait," she said. "There's a car coming."

I looked at the powder-blue Lincoln way up the road, poking along in the southbound lane. We could've been back and forth across the road half a dozen times before it got to us, but I knew it wouldn't do any good to say so. It moved slower and slower until it rocked to a stop a few yards away. A shriveled-up old woman looked at us from under the arch of the steering wheel and pecked at the air with an arthritic hand.

Tammy smiled and waved. "See!"

And I said, "She needs shocks."

We crossed the beach road and into the shadow of the Fleur de Mer, the expensive oceanfront condos, and at five stories, the tallest thing for blocks. It's amazing how the real estate can change from one side of the street to the other down here. Tammy drug her fingers along the security gate painted to look like old copper.

She suddenly giggled. "What's Clyde call this place again?"

"He calls it Fleur de Merde. French for 'turd blossom.'"

She hooted and said, "'Turd blossom!'"

"He used to could see a little slice of ocean from his upstairs window. Back when it was just the two cottages they tore down."

We cut between two palms into the parking lot of Cherie Down Park and even though it looks like a girl's name, all the locals say it like, "cherry." It's a public park with beach access and outdoor showers and bathrooms and a little boardwalk that runs both directions through the dunes. It's snowed over with people on the weekends, but during the week we pretty much have it to ourselves except for the homeless guys that hang out in the picnic shelter when the sun starts going down. Three feral cats live under the boardwalk up at our end, and one's missing his tail. The Cat Lady brings them dry food and fresh water every evening, and Tammy babies them the rest of the time.

Tammy whistled and clapped her hands and called out, "Flopsy! Mopsy! Cottontail!" and all three of them bounced out of the bushes and across the pavement like they'd been waiting. I think the mostly black one is Flopsy, and the mostly white one is Mopsy. I could have those two mixed up, but I know the calico with the missing tail is Cottontail. Cat Lady calls them something else, in her thick German accent, but I don't remember what. She could probably call them Balled, Blued, and Tattooed for all they care, just as long as she keeps showing up with those plastic milk jugs full of food.

One time I asked Tammy why she calls the one with no tail Cottontail. She explained that she thought he should actually be called Fierce Bad Rabbit, after a fierce bad rabbit that got his tail and whiskers shot off by a mean old farmer, but since his little nub of cat tail looked not unlike a rabbit's, being white on the backside, she thought Cottontail was better, and more appropriate for a cute, sweet little kitty. I didn't ask about Flopsy and Mopsy.

I pushed the black one away from my ankle and said, "You'll get fleas."

"You say that every day."

"Then one day I'll be right," I said.

She kept scratching Cottontail under his chin. "You don't have fleas. No, you don't. Sweet kitties don't have fleas."

"Yeah, you'll look pretty funny when we have to shave off all that pretty blonde hair."

She looked up and said, "I'll look like you."

I rubbed the stubble on my head and said, "But I don't have fleas. Not yet anyway. I just don't have enough hair to bother shampooing. Except on my back."

She stood up and clapped her hands again. "Off you go, off you go. We have to go see the mayor. Maybe he'll give me a fish to bring you."

After a few more passes through her legs, they chased each other off into the low bushes. It would be no mean feat to talk Clyde out of a fish, especially for a cat, but Tammy had a better chance than most. I paused on the sidewalk, just before the wooden steps of the dune crossover, at the leaping dolphin. Someone, back when they poured the sidewalk, drew a bottle-nose dolphin into the wet concrete. And in some secret ritual, sometimes three times a day, coming and going, she traced the line of its belly with the big toe of her right foot. But not today. I waited a moment longer, watching her pretend it wasn't there, watching her pretend she'd never cared about it at all, that the awful weight of superstition can be shook off just like that. We walked up the steps and caught the first breeze off the ocean.

I saw the decking nail sticking up on the crossover. "Damn. You forgot to tell me to bring the hammer."

And she said, "Don't forget to bring the hammer."

"Funny kid."

There was a homeless guy I'd never seen before, sunburnt brown with knotted hair like dirty rope, squatting in the shade of a bush at the edge of the dunes.

As we stepped off the boardwalk into the sand, she said, "Why do you call him that?"

"Call who what?"

"Clyde," she said. "Why do you call him the mayor?"

"Clyde? 'Cause he's the mayor. Of our street anyway. Knows everybody. Never too busy to stop and talk. Been here the longest. He has tools and ladders and leaf blowers, and he's pretty good about lending them out if you don't take advantage. Worked at NASA forever, and if he doesn't know how to fix something, he can figure it out right quick. Just a good guy."

We made our way down to the damp, hard sand close to the water and turned up north toward the jetty.

"Is he your best friend?" she asked.

"Well, I can't say I ever thought of it that way before, but he might just be."

When we met, Clyde was just an old guy across the street who treated me better than I deserved, but now we're friends. I *had* a best friend, back when I worked the line, pumping Jet A and 100 octane up at Lake City Gateway Airport, and before that up at a garage in Georgia, but that ended even worse than most things.

"Is that why he helped try to fix the A/C?" she asked.

"Yeah, but it just cost too much."

"And why you're helping him fix his outboard?"

"Yep, if the parts ever get in. That's an old, old outboard."

Then she said, "Is that why he give you that bag of oranges last night? Because you're best friends?"

No, he gave me that bag of oranges because he felt bad and he wanted to do something, and Vera probably put the bag of oranges into his hands to give us. But I only said, "No, not exactly. But they're good, aren't they? I should've brought a couple."

"We'll never get through them all before they go off," she said. "Maybe we could put some up."

"You know how to do that?"

"I used to help my grandma put up pickles and green beans and those little plums no bigger than walnuts." She waved a hand in front of her nose at the memory and said, "Whew, that vinegar smell will light you up. Can't be much different. I bet Doris could help us figure it out."

And I said, without thinking, "Your mom know how to do that stuff?"

She looked at me like I might have lost my mind. "Pere,

you ever had mac 'n' cheese made without margarine? I mean, besides boiled macaroni, there's not but three ingredients— milk, margarine, and that pack of orange powder. There's not but three ingredients, but you really need all three."

"We ate out a lot."

"I learned to cook a few things early," she said.

Toward the end there, it's not like she was eating much anyway.

"You know your way around the kitchen," I said. "You're a good cook."

"Pere, I don't know that you're a good judge. When I got here you were living on hard-cooked eggs."

"A man could do a lot worse than hard-cooked eggs." Especially since all you need is water, a pan, and eggs.

She looked up at me. "Then you must not've ever had to live with somebody on a diet of hard-cooked eggs."

"You get used to it."

And she said, "Not the smell."

I thought about that for a minute, since it was the first I'd heard of it, then said, "Yeah, I can see that."

"And you may want to get your cholesterol checked at some point," she said. "I know you need sugar and lots of boiling water."

"Sugar?"

"To put up the oranges. We need sugar and lots of boiling water," she said.

"Hell, we'll prob'ly have to buy a bunch of jars and lids and pans and shit and by then we'll be tired of eating them anyway."

She squinted off at the water. "I guess that's one way of looking at it. Vera might lend us pans."

I couldn't imagine such a thing and said so. "I don't know. Vera and her pans."

We walked along in silence for a moment, low waves slapping the sand.

"I had a best friend," she said. "Back in Ohio."

4

BEST FRIENDS

Her best friend back in Ohio was named Becky, and as she padded along the firm, damp sand right up against the water, I got to hear all about her.

"She lives in town," Tammy said. "She's the last bus stop on the way to school and the first stop after, but we been friends forever, probably since third grade. She lives in a real house that never had wheels, and both of her parents are still together. Her mom is a nurse's assistant and her dad runs a tire store out on Route 4, but he doesn't own it because if he did he'd do a bunch of stuff different."

She stopped to pick up a small white shell, and after turning it over carefully in her hands, she flicked it into the water. "She has really short hair that's almost white and glasses. She asked for contacts last Christmas, but Santa couldn't afford them. Grandma thought she was an albino but she's not, not really, just a little bit. She's really pale and has to be careful about sunscreen and sunglasses. That might be why she likes dolphins so much. She has a big stick-on mural of a jumping dolphin on her wall that her mom found at Big Lots. I wanted one too, but they were sold out by the time Grandma got there."

She scanned the deep water for dolphins, then said, "She didn't have cats 'cause her dad's allergic, but she had an aquarium with gerbils under that dolphin that always smelled like pee and she called them Justin and Taylor, even though I don't think she knew one way or the other until they had seven little babies. We watched them every day and they were ugly as sin but cute too, and Justin and Taylor took really good care of them until one day after school four of them were gone except for some little paws and one with half its tail bit off. Becky thought Justin ate them, and I thought it was Taylor, but our science teacher at school, Miss Mackley, she said it could have been anything, like not enough food or something scared them, or the babies were sick or something new they weren't too sure about. It might have been our fault, 'cause even though her dad told us not to, we put a toilet paper roll in for them to play with, even though their eyes weren't even open yet, and Becky's mom bought that really nice toilet paper like Vera gets that smells like old lady perfume and doesn't rub you raw."

I never paid too much attention to toilet paper as long as it does the job, but I know Clyde places a lot of stock in it, especially when his piles are flaring up. She looked at me for long enough that I guess I was supposed to say something, so I said, "Yeah, they got nicer toilet paper than us."

She snorted. "That's not saying much, Pere. We got McDonald's napkins."

"The price is right."

"Maybe for *your* crack," she said. "We wanted to take the other three babies out, especially the one with its tail bit off, but Becky's dad kept saying, 'Nature sorts these things out.' I don't know if he knew what he was talking about or didn't want us to go through the heartache of trying to feed those babies with an eye dropper just to have them die on us. Or more than likely, he didn't want to get stuck doing it when we got bored."

That sounded like the best guess, but I didn't say so.

She took a deep breath. "Becky named that one with no tail Stubbins. I wouldn't have named him Stubbins, but he wasn't mine and Grandma wouldn't let me have one 'cause she said they're just rats. Stubbins caused the only really big fight Becky and me ever had, even though it wasn't his fault. When they got big, big enough to give away, Becky's mom and dad said she could only keep one, which seemed kind of mean to me that she'd have to give away either Justin or Taylor 'cause she'd had them both all along, but I guess once they get started they're nothing but baby gerbil-making machines and they weren't counting on that. Tommy Pafford wanted one, and he wanted

Stubbins, even though Stubbins was kind of clumsy with that tail half gone, but Tommy had nine fingers and I think that's why he wanted him. I didn't mind. I liked Tommy. I liked him ever since we were in a class play together about mythology. He was Prometheus and I was Io and I think he liked me whether I was a beautiful princess or in a cow suit watching him get his liver eaten by a Halloween crow taped to his belt. That cow suit looked really good, but it wasn't anything but white sweats with sticky black felt spots and ears that stuck out that Grandma threw together like it was nothing."

I don't remember much about mythology, if I ever learned anything, so I said, "We just put on plays about pilgrims and Indians, and I was always an Indian."

"I *liked* him liked him, but Becky didn't know 'cause I had not told her. And Becky tried to sell that gerbil to him for a kiss, even though they were free to a good home, and like her dad said, 'A good home is one that'll take a gerbil.' After Stubbins was down in his Folger's can in a handful of cedar shavings for traveling and everything, Becky asked Tommy for a kiss, just like that, 'How 'bout you kiss me for him?' But he didn't. When she told me all that is when I got really mad 'cause she said he must be a gay or something and I said maybe he just didn't like kissing a ghost and then she got really mad 'cause she's super sensitive about that. But then she said it didn't matter 'cause she didn't even like Tommy, she just wanted to see what getting kissed on the mouth was like and it seemed her best chance, him having nine fingers and all."

That made sense, I guess, to ten-year-old girls at least, and I said so.

"Are you looking?" she asked.

For shells, small white ones, with wave-worn holes in the high, narrow end. I wasn't, but I said, "I'm on it."

And in a quiet voice, like she was talking to herself, she said, "I'll call her later and tell her about the Turd Blossom Hotel 'cause it's the funniest thing ever and she'll think so too."

We each picked up a few shells—too big, too brown, too

chipped, cracked, or broken. She's working on a necklace and we have to find one shell a day, no bigger than the nail on my ring finger. Clyde gave her a handful of silver swivel-snaps from his tackle box, and Vera found a length of black cord. Our hearts not really in it, we tossed them back in the water.

"We were best friends when I left," she said. "She didn't care I still slept with Buddy like some little kid."

5

STRESSED FLOUNDER

The beach hooks out into the ocean and ends up against the rocks piled to make the jetty for the port channel. The gambling ship was still in, and we could see people switchbacking up the covered gangplank.

"See, the gambling ship's still in," I said. "They're just now hustling the geezers on. Holding them upside down and shaking all their money out like on the cartoons. We got plenty of time."

There's a boardwalk along the top of the rocks and a metal fishing pier out at the end over the water.

Tammy pointed. "There's Clyde." Clyde was in his regular spot out on the pier, his massive back to us, putting a serious strain on a little canvas sling chair. As we walked along the weathered boards, she said, "Don't drag your feet, you'll get a splinter." Then she ran ahead to clap her hands at the tame gulls and check the white five-gallon buckets of each fisherman. She yelled, "Hey, Clyde!"

And Clyde called back, "Hey, Tammy."

Tammy looked into his bucket and danced away in a shuttering spasm. "Ew! Ew! Ew!"

She looked into the bucket again and turned away, stamping one foot and covering her eyes. Clyde laughed. "Jumpin' Jesus Christ on a rubber crutch!" she said. "I can *not* believe that. That is sooo gross. Pere, it's a flounder."

I looked into the bucket and shrugged.

"A *flounder*," she said. "One of those nasty, two-eyes-on-one-the-same-side-of-the-head fish."

"Yeah?" I said.

"Ew! A flounder! Can you imagine such a thing? Can you imagine anything so…so…so unnatural?"

Clyde smiled at his fishing rod.

She said, "They're not born that way, you know. They look just like all of the other fish when they're little. And then that eye…" She made a little basket with the fingers of one hand and held it up to her eye. "It starts moving. R-e-e-e-al slow." The basket of her fingers started moving slowly across her face. "And it wanders across one side of its head…all the way over to the other side of its face. Can you just imagine? Can you just imagine waking up one morning with both your eyes on the same side of your nose?"

I thought about it a moment. "Back in my drinking days, I believe I did a time or two."

Clyde and I both laughed, but Tammy just stared at me. She said, "Now, what's that supposed to mean? Percival, I swear, sometimes the things that fall out of your mouth are God's own mystery, they surely are. That's not a thing to joke about." I tried to look ashamed, and she looked in the bucket again and said, "I've ate deer, but I've never been hungry enough to eat flounder. Tell me you're not going to eat that."

"They may not look good," Clyde said, "but they taste good." Then he looked at me and said, "Kind of like that old joke, 'You looks bad.' 'But I feels good.'"

And I said, "Oh, yeah."

"You've had venison?" Clyde asked Tammy. "Venison steak, marinated in a little red wine vinegar overnight, slap it on the grill with salt and pepper. *That's* good eatin'."

Tammy raised her eyebrows up and said, "Have *I* had venison? I'm from Ohio, Clyde. We're snowed over with deer up in Ohio. There's so many deer, and no natural predators except cars, that they're begging people to shoot them 'cause they ain't got enough to eat to get through the winter and they don't even much care what you kill them with. Grandma read that over in Cincinnati they were selling bow hunting permits for the city parks. Make you think twice about going on a swing set there. Every night there'd be eight or ten in the field behind us—bucks and does, and one time a momma had triplet fawns.

Dad didn't hunt, but some of his buddies gave him rolls of venison breakfast sausage and it tastes way better than regular old sausage on a cold winter morning."

"I bet," Clyde said.

I used to deer hunt when I lived up in Virginia, but mostly just to sit in the woods around a campfire and get drunk. The bucks didn't have much to worry about from us.

Tammy looked in the bucket again. "You don't have to eat that, Clyde, We got lunch meat and government cheese. You can bring Vera."

"You know Vera doesn't leave the house," Clyde said.

I pointed back down the pier and said, "Go run some gulls."

Tammy ran back down the pier, bent over and clapping low to the ground, the gulls so tame they just hopped a few feet until she rushed them.

"Speaking of Vera," Clyde said, "Tammy better watch that rubber crutch stuff around her. I been fighting the good fight every Sunday since she got here to keep her from being dragged off to church and cleansed of her wickedness."

I looked back down the pier at Tammy and said, "There's not much wickedness in that one."

"Tell that to the wife."

"How'd that joke go?" I asked.

Clyde smiled to himself. "How'd that joke go? Well, let me see. It was two ole boys. What were their names?"

And I said, like I'm supposed to, "Was it Rufus and Roy?"

And Clyde said, "I believe it was."

And I said, "Always is."

"Seems like. So Rufus and Roy are out working the fields, and they take a break. Roy looks to Rufus and says, 'You looks bad.' And Rufus, he says, 'But I feels good!' 'But you looks bad. Real bad.' 'But I feels good!' Roy thinks on it a minute and says, 'I'm run up to the house and get the doctorin' book.' So back he comes and sits there, pouring over that book for a while, 'Looks bad, feels good. Looks bad, feels good.' Finally, he taps a page, 'Rufus, says here you's a pussy!'"

I'd remembered it halfway through but I laughed like I hadn't. "That's it."

We both stared at the end of his pole for a minute, watching it flex with the current.

Without taking his eyes off the end of his pole, he said, "You tell her?"

I didn't much want to talk about it, but he knew anyway. It was their phone Missy called collect on. After Tammy came down and I quit working steady, that prepaid cell phone was eating me alive. When the minutes finally ran out, I called up Lowell Correctional and changed the emergency contact number to Clyde and Vera's. Missy calls collect every Sunday at four to talk to Tammy for twenty minutes. I used to try and think of something to say, but now I pretty much just say hi and hand the phone over. But everybody knows about those calls—last night's was something different.

"Midnight phone calls are never good," I said. "You figure that out younger than her. She watched me standing in your driveway on the phone for an hour. Hell, she prob'ly heard her mom crying all the way across the street." I watched Tammy kick something off the edge of the pier into the water. "She's got enough people lying to her."

"How'd she take it?" Clyde asked.

"It went hard with her last night. But today, nothing."

"Some children are an open book," Clyde said, winding his line in a couple of clicks. "It's all right out there. We've got two like that. Our oldest and the boy. But our youngest? She's just like Vera. And they're not ready until they're ready."

I nodded and waited for more, but when I figured out there wasn't any more, I started laughing. "Goddamn, Clyde. Thanks for clearing that up for me."

He blushed a little under the brown and said, "No problem."

"No shit, you ought to write a book or something"

One of the charter fishing boats from the marina was heading out, and the captain took off his hat and waved it up at me. "Pere! Hey, Pere!" he yelled. And when I waved back, he yelled,

"When you coming back to work? The place is falling apart without you, and that Cubano kid could fuck up a wet dream. He put beer and ice in my live well."

"Soon!" I yelled back. "I just got some stuff to sort out."

The captain nodded big and yelled, "And he can't back up worth a damn either. Takes him about six tries with the boat trailer all over the place, like a broke-dick dog trying to fuck."

Clyde laughed. "'Broke-dick dog. I ain't heard that in a while."

Then the captain pointed at me but yelled to Clyde, "You know your buddy there? He backs up like a fucking French army tank. No lie. Big or small, long or tall, Pere don't care. He'll get it in the water in just one shot. Guaranteed."

I'm good at going backwards. I'm not sure why. He throttled up and we waved once more.

"Manatee!" Tammy yelled. She had her feet up on the second rail from the bottom and was bouncing up and down while she pointed with her free hand. The manatee was rolling slowly at the surface, grey and slick.

She stopped bouncing and called, "Is it a mommy or a daddy?"

"I don't know," I yelled.

"How do you tell?" she yelled back.

"Ask Clyde. He knows everything."

"Hey, Clyde!" she yelled.

Clyde said to me, "You're a funny guy."

"Hey, Clyde! Is it a boy or a girl?" Tammy yelled again.

"I don't know!" Clyde yelled back. "You've got to be underneath it."

"What if you're underneath it?" she yelled.

Clyde sighed and yelled back, "Next time you're underneath one, come and ask."

Tammy yelled, "They used to think they were mermaids."

"That'll give her something to look up on the internet this afternoon," I said.

"I don't want to hear about the intra-net," Clyde said. "The intra-net is the new sucking sound I hear every time I open the bills. EBay and the intra-net shopping. Little Chinese people working 'round the clock to keep the container ships coming to our condo. I'm sorry I ever bought her that computer. She said she didn't want one, and I should've listened. Now she never gets off it. Solitaire and shopping, shopping and solitaire. It used to just be the catalogues. I think *Carol Wright* and *Lillian Vernon* legally adopted her when I retired. We're the only house in Florida filled with those stuffed cats with the really long tails you put in front of doors to block the winter drafts."

"Like those ones in the kitchen?" I asked.

"Kitchen? Yeah, the kitchen. Kitchen and every other room. We even got them on the closet doors so the clothes don't catch a chill. There's one in the garage that looks like an Italian table-cloth. I'm not lying. I kick it behind the storm shutters every chance I get, but she always drags it back out and dusts it off. I'm too ashamed to tell you how many. And if I ever open a credit card bill and, in a fit of blind rage, choke the life out of my loving wife, Vera—not that I'm going to, or I want to, or I lay awake in the wee hours contemplating such a wicked, wicked thing—but if such an unimaginable tragedy were to occur, it will occur with the really long tail of a stuffed cat."

And I said, "Got it."

"You looked at a *Carol Wright* catalogue recently?"

"I don't get much mail."

"No, you're 'bout off the grid," he said. "Well, I try to get the mail before Vera, and shitcan the catalogues for obvious reasons. And I saw the *Carol Wright* and I thought to save it for Tammy, 'cause I always liked looking through them when I was a kid. So I'm paging through all the usual weird stuff you'd never see anywhere except your grandma's house, and then I get to a two page spread and I'm here to tell you, *Carol Wright* has changed, or Grandma has changed or something. 'Neck' massagers to shame a horse, vibrating male-enhancement rings, five-attachment fingertip fun units, all-nude yoga, Girls Gone Wild, Boys Gone Wild."

"In a *Carol Wright* catalogue?"

"Can you believe it? Made me scared to look in *Lillian Vernon*. I threw it in the trash." Then he looked at me sideways and said, "Right after I ordered that all-nude yoga."

He laughed out loud and I smiled and when it was quiet again, I said, "You know, maybe those long-tailed cats have not a thing to do with winter drafts."

He rubbed his chin for a moment in mock consideration, and then said, "You think?"

"There's a new homeless guy hanging around the park."

"One of Tampon John's bunch?" Clyde asked.

"I don't think so. I've not seen this one before. Blonde and grey hair twisted up like rope and burnt up by the sun. He's been outdoors awhile. A couple of teeth."

"Hell, that could be any of them," Clyde said. "I'll keep an eye out." I tapped the bucket with the side of my foot. "Don't stress my flounder."

"When I get back to the house, I'm going to give you a couple of bucks for the phone."

He spit through the rails. "Don't be dumb," he said. "If I had a heart attack and you called 911, would you want any money?"

I thought about it and said, "No, 'cause I'd have to borrow your phone to do it."

"No, Pere, it's what friends do. It's what neighbors do. What the hell do Vera and I have to spend our money on? More long-tailed cats? It was an emergency."

"Yeah, but that was a 'collect' emergency. Vera was worried about that phone bill."

He shook his big head and said, "No, she was worried about the *phone*. She loves that cord. You had it stretched all the way out through the garage to the street."

"That's got to be close to thirty feet. *Carol Wright* purchase?"

"*Lillian Vernon*," he said with a smile. "Discontinued color."

We watched Tammy flicking little bits of something off the pier into the water.

"I had to get out past that rotting bait smell in your garage," I said.

"Yeah, that's why she won't let me keep the boat in there anymore. But we still can't get the stink out."

"It smells just the same up here when the wind dies down." I asked, "Don't you ever get tired of it?"

He said, "For the first twenty years we were married, I had her convinced it was aftershave."

We both jumped when his tackle box started ringing. "What the Sam Hill?" He opened up his tackle box and lifted out the top tray. There was one of those clamshell cell phones with the big buttons like they sell on TV for old people. He opened it and shouted, "Hello?…Vera?…Well, where do you *think* I am?…That's right…I *don't know*!…When I'm done! Okay… Okay…Bye." He clapped the phone shut and stared at it in his hand. "Vera." Then he shook it like there might be water trapped inside. "When my boy brings that boat trailer back, he's going to have a mighty uncomfortable ride back down to Pahokee when I shove this up his ass." He shook his head. "I can't believe she snuck that in my tackle box."

I'd bought my dad one too, back when he was getting bad. It was a Lady Bug or a June Bug or a Stink Bug, but I could never convince him to keep it with him or turn the damn thing on. He said he was saving it for an emergency, and there was no explaining to him that if there was an emergency, he'd need it on him and without a dead battery.

"He's prob'ly just worried about you," I said. "Like if you're out on the road driving."

He eyeballed me. "You looking for a mighty uncomfortable walk back to Cherie Down Park?"

I held up both hands and laughed. "I got no dogs in that race."

He looked like he might chuck the phone in the canal, but he put it back in his tackle box and latched it away. He asked, "Is she going to be okay?"

I didn't know if he meant Tammy or Missy. And I guess I knew it didn't matter which. "It's pretty much all over but the crying," I said. "They're going to get her back on her regular meds."

"You going up? You can borrow the Buick. Tammy could stay with me and Vera."

"Clyde, much as I'd love to blow the cobwebs out of that Buick up the turnpike to Ocala, they'd suspend *your* license just for letting me sit behind the wheel. The politicians up in Tallahassee ever push those pink DUI plates through, they'll have little photos of my head on them instead of those two oranges. No. They take a dim view of swapping meds up at Lowell Correctional. Trouble in general. You know."

I wasn't for sure, but I think Clyde was the only one of us that hadn't done some time, even short time. There's a postcard on the refrigerator of those two license plate oranges, right under the one of Swampy the World's Largest Alligator up in Christmas between Titusville and Orlando.

"That doesn't seem right, all things considered," Clyde said quietly.

I squatted down on my heels, my hands close enough together that they might almost be holding something. "Took the life right out of her, Clyde."

Tammy came running up the pier. "It's moving! It's moving!" she yelled. "The gambling ship is heading out!"

6

SHIP OF FOOLS

We watched the gambling ship moving slowly up the channel, and Clyde said, "Ship of fools."

Tammy pointed to the charter boat in the distance. "That charter captain yelling at you is funny. He cusses like you wouldn't believe. He tried to tune it down when I was first around but I guess once you're in the habit of dropping the Big F bomb in front of every other word, that's not easy to break. Grandma'd be sticking one of her old red bars of Life Buoy in his mouth like the biggest, nastiest breath mint in the world. I know."

Clyde laughed out loud. "I forgot about Life Buoy."

"Grandma wouldn't care much for that gambling boat either, seeing as how she didn't think much of gambling. We'd always get stuck behind somebody at the Stop 'n Rob playing their numbers, and they always play ten different games, you know, like Pick 3 or Pick 4 or Pick 5, Rolling Cash, Second Chance with a kicker, whatever that means, and Grandma would pretend she was talking to me but talk so loud everyone *but* me turned around when she said, 'Tammy, right there is a stupid tax. It certainly is.' One time she said it to a guy with lightning bolts tattooed on his neck buying cold medicine and lottery tickets and the Paki couple that ran the place pretended they were deaf."

She stopped like that was the end of it, until I asked, "And what happened?"

She shrugged. "He snapped his little stack of lotto cards against the Sudafed box and said, 'What're you yapping about, you old b-word?' But he said the b-word. Grandma pointed at his neck and said, 'Do you even know what that means, you ignorant trash? If *your* father fought Hitler's SS bastards, you might.' Then he looked at me and said, 'You best get old granny home.' Grandma snorted a laugh through her nose, then she reached in her purse and said, 'Speak to my grandbaby again, the last sound you hear'll be the air rushing out of that empty head of yours.'"

Clyde looked worried. "What was in the purse?" he asked.

Tammy said, "Her pocketbook pistol—a five-shot Smith & Wesson hammerless Airweight. Short barrel, maybe inch and a half or two inches. .38 caliber."

"That'll do it," I said.

Clyde said, "I didn't even know they made a hammerless revolver."

"She didn't want it getting hung up in her purse. That's why she had the wood grips instead of the rubber." Tammy tugged at my elbow. "I know you told me this before, but how come they're all just standing around? Shouldn't they be gambling or something?"

I said, "They're not allowed to start gambling until they're a couple of miles out. But I couldn't tell you why."

"Three miles off shore," Clyde said. "State law. Any closer than that they figure folks might try to swim back when they have a few bucks left."

"Hell, this is when your mom raked it in. All they have to do for close on an hour is drink and they still have money to tip."

Tammy closed her eyes in concentration. "Did she like this job? I can't remember."

I thought about it and said, "Like it? I guess. The shoes hurt her feet, but the money was pretty good. She didn't much care for the uniform." It wasn't much more than a fancy one-piece black swimsuit, hose, and strappy heels.

"Why not?" she asked.

"Why not? Well, mostly 'cause there wasn't much to it. What'd she always say? Didn't leave much to the imagination."

But by God she was beautiful.

Tammy said, "I don't know why that would've bothered her,

you should have seen what she wore to my second-grade Meet-the-Teacher night."

"You must've liked it well enough," Clyde said. He turned in his chair to Tammy and said, "He met your mom at work you know."

"You *met* her, met her?" Tammy asked. "Like the first time you ever saw her? Was on the boat?"

I watched the diesel smoke from the single stack pulled away to the south. "That boat, yep. On a Saturday night."

She looked hurt and asked, "How come you never told me that?" I couldn't think why and said so. She watched the boat coming slowly up the channel along the jetty. "But we're up here most every day," she said. "We've seen it go out like a million times."

I knew it had something to do with me being somebody else back then, somebody that wasn't me now, somebody that she never had to know. Not that she didn't know somebodies like that. But all I said was, "Yeah. I'm sorry."

She looked at her feet and worked her toes carefully over the edge of the pier. "Was it love at first sight?"

"Something like that. I was up in the show lounge, enjoying the 'Tribute Performers.'"

"Like Barry doing his Neil Diamond?" Tammy asked. "I wouldn't walk across the street to see the real Neil Diamond much less a fake Neil Diamond. Barry played me a bunch of his songs that one day and some of them sounded kind of like I might have heard them when Grandma played the radio or walking around music at the Wally World, but that doesn't mean I'd listen to it unless you tied me to a chair."

≪

It's funny she said that about being tied in a chair. I *was* in the Show Lounge, up on the top deck, which is just a big bar with a little stage and a few spotlights. And there *were* Tribute Performers—a chubby hillbilly in white polyester stretch pants and a red wig trying to convince everybody she was 'Reba' by braying, "Y'all." There was a light-absorbing Haitian emcee in mirrored sunglasses named Bertrand, and Missy was making the rounds through the crowd with one of those little cork-lined trays. Of course at the time, I didn't know it was Missy yet. And I was right up against the stage, roaring drunk.

When Reba started in on "Fancy," I stood up and yelled, "Jesus Christ, you lip-sync like a fucking kung-fu movie. Give me that cheap-ass wig, I'd look more like 'Reba' than you."

Missy passed close behind me, and I dropped my head back so I was looking at her upside down. "Angel, I could sure use another drink," I said. "Reba and the Buzzkills here are sucking the vodka out of me faster than you can pour it in."

When "Fancy" finally ended I stood and clapped. I yelled, "Honey, when those control-tops finally cut loose, you got 'Wynona' written all over you."

I was always the funniest guy in the room. At least to me.

Reba backed through a service door waving like a queen, and the Haitian emcee took the stage clapping gently. He said, in a heavy accent and with no emotion at all, "Thank you, Reba. Wasn't she great? She'll be back for our second show."

And I jumped up and yelled, "Threat! Threat! Did you hear him threaten me?"

Everyone ignored me except Bertrand, whose mirrored sunglasses shifted ever so slightly in my direction. I sat down.

"Now. Without further adieu," Bertrand said. "Ladies and gentleman, the one, the only, the incomparable Jazz Singer himself, Mister Neil Diamond."

Bertrand made an odd, kneeling flourish and "Neil" burst through the service door. Neil is a balding Jewish guy named Barry, and he had his pudge packed into the same blue sequined shirt he wears every show. We're friends now, and he rents a sin-gle-wide over in the Whispering Pines Trailer Park. He always had Kool-Aid for Tammy back when we used to go to visit.

But that first time I saw him, I said, "Neil Diamond? Neil *Diamond?* You look like a fucking dentist." Then I hooked a finger in my cheek and said, "Can you look at this back molar? It hurts!" But it came out sounding like, "'An 'ou 'ook at 'is 'ack 'olar? It 'urts!"

And all of the sudden, my arms were pinned behind my back and the emcee was hissing in my ear, "Show's over, Billy Bob."

He turned me toward the service door and I was looking down into Missy's front porch, and the nametag in the side-yard that read, MISTY. But I didn't read it right and I said, "Lord, Missy, you got some pretty eyes."

She smiled and said, "Be nice."

Bertrand shoved me through the service door and down a maze of narrow corridors to the security office. He pulled me down into a steel chair and then patted me on the head like a dog. "Are you going to be a nice drunk," he asked, "or do I get to handcuff you to the chair?"

I hopped the chair a couple of times and said, "You can handcuff me if you want to, but it seems like if you were serious, you'd have it welded down."

He took off his glasses and considered himself in their reflection, then he put them back on without ever looking at me. "If *I* was serious," he said, "I'd have a drain in the floor."

Even in my drunken state, I took a minute to think about exactly what that might mean. Then I eyeballed him and said, "Hell, buddy, I been ankle deep in blood before this. In an ambulance. Up in Lake City. At the airport. Maybe I'll run your drain idea by the EMTs." And just the memory of that day sobered me up as fast as it did the day it happened. "And that was my friend."

Bertrand reached into his back pocket and pulled out his wallet. "Let me show you something, my friend."

I figured we might as well get to it, so I said, "I got something in my wallet too. And you ain't *my* friend. You're just some rent-a-spade keeping the blue hairs from breaking a hip fighting over their favorite nickel slots."

He whistled without making any sound, and I got my tongue tucked in back and my jaw locked down tight as I could. But before Bertrand had a chance to knock me into the corner, Missy stuck her head in the door. "Bert?"

He sighed and asked, "Miss Misty. How can I help you?"

"Mister H. wants you back upstairs. Barry's about to sing 'Coming to America.'"

Bertrand slumped back into his chair and shook his head sadly before standing right up again. He tucked his wallet back into his pants. "Please, call me Bertrand," he said.

"I can stay," she said. "I'm on break."

After he left, she sat down across from me with her ankles crossed and the little drink tray on her lap.

She said, "I'm not on break. Not yet. But Tina's watching the floor." I tried to think of something not stupid to say, but it took so long that she started wiggling one leg up and down. Then she said, "He's not bad. I mean, he did eat somebody once. Part of somebody. But he's always been a perfect gentleman to me. Can I get you something? Besides another vodka and grapefruit juice. Coffee? Coke? Something from the buffet?"

"Until just a second ago, I could've hit that buffet."

"You're not missing much. Bait shrimp and hardboiled eggs."

I asked, "You're joking about him eating somebody, right? Messing with the drunk guy?"

"No," she said, shaking her head.

"How do you come to know something like that?"

"He's got a picture in his wallet. It was in *Time* or *Newsweek*. Down in Haiti. He's eating a piece of somebody off the blade of a knife. Somebody that supported the wrong guy. And he's wearing those same sunglasses. I'm surprised he didn't show it to you. He shows it to everybody."

"Hasn't he got any pictures of his kids?" I asked.

"Oh, yeah!" she said with a smile. "Three little boys, cute as can be. All look just alike. Stair steps, one, two, three. I just got one, a little girl—"

"Wait!" I interrupted. "Don't tell me." I rubbed at my temples in deep concentration and said, "I'm sensing a…Is the first letter a *T*?"

She stood up and said, "Why, yes it is. Like 'tattoo.' Like the one you read on my back in this stupid outfit. You must not be *that* drunk. I'm going to have to get one of those bumper stickers for my ass that says, 'If you can read this, you are following too close.' I swear to God, I'd get to wear more clothes working at Hooters."

She stomped out of the little office and slammed the metal door.

I yelled, "A Coke would be nice," but if she heard me, she didn't come back.

I spent the next couple of hours in that little office. I thought about leaving, but it didn't seem like I'd find any place to hide out on a ship that small that Bertrand wouldn't already know about. And I also wasn't sure what would happen if I ran off and he caught me. I felt the propellers shudder to life and the floor tilt gently as we made the wide turn back to port. I heard racks of glasses rattling by in the passage way as everything was closing down. That's when she came back to get me. She had a zip-up hooded sweatshirt over her uniform.

She said, "Come with me."

"It's not his dinner time, is it?"

"He doesn't care. As long as you don't start any trouble in the next twenty minutes so he can get home to the wife and kids."

I stood up and asked, "Where are we going?"

"Up on deck. A secret place. All of the yellow lights are on."

I followed her legs along narrower and narrower passage ways, through a door marked Do Not Open, up ladder-steep stairs, and finally out onto a small observation deck, maybe four feet square, in the shadow of the smokestack. The ship was curtained in strings of little Christmas lights, but all in yellow. "I come up on whichever side the wind is blowing from," she said, "then you don't smell the diesel. Nobody ever comes up here."

We stood in silence and watched the thousands of lights shining off the dark sea like gold.

She asked, "Have you ever seen anything so beautiful?"

And I hadn't, but I didn't say so, not then. "I didn't mean anything. About your daughter."

"Tammy. She's eleven. She lives up in Ohio with her father. But she's coming down when school gets out."

And then I said, "Look at the lights on the water."

She leaned her head over slow as lazy smoke and rested it against my shoulder. She whispered, "That's it. That's what I love. That shimmering on the golden sea."

⁓

Tammy stood on the rail of the pier to look closer in my face. "She said that?"

I was still lost back there, so I asked, "What?"

And Clyde asked, "She said that?"

"Oh, yeah. Right off. She couldn't wait for you to come down. She talked about you all the time."

Tammy shook her head and said, "No, about the lights. She said that about the lights? 'The shimmering on the golden sea'?"

"Yeah, that's what she said. Just exactly right."

Tammy looked off over the water. "The shimmering on the golden sea."

I repeated, "The shimmering on the golden sea."

Tammy said, "That's really beautiful."

"Yes, it is," Clyde said.

"The prettiest thing I ever heard anybody say. Like she opened her mouth and a hummingbird flew out. My heart skipped a beat. It really did."

Tammy thought about that and Clyde said, "And that's how he met your mother."

"That's how I met your mother."

And Clyde added, "More or less."

"Yeah," I said. "More or less."

"The big cruise ships are going out tomorrow," Clyde said.

I nudged Tammy. "You hear that? The big cruise ships are going out tomorrow. Want to come up and yell at that Disney ship to throw us a rope?"

Tammy shook her head.

"No?" Clyde asked. "They got all-you-can-eat ice cream. Soft-serve like up at the Circle K. Chocolate or vanilla or mixed.

Free. Twenty-four hours a day. You just walk up and help your-self."

"You just walk up and help yourself?" Tammy asked.

"That's right," Clyde said. "Just walk up and help yourself."

She thought about it for a long moment, then said, "No, I don't think so."

"No, you're right," I said. "We'll all go together. A three-day cruise to the Bahamas. When she comes home."

Tammy kicked gently at the railing, and without looking at me, said, "Not all of us." Then she gave Clyde a little wave and wandered off down the pier.

No, not all of us.

I called after her, "Did you want to ask Clyde for a bait fish? For the kitties?" She just kept on walking.

Clyde nodded his head at Tammy's back and said, "It's not right, is it?" But not like he didn't know the answer. He opened up his cooler and handed me his last three little shiners, and we both looked at them lying in my palm, cold and slick with rainbow sheen, the surprise of death still in their eyes.

I closed my hand and said, "I'll see you later." Then I followed Tammy down the pier, the distance between us not shrinking at all.

7

FRIENDS LIKE THAT

Once we got back down on the beach, I followed ten steps be-hind, listening to her on that broken cell phone. "I don't know why Pere didn't tell me he met Mom on the gambling boat. I don't. I'd tell him something like that. I would. It doesn't seem like they'd have hit it off… I know! But Mom cleaned up good, when she was clean. She used to be really pretty, right?"

It seems like there was a time when I could figure out when I hurt somebody's feelings, but maybe a ten-year drunk and watching Missy spiral down the hole killed that off. Or maybe a little girl's feelings are something too fragile for my calloused hands.

"Remember Grandma had her high school picture on the knick-knack shelf?… No, the one over the sofa. I'd look at it and wonder when it all went bad. Grandma did too, but on the inside. I used to watch her dust it without looking at it, like she wanted to put it away in that box in the closet, but if she did, it would bring bad luck, like she'd curse the future, curse it as sure as Chief Cornstalk cursed Point Pleasant across the river in West Virginia before they killed him, and his restless spirit called up Moth Man, and he made that silver bridge fall down… No, it was for sure the Moth Man. Everybody saw him… I hope it wasn't me. Grandma said it wasn't, but I'm not sure she wasn't just trying to make me feel better. Grandma said she'd cried a million tears trying to figure that one out, trying to figure out that spark of time when her sweet little girl turned into a druggie. And she said a million tears didn't mean a thimble of spit to a druggie."

Grandma had that right.

"I don't know why he didn't trust me with his secret,"

Tammy said. "Maybe he wanted to keep that little piece all for himself. I don't know. And I don't know why we can't all go on the Disney cruise. And I don't know why we never will. And I don't know what's going to keep them together. I just know I'm not enough, not near enough."

Then the wind shifted and carried Tammy's small voice away from me, out over the low waves and blue-green water. After she shut the phone and shoved it down in her pocket, she slowed up enough to let me catch up. The daily duel of banner planes was already underway, and they crisscrossed just offshore. The yellow Piper Cub heading south towed the banner that read, *Go Cart Golf Rock Wall Laser Tag*, and the little old-as-dirt 152 heading north read, *Graphic Body Boards $2.99*. After what happened up in Lake City, it took a while before the sound of a propeller didn't make me break out in a cold sweat.

"Haven't they sold all of those two-ninety-nine body boards by now?" Tammy asked. "They need something else."

And I said, like I do every day, "What's 'golf rock'?"

She was supposed to say, "What's 'wall laser'?" But she didn't. She just smiled a weak smile and shielded her eyes to scan the ocean.

"See any?" I asked. She shook her head. "Maybe they're further out."

"No, not a thing," she said. "And none yesterday either."

"They never stay away long," I said. "Just when you think they're not coming back, there they are."

She dropped her hands and said, "Tell me about the sick one."

"The sick one? Well, the rest of them were out past the sandbar, where they usually are. But the sick one was right there. Couldn't have been in eighteen inches of water. His belly was in the sand and the low shore lap was breaking right across his dorsal. I could've knelt down and stuck my finger in his blowhole from right here. And this other one—"

She interrupted and said, "How do you know it was a boy?"

I looked at her. "I don't. Might've been a girl. Prob'ly was.

So this other one, like a nurse, he keeps coming beside her, nudging her out with his shoulder." I nudged her with my elbow toward the water. "Just enough so she doesn't get beached. But no more. It's like she doesn't have an ounce of energy to do anything but that, and only just that if she's got a little help. And they go along like that for the longest time, him nudging her out just enough to keep her from beaching.

"I walked along with them most of a mile. Then out past the sandbar, in the dark water, the rest of them found a school of fish and began to feed. So they send in a messenger, one that swam straight in for the beach, straight for the sick one and her nurse, and he comes whipping up on the outside of her. And together, the messenger and the nurse, together they work her out to sea, out to where she could feed and get healthy."

Tammy thought about it for a minute, glancing out to the dark water. "Did that really happen?"

"Hand to God. Word for word. The strangest thing I have ever seen in the animal kingdom, and I once saw a Rottweiler commit suicide. Looked me dead in the eye, then jumped the guardrail and took a sixty-foot header into the Indian River."

She started walking on her heels, poking circles in the wet sand, then looked back out to the ocean and said, "You think she made it?"

"Friends like that, what do you think?"

We walked along in silence until we came to the wooden steps of Cherie Down Park. Tammy looked away and said, "Hummingbirds have flown out of her mouth before, you know. Stuff like that 'shimmering on the golden sea.' One time she saw some geese, real early in the morning, on her way back home from somewhere. We call them Canadian geese up in Ohio, but Doris says they're really called Canada geese, but either way, she saw a bunch of them flying low in the first light of dawn. She said, 'I watched them till you couldn't see nothing but the silver on the tips of their wings.' She said that, real slow and dreamy. I don't know, maybe she was high."

I opened my hand to show her the three little fish.

She smiled."One for each kitty." She picked them up by the tail one at a time, lining them up along her palm. Then she ran for the steps, her feet squeaking in the dry sand.

"Thank Clyde when you see him," I yelled after her.

And she called back, "I will."

The cats were on the dune crossover waiting for her, just like they'd made a plan. She did a weird little dance, shuffling backwards in a tight circle, trying to herd two away while she fed one a fish. When I made it to the crossover, I saw the new homeless guy hunched down behind the bushes between the dunes. He was watching her, one hand working at the crotch of his pants. I pretended not to see him and helped Tammy sort out the cats.

Tammy said, "Watch Flopsy and Mopsy!" They just snap at theirs enough times to choke 'em down."

And they did, the way cats'll do, working their jaws wide with their eyes near shut.

"It looks like they got caramel apple stuck in their back teeth but no finger to dig it out with," she said. "But Cottontail, he puts everything on the ground to eat it and I don't know why."

Cottontail took his little baitfish and backed up a few steps before he set it down to work on it, and I helped Tammy keep Flopsy and Mopsy from trying to steal what wasn't theirs.

She said, "Miriam the Cat Lady said he does that with the dry food she brings so I'll have to tell her he does it with everything."

As we crossed through the parking lot, I said, "Cat Lady won't like it."

"Miriam? Miriam won't care. Miriam loves kitties."

"I don't know how happy she'll be when they're too fat and happy to eat the supper she brings."

"You ever notice she always wears long-sleeves?" Tammy asked. "Even in this heat? Shorts and long-sleeves." She pursed her lips and shook her head from side to side, like it was a riddle she might not ever figure out.

After we crossed back over the beach road, we stopped

at the pink and blue access lid next to the sidewalk. Duane's Chevy was backed into their yard up the street. Tammy looked from the access lid to Duane's Chevy and back again. She said, "Grandma got Buddy at the Dollar General and he had a mane and tail you could comb and a horn that shone rainbow colors depending on how the light hit it, and it used to be that if you pressed his left front hoof, he'd neigh like a horse, even though I wasn't sure unicorns neighed until the battery died." She looked up the street. "Duane kind of reminds me of Dad, you know. Not like he's bad or anything, just like he's all half-assed and hard luck and dumb enough to think the bottle is going to fix any of that."

Yeah, like I didn't know about being half-assed and bad luck, like I didn't know about being dumb enough to think the bottle might fix it. But I just nodded.

"You should have brought Buddy down in that bag of clothes," I said. She had a black trash bag half full when we picked her up at the bus station.

"I didn't pack that bag," she said. "Dad did. If I'd a packed it, it might've had clean clothes in it. And another pair of shoes. I don't know what he told the school. Maybe it got too hard for him to hide his semi from the Repo Man with me hanging around his neck. He just woke me up one morning and that trash bag was already knotted by the door. He said, 'You're going down to your mom's for the summer.' I didn't believe him, but he was still drunk or hungover or both. I mean, Mom talked about it a bunch of times, but I can't say as I ever really let myself believe it. I didn't get to say goodbye to Becky or Tommy Pafford or even Jimmy the Retard, and when I got here and dumped out that bag, all the clothes were dirty. Buddy's still in Ohio, probably still tangled up in the sheets if I know Dad. Or if he took off and the bank already took the house, Buddy's under a mountain of garbage at that dump south of town."

When we got up to the condo, there was a three-foot section of palm trunk on the ground and a thin cord running from Duane's bumper to the trunk left standing. He was in the truck revving the engine, and Pearl was on the little concrete stoop with her arms folded.

Pearl yelled, "Is that my good clothesline?"

Duane eased out the clutch and the line pulled taut. Then half his bumper folded back and when the truck lurched forward, the line snapped.

Tammy whispered, "Like you couldn't see that coming."

Pearl went inside and slammed the door and Duane just drove off, the rusty bumper sticking straight out behind him like a possum's tail.

"Run inside and get a list together for Publix. I'm going to grab the hammer and run back and pound that nail down."

"We could do it after lunch," she said.

"No, we'll go see Doris. I want to take care of it while I'm thinking about it. We need big marshmallows."

"Is it that hammer that looks like a tomahawk?" she asked.

"Yeah, it's a sheetrock hammer. For drywall." It wasn't the right hammer, or maybe it was, but it was the only one I had left.

"We watched a movie in history class about Indians and pioneers, and this one mean Indian had a tomahawk hidden in his blanket. and when he let it slide down through his hand it was scarier than when he hit the soldier in the head with it."

After she went inside, I opened up the garage and got my old sheetrock hammer with the two-inch blade on the back. When I came out of the garage, Tammy called to me from her bedroom window upstairs. "Tampon John, he sleeps in the bushes right near that sticking up nail."

I wasn't sure what she meant, but I nodded and waved before I walked off down the street. I watched Tampon John wake up one day, and it seems like it takes him a while to figure out where he is. And even when he figures it out, it's not like he's in the same place as the rest of us.

I walked on over to Cherie Down Park and found that nail sticking up on the dune crossover. It only took one whack to drive it back down, but you can't hit a nail just once, so I hit it again. Tampon John didn't pop up like a whack-a-mole, so I figured he was in another bum nest further down the beach. I found the new one laid out on the picnic table under the shelter, a Tall Boy wrapped tight in a brown paper bag tucked between his legs. I sat on the bench and tapped lightly on the table with the hammer until he opened his bloodshot eyes.

I said, "Wake up, Crap Pants. It's moving day."

8

GOLDEN RAYS

Tammy wanted to go by Cocoa Beach Pier on our way to Publix. It's only a couple of blocks out of the way and it seemed like a better plan to do it when we weren't hauling bags of groceries. Cocoa Beach Pier is an old-school wooden pier, with bars and shops and restaurants tacked along it out into the water, not like the empty metal fishing pier up at the jetty. It looks like it's ready to fall into a pile of rotten lumber, but it's looked like that ever since I've been down here and it's probably looked like that the last fifty years. There's always one of a couple of different guys in the parking lot handing out brochures for the resort condos, trying to sign the tourists up for a free dinner and a presentation. The one today looked like an ex-car salesman that couldn't get ahead of his coke problem, and they've all learned not to waste their breath or their full-color brochures on me and Tammy.

I convinced her to wear Missy's old flip-flops, not because Publix enforces the 'no shoes, no shirt' policy, hardly anyone does down here, but for the walk down. The high tide mark of broken beer bottles tossed by college assholes gets thicker the closer you get to Cocoa proper. I was one of those assholes for half a semester at Virginia Tech in Blacksburg because my dad got some benefits for going to 'Nam one too many times. He was so old by the time he had me, I think his dick was the only thing that still worked. A counselor told me my "talents lay elsewhere," which was code for "Pack your shit." Apparently, drinking, fighting, and fucking were not areas of study in which they offered degrees, which surprised the hell out of me because I thought that's what college was all about. And it was too bad because while I hadn't missed a single chance at those three, I seemed to have missed every other class. "I like Greyhounds and breeding," I said. "How 'bout a major in Animal Husbandry and a minor in Phys Ed?" But the counselor didn't know a Greyhound was my favorite drink back then, vodka and grapefruit juice, so she didn't get the joke. I liked my freshman English teacher, and when I told him I was leaving, he said, "You're smart. It just remains to be seen whether you're smart enough to get your head out of your ass." Then he cleaned his eyeglasses with a real cloth handkerchief before he said, "I'm guessing that's not the first time you've heard that." Not the first, or the last either.

Tammy scuffed the oversized pink sandals along the thin layer of sand covering the concrete lot. She said, "Don't you love that sound? I do."

I steered Tammy over to my left, and we walked up the plank ramp, past the usual creeps camped out on bar stools along the railing to the right, nursing Coronas with lime and staring at the teenaged girls playing volleyball down on the beach. Or maybe they're watching the teenaged boys. It's hard to say. There's a gift shop on the left, and as we passed by the glass door, I gave the Russian girl behind the counter the one-fingered salute and yelled, "Oxana! You're number one!"

She flipped me off with both hands, her fake nails flashing purple, without ever looking up from her magazine.

"Keep that up," Tammy said, "and you're going to get us in trouble. It wasn't much of a necklace anyway."

"Not the point. If you're going to sell something, you ought to stand behind it. If you're going to sell crap, you best figure folks aren't going to be too happy about it."

It was a shark tooth necklace, with a tooth not much bigger than a house cat's. Tammy liked it well enough, and it was all we could afford the first time I brought her here. That very next morning, after she fixed my thermos full of coffee for work, she went upstairs to get a shower and I heard the black beads bouncing off the sheet linoleum like so many ball bearings. She'd yelled, "Pete!" and by the time I made it up the stairs, she was standing in the open doorway of the bathroom in frayed underwear, with a handful of loose beads cupped in her hands like a baby bird.

We took it back that afternoon but nothing I said would convince Oxana to give Tammy a new one or refund our money. She finally threatened to call Brevard's finest, and I threatened to call INS and that's how we arrived at our current Mexican standoff.

We cut through the enclosed hallway that runs sideways between two restaurants, past a burnt-red tourist woman waiting for the bathroom. When we got out the other side, Tammy said, "She'll be hurting tonight."

There's a long, open run of pier for the fishermen out over the water, with a thatched tiki bar at the far end. I think they always charged to fish, but it used to be free just to walk out and see the sights. Now you have to pay a buck. Standing Bear was manning the little blue-striped admission tent. He's a Seminole, and must be close to six foot, six. Tammy says that standing in that little tent, he looks like pictures of the guards in front of Buckingham Palace, except that he's as big as they are with their fur hats on. He hunched down to look out from under the rolled-up plastic curtains. I put two dollars up on the counter and he waved it away, like he always does if the boss isn't around, and nodded us through.

Tammy said, "Thanks, Mr. Bear." And he nodded again.

A few day drinkers were keeping the barmaid company out at the tiki bar, and one fisherman had three rods going. There's a three-foot-high plastic tiki statue with flashing orange eyes behind the bar. Tammy walked two fingers along the railing and watched the water get a deeper blue-green.

I asked, "Any manatees?"

"They like the rivers and canals," she said. "Shallow water, but not this rough stuff along the beach."

I didn't know that, and I said, "Guess that's why we never see any out here. How 'bout dolphins?"

"No, not yet," she said, "but they usually like it a little further out."

I said, "We're batting a thousand."

"Not even many surfers today," she said.

A few were bobbing in the gentle swell, hoping against hope for a decent wave. The bottom half of the wooden pilings, the part down in the salt water, are wrapped in concrete blankets like giant corn dogs. And despite big red and white signs that read, SURFERS STAY 200 ft FROM PIER, the whole point seems to be to surf through, in, and around the pilings. A peroxide blonde, who looked like she ought to be wearing out the shocks on the back of a Harley, was holding down a weathered bench and sunning her tattoos. A chubby girl, probably Tammy's age but three times bigger, stood behind the bench and passed her hands slowly in front of the woman's closed eyes.

"Goddamn it, Angel," the woman yelled. "Stop blocking my sun."

"'Goddamn it, Angel,'" Tammy whispered with a giggle. "That's funny."

The woman yelled, "Ray, will you do something?"

Ray must have been one of the bar flies or the fisherman, but he wasn't speaking up.

Tammy stopped and pointed down at the water. "Look at that."

There were six stingrays, each maybe two feet across, gliding easily along in formation. Tammy stood up on the middle rail so she could see better. "They look like sheets of gold," she said. And they did, like squares of some heavy gold fabric, lined up like diamonds, their edges curling in the current. "They look like slow-motion Tinker Bell, if she flew underwater."

I couldn't remember who Tinker Bell was, but before I had a chance to ask, she said, "Where do you suppose they're going?"

And just then they banked, headed out to sea, and then came back around in a lazy circle.

Standing Bear's shadow blocked out the sun, and he said, "I'm supposed to tell you she can't stand up on the rail like that. She don't have to get down or nothing, but if somebody was to ask, I told you so." Then he nodded at me and I nodded back.

Tammy squinted at him and said, "What are they?"

Standing Bear shrugged. "Stingrays. Some people call them golden rays. Most people call them cownose rays. Depends."

Tammy pulled her mouth to one side. "They'd don't look much like the cows we have in Ohio."

"The front of 'em, looks like a cow's nose," Standing Bear said. "There's bullnose rays too. But not like cows and bulls. Not like the bullnose are the boys and the cownose are the girls. There's girl bullnose and boy cownose. If you understand my meaning."

"I know where calves come from," Tammy said, "if that's what you're worried about. You mean they're different species."

He frowned. "Yeah. That's the short path."

"I thought they hung around under the sand in the shallows waiting to get stepped on," I said.

He shook his head. "No, these are flying rays."

Tammy said, "It does. It looks just like they're flying."

The three of us watched them ride the currents.

Tammy shook her head and said, "I wish I could do that."

Standing Bear asked, "You can't swim?"

Tammy frowned at him. "Yeah, I can swim. I'm a good swimmer. But I can't fly."

She's really not that good a swimmer, but she never goes out very far either. The rule is she can't swim unless I'm right there watching. If she ever gets in trouble, I know I can get her out because I may not swim pretty, but I can get where I need to no matter how long it takes.

She watched the rays. "Do you have the flying dream?" she asked. "The one where you just kind of lean forward and your feet float up? And you just glide along, slow as walking, about so high?" She held one hand up to her skinny shoulder. "I used to have it all the time, and I was always at school, in that long hall between the office and the cafegymtorium. I'd just start floating along and nobody even notices, and Becky's still talking my ear off about some new boy like I'm not lighter than air, like I'm not just a soap bubble before it pops."

"Yeah, I've had dreams like that," I said. "But Becky's not in them."

And Standing Bear said, "She's not in mine neither."

Tammy gave me a half-smile, but never took her eyes off the rays.

I always wanted to fly, that's one reason I ended up in Florida. My dad was a pilot for the army, not one of the hot-shot navy fighter jocks, and flew a low 'n slow Cessna O-1E Bird Dog not much bigger than the banner planes. But he got clipped by a medevac chopper and didn't get rid of his last Willie Pete rocket before he hit hard. He put his head through the plexiglass windshield and blacked out for a minute during the fire, but he walked away from it, which is something. He had some burns on his right side so he was never without a shirt in the summer, and I guess he got a Purple Heart because it says so on his gravestone, but I never saw it.

I didn't have the heart to tell Tammy that real flying wasn't much like the flying dream, especially in a small plane. I got some hours in up in Lake City. It's noisy, and you can feel the engine in your hands and feet and even up through your seat. You can smell the oil in the exhaust, and it's always too hot or too cold, but I used to think it was the most fun you could have with your pants on before the accident. Hell, up in Virginia I'd spot for a guy scoping his pot plants over the border in Kentucky just to go up.

Out next to the tiki bar, the fisherman started yelling, his rod bent almost double. We watched him fight whatever took his bait.

Tammy turned to Standing Bear and asked, "What's that tiki man mean?"

Standing Bear's eyes shifted ever so slightly, from the fisherman to the flashing eyes of the tiki. He said, "Mean? It don't mean nothing. Just a tacky totem for the tourists."

Tammy thought about that, then said, "But they meant something to someone, didn't they? Like gods and spirits? A long time ago?"

"Yeah, I guess," he said. "Maybe not so long ago. But not us."

I wasn't sure which "us" he was talking about, but I know it didn't matter. The fisherman dipped the end of his rod and worked the reel until a cownose ray broke the surface. It wasn't gold at all, but putty-colored on the top, like the rubbing compound I used to use up at the marina, and white on the belly.

Tammy frowned. "Is that one? It's not gold at all."

Standing Bear pointed the fingers of both hands at the ocean, and said, "The sun's rays, they hit the water and make them gold."

"Refraction?" Tammy asked.

He frowned with his eyebrows pinched close. "You mean reflection? I don't think so. But maybe."

The chubby girl stood next the fisherman, looking over the rail at the dangling ray. She yelled, "Momma! Come looky here! Daddy caught him a stingray."

The peroxide blonde shrieked and jumped up from her bench. "Angel, come away from there!" she yelled. "Ray! Ray! Cut it loose! You'll get stabbed through the heart like that alligator guy on the TV."

Ray the fisherman leaned his pole against the railing and held the line, then looked over the rail at the dangling ray. He said, "I don't know that this one's big enough to shoot me in the heart, honey."

Honey the peroxide blond stood at a distance, holding Angel under one heavily tattooed arm. She yelled, "I bet he told his wife the same thing."

Ray gave the line a little tug and watched the ray twirl putty and white. He sighed. "Damn if that ain't a brand-new tandem bottom drop leader rig." Then he cut the line with a black-handled folding knife. The cownose ray dropped back into the ocean, trailing loose spirals of monofilament catching the sun. The six down by us twitched at the splash.

Standing Bear shook his head in disgust. "If you aren't going to eat it, at least get the hook out."

"Eat it?" I asked. "I've never been that hungry."

Standing Bear shrugged. "You can eat the wings."

"*You* can eat the wings," Tammy said.

Standing Bear shrugged again. "I bet when an Indian told the pilgrims they could eat lobster, they said the same thing."

Tammy pointed and whispered, "Holy Christ!"

From the darkness of the deep water, like ghosts of gold, more cownose rays drifted up, probably fifty all told, and joined the others. We watched them in silence, carving lazy *S*s out toward the cape, until we couldn't tell them from the sunbeams off the water.

Tammy leaned her head against my arm like she was too tired to hold it up, and said, "What's a group of rays called? Is it a pod? Or a school?"

I didn't have any idea, but Standing Bear said, "A school." And he sounded like he knew.

9

BLUE HAWAII

We got a ha-ha cart. We didn't know it was a ha-ha cart when we wrestled it from the corral at Publix, but we figured it out pretty quick. Tammy stood backwards on the tubing around the low shelf and hooked her arms behind her into the basket. As we rolled across the parking lot, it rattled up and down from a missing chunk of rubber on one wheel.

She looked back at me over her shoulder and let her head wobble loose in time with the wheel. "Pere, they got us again."

I asked, "Is this like your flying dream?"

She hung her head. "No, not much."

"How do you suppose they know we're coming?" I aimed for the long line of propane grills chained one to another, and as the entrance doors slid apart, I said, "You ready?"

"Oh, yeah," she said.

I rolled us into the cool fog of air conditioning and snaked through the tall buckets of bright flowers at the edge of Produce. Goose bumps came up on the backs of her arms.

She shuddered and said, "That's the ticket." She held the top of the basket with both hands and leaned out far in front of the cart, looking for all the world like a hood ornament on some old, expensive car. She whispered, "Aisle eight."

I slowed up and said, "Watch it there, Danger Ranger. Want any bananas?"

She considered the bananas, all looking a few days too old already. "We got oranges."

"True enough. Oranges we got."

She whispered, "Eight! Eight! Eight!"

Aisle eight used to be the cookie aisle, but then they rearranged everything a couple of weeks ago and now it's candy on one side and feminine hygiene products as far as the eye can see down the other. But the draw of aisle eight isn't the candy, but the rolling, uneven floor, probably from a cracked slab shifting in the sand, badly repaired and tiled over with commercial linoleum. We found it on our first trip, and now pushing her down the empty aisle at breakneck speed on the way to see the Cookie Lady is the start of our Publix ritual. I waited at our end because Lardass was sorting through the chocolates. She seems to be here every time we are, curtained in tropical flowers, with her saddlebags overflowing her little three-wheeled electric scooter and one of those aluminum grabbers to reach things on the high shelves. Sometimes we see her out in the parking lot in a blue-sign spot. She backed down the aisle, rolling bags of chocolate-covered everythings between her thick fingers, beeping like a garbage truck all the while.

"Good thing we got nowhere to be," I said.

Tammy straightened back up. She looked from one side to the other and shook her head. "I don't know, Pere. Candy and Kotex don't seem right."

Lardass beeped her way through the chocolate-covered peanuts, the chocolate-covered raisins, the bridge mix, and seemed to settle on the turtles.

I said, "Jesus Christ. I can feel myself growing old."

"Shhh. Don't be mean."

Lardass turned her head around as far as the donut of neck fat would let her, then she jerked the little handle bar around to face us. She smiled. "I'm sorry. Am I in your way?"

I wanted to tell her that she was in my way and everybody else's, that she was in her own way, that I didn't know how she rated a wheelchair sticker just because she couldn't put her fork down, that if I was an old soldier who lost a leg to a shit-dipped punji stick, I'd be pretty goddamn pissed if I saw her offloading in the last handicapped spot. I wanted to tell her that if you need a custom van with a forklift, an electric scooter, and an aluminum grabber just to haul your fat-ass around the grocery store, maybe the grocery store isn't where you need to be. Instead, I just waved one arm, like I used to at all the retirees that bought too big at an Indiana boat show and still thought they had a chance of getting it in the water without me.

As she hummed by, Tammy smiled at her and said, "I like your dress."

Lardass stopped and smiled up at Tammy hanging off the cart. "Well, aren't you sweet? I like your sandals. They've got pink flowers too. Are they your momma's?"

I looked through the wire mesh of the cart at the dirty flip-flops two inches too big.

Tammy nodded, then pointed at the dress. "It's Hawaiian, isn't it?"

Lardass looked at her lap and said, "Well, I suppose it is."

"It's a mu'umu'u," Tammy said.

And Lardass said, "You're right! It's a moo-moo! I just love them."

Tammy squinted one eye at her. "Know how it's spelled?"

"Like a moo cow?"

Tammy smiled. "No. That's what everybody thinks. M-o-o, or m-u-u. But it's m-u, apostrophe, u-m-u, and another apostrophe, and one more u. Mu'umu'u, it means 'cut-off' in Hawaiian."

Lardass considered the vast expanse of material. "Cut-off? I don't think they cut much off this one."

Tammy hung out from the cart at arms' length. "It's a shorter version of another kind of dress, a dressier dress. That starts with an *h*."

Lardass looked at Tammy and said what I was thinking. "How'd you get so smart?"

Tammy pulled herself upright and shrugged her shoulders. "I think I'd like Hawaii."

Lardass smiled weakly and petted the handle bar of her scooter like a cat. "I think I'd like Hawaii too," she said. "But I guess central Florida is as close as I'll ever get."

Tammy turned to her and said, "They use the same word if you lose your leg. Mu'umu'u."

Looking for all the world like she might cry, Lardass asked quietly, "Like to diabetes?" And she said it like *die-a-beat-us.*

Tammy shrugged. "I guess." Then she turned to me and said, "Let's go, Pere. Before all of the free cookies are gone."

10

COOKIE LADY

The broken wheel made the ride down aisle eight more exciting than usual, like a car with one tire badly out of balance getting up to speed. Tammy opened her mouth and said, "Ah," the whole way, the sound wavering like when she talks into the fan at the condo. We swerved to a stop in front of the bakery case and Tammy frowned at the paper plate full of crumbs sitting on top.

She said, "I think they were chocolate chips, or maybe even sugar cookies."

Sugar cookies are her favorite. I said, "Free cookies never last long."

She pulled her mouth to one side and said, "You said a mouthful there."

"Lardass back there probably ate 'em all," I said. "And that grabber, she's got it moving so fast it looks like a robotic arm spot welding a new car on the line." I held my hands flat and straight and pretended to throw cookies in my mouth as fast as I could.

"Don't be mean," Tammy said. "She can't help it."

"She might be able to help it if she stayed out of aisle eight." I looked over the case at the stainless work tables and ovens. "You see the Cookie Lady? Maybe she's on break. Let's do our shopping and check back."

Tammy shifted her clumsy sandals on the chrome bar to turn around to face me. It's a point of pride for her to never actually touch the floor in Publix. "I think when they're gone, they're gone," she said.

I turned toward the dairy case and asked her, "How do you come to know so much about Hawaii?"

"The internet," she said. "When Doris and me were finding out why all the coconut palms are dying. We went from one thing to another and suddenly we're in Hawaii. You know, sometimes you just end up somewhere and you're not even sure how you got there."

I wanted to tell her she'd just described most of my adult life, but it'd probably sound more sad than funny so I didn't. Not wasting time so much as killing it, day after day after day, until suddenly it's ten years later and everybody's dead and all you've done since getting kicked out of college is work one shitty job after another, slowly working south for no particular reason. Until I met Missy, I just figured I'd eventually fall off the tip of Florida into the sea and get run over by a '53 Ford Customline jerry-built into a boat filled with four hundred Cubans.

When I stopped in front of the milk, she said, "Pere, It's a hundred degrees out there. Don't get the milk first."

"What's it matter?" I said. "It's cold enough to hang meat in here."

Tammy let her head fall forward and shook it sadly from side to side. "I don't know how many times I've said this before—canned goods first, then your dry goods and perishables, *then* your meat, dairy, and frozen foods."

"Did your mom teach you that?" I asked.

She barked a laugh. "No, she'd get the milk first too. Grandma Sue."

"Sounds like Grandma Sue had a system."

She smiled. "Yeah, Grandma Sue had a system for everything," she said. "There's a right way and a wrong way and it doesn't cost a thing to do it the right way. As a matter of fact, it usually costs you more in the long run if you try to half-ass it."

I wish I'd been smart enough to listen when somebody tried to tell me that at her age. It might've changed more than I had the heart to think about. Grandma Sue was Missy's ex-mother-in-law, and Tammy and her dad were living with her until late last year when she died in her sleep still holding the remote. I'm betting the modular home dealer called the note and that's why

Tammy got pushed on a bus to Florida. He couldn't even keep up the payments on his semi. Missy cried when Grandma Sue died but couldn't get off work to go up for the funeral. She'd said that before Tammy came along, Sue was the best part of that marriage.

A young mother, pimpled and pierced, wheeled past us. The baby, sitting on the green flap of the little folding shelf, had fake diamond studs in her ears and was suckling on the metal-ringed end of a plastic-wrapped tube of breakfast sausage.

Tammy made a face and whispered, "She knows that's raw, right?"

"Pork baby," I whispered back.

I laughed but Tammy didn't. I guess even a pork baby was better than no baby at all.

She shook her head. "Who'd poke holes in a baby's ears?"

"Good question," I said—another one of the ten million I didn't have an answer to.

Tammy put her face down in the cart and said, "Seems like if you were lucky enough to have a baby, you'd want to make sure they didn't get hurt, not hurt them."

I was going to use Clyde's line about how you need a license to fish, but not to have kids, but today wasn't the day, so I just said, "Okay, what should we get first?"

She pointed behind me. "Corn."

We stood in front of shelves and shelves of canned vegetables and considered all of the different kinds of store-brand corn: creamed corn, yellow corn, white corn, yellow and white mixed corn, yellow hominy and white hominy. It took her some explaining to convince me that hominy was really corn. We decided on mixed, but not until she figured out whether it was any cheaper to buy one can of each and mix them ourselves at home.

I looked down the aisle and said, "Baked beans? We could make beanie wienie."

She raised her eyebrows at me. "Beanie wienie?"

"Don't tell me they don't have beanie wienie up in Ohio.

You take baked beans and slice up a hot dog in them? Maybe a little chopped onion."

She looked disappointed. "Oh. Franks and beans."

"Okay, franks and beans," I said.

"I don't know, Pere. You know beans make you a little…" Then she fanned one hand in front of her nose.

I shrugged. "They're beans."

She looked down the aisle for a long moment, then said, "What the heck. Let's get some. I'll cook you beanie wienie."

We turned down the next aisle to get toilet paper. She drug her fingers lightly along the rolls of paper towels, and as they changed over to blocks of dinner napkins, she said, "Are these sanitary?"

"What?"

"Are these sanitary?" she repeated.

"I'm not sure what you're asking," I said.

She poked the packages with one finger as we rolled by. "Sanitary? Are these sanitary napkins?"

I slowed down and said, "Uh, these are napkins. And I guess they might be sanitary. But these aren't sanitary napkins." She looked at me like I didn't know what in the hell I was talking about, which I really didn't. "Sanitary napkins are woman-problem things. Aisle eight stuff. I think they call them something else."

"Tampons?" she said, glancing at me. "Are you talking about tampons?"

I didn't think I was. I said, "No, I don't think so. They're something else. But for the same thing. You said they didn't belong in the same aisle with the candy."

"Kotex?" she asked.

I nodded.

She looked concerned and asked, " Really? I don't think so."

"I don't know," I said. "Maybe you prob'ly ought to ask your mom when she calls."

"Is she still going to call? On Sunday?"

"I don't see why not."

"I thought since she called last night…"

"She'll call," I said.

"But isn't she in the infirmary?" Tammy asked. "Maybe they won't let her call from the infirmary."

I hadn't thought of that, but I said, "She'll call."

Tammy clutched her fingers through the front bars of the basket. "I guess I could ask Doris."

"Either one."

She looked down and said, "Maybe Mom's using them right now. For the bleeding. Do you think she's bleeding?"

I just shook my head, because if I let myself think about it, she probably was, but I didn't want to think about it.

Tammy one-handed a six pack of toilet paper into the cart as we wheeled by. "Just once, I'd like to get the good stuff. You know the toilet paper in Vera's bathroom? It's got ripples and lotion and layers and feels like a towel fresh from the dryer."

That sounded pretty good, and I said, "You spend an awful lot of time thinking about nice toilet paper, don't you? You think that Becky girl knows you were just friends with her because you liked taking a dump at her house?"

"That's not true," she said. "And don't you know you shouldn't poop at other folks' houses unless you just can't help it?"

I looked at her like she's just said the craziest thing I ever heard. "Who filled your head with that nonsense? That's *all* I do at other folks' houses."

When we wheeled out of the far end of the aisle, Cookie Lady was waving at us from behind the bakery case. "C'mere," she yelled, holding up a sugar cookie in a little square of waxed paper.

I yelled back, "Where you been?"

"Watching my grandbabies," she said. "So my girl and Useless could go up to Atlanta."

I think Useless is her son-in-law, or maybe just the father of her daughter's newest baby. She reached across the case, and Tammy leaned over its arched glass front to take the cookie.

"There you go, sweetie," the Cookie Lady said. "Don't you ever get off that cart?"

"Not if I can help it."

"I hid that away 'cause I thought you might be in to see me. Just had a feeling."

Tammy smiled. "Thanks."

"You're welcome." The Cookie Lady turned to me and said, "That one in the electric cart? She can jump up quick enough for a couple half dozen free cookies."

"I believe it. What's in Atlanta?"

Cookie Lady made a face like she'd stepped in something. "A bunch of thumpity-thumping rap music, I guess. Seems to me like if he can drive eight hours to a rap concert and buy the tickets, maybe he could find some child support."

"You couldn't pay me to go to Atlanta," I said. "I was there once and didn't leave anything."

Cookie Lady snapped two clear plastic gloves from a dispenser mounted on the wall. She rubbed one between her thumbs and blew in it to open it up. She said, "I always thought they should give Sherman another whack at it myself."

11

ALPHA-MEGA-TURD

On the way back from Publix, we stopped every half block so Tammy could rearrange the bags she was carrying. I had the milk and hot dogs, the baloney and fish sticks, the cheese puffs, beans, and corn. She had the bread, eggs, and marshmallows in one bag, and the toilet paper in the other.

Tammy asked, "When were *you* in Atlanta?"

I thought about it. "It's been a few years back. I worked at a garage in Monticello, a little south."

She scrunched one eye at me. "Monticello? That's in Virginia, not Georgia. We studied it in school and the beds were really small."

I shook my head and said, "The one I was at was in Georgia." I was drunk the whole time I was there, but I do remember what state it's in.

"Thomas Jefferson?" she asked. "Founding Father? Author of the Declaration of Independence? That's Virginia. I bet you a million bucks."

"Even if you had a million bucks, which you don't, I wouldn't take your money. Monticello, Georgia—the county seat of Jasper County!"

She just said, "Oh."

I didn't tell her that Monticello's main claim to fame was that when the rest of the country was driving Model Ts and worrying about WWI, they lynched a whole Black family including two girls just over some moonshine. That, and some country star you don't even care ran to pork because she has such a pretty face. I mostly did tires and oil changes, batteries and mufflers—anything that nobody gave a shit whether I was sober or ASE certified. That's where I met my friend Lee, and when he ended up down in Lake City, I went on further south for another two dollars an hour.

I didn't want her to feel dumb so I said, "It's probably like Washington or Hamilton. There's one, big or small, in every county in every state this side of the Mississippi. And I'm like that Johnny Cash song, 'I've been everywhere, man.'"

She smiled. "Grandma Sue *loved* Johnny Cash."

"'A Boy Named Sue'?"

"Well, duh. Because—"

I jumped in and said, "Because she was a boy?"

"No, she wasn't a boy," Tammy giggled and said. "Because her name was Sue. And 'Dirty Old Egg Sucking Dog,' 'cause she *had* an old egg-sucking dog named Jasper, and he smelled all the time, even right after he had a bath. Then Dad had to take him out in the woods and shoot him 'cause he was puking up blood. Dad said he buried him, but I never saw him with a shovel so I didn't go back in *those* woods."

That sounded about like her dad from everything I'd heard from Missy. Why do a good job when you don't have to?

Then Tammy said, "But she really loved the love songs, like 'Ring of Fire,' and 'I Walk the Line.' She could sing along and she had a really pretty voice."

"Hell, anybody don't like those songs has something wrong with their brain."

"I like 'Hurt,' even though he didn't write it." She asked me, "Have you seen the video?"

I pretended to think about it and said, "No, I don't think so."

"It makes you cry. He's old and sad and there's all these photos from when he was young and happy and it makes me think of Grandma." She thought about that sad thing, or something very much like it, and finally said, "I'll show it to you. On the computer. When we go see Doris."

I stopped to rearrange the bags I was carrying and give her a chance to catch her breath.

After a moment of rubbing at her skinny shoulders with her hands crossed against her chest, she said, "I don't know, Pere.

A couple years at the wrong Monticello don't seem like you've been *every*where."

"I worked up by you for a couple summers, over in Cincinnati, at that big swimming pool east of town,."

She hung her mouth open for a minute, "*You* worked at Coney Island? I been there, with Becky, on a little blue bus from her church."

I frowned. "Coney Island? Was it called Coney Island? I thought that's in New York."

"Yeah, it's called Coney Island," she said, "like the one in New York. You're probably thinking of Sunlite Pool. They call the pool Sunlite Pool."

"That's right! Sunlite Pool. 'World's largest recirculating pool!' Or something like that. I spent a couple summers fishing turds out of there and hosing vomit off the concrete walk around it. What is it with you kids crapping in the pool? Who knows? I might've fished out one of your floaters."

"I didn't poop in the pool! It was just last summer."

"You want to hear something nasty?" I asked.

"Something *else* nasty? I don't think so."

"Okay, so those lifeguards? They spent one whole summer having a giant turd contest."

She made the face I thought she'd make.

"No lie. When someone pinched a contender, they had some super secret announcement they'd make over the PA, like, 'Would all available guards and porters report to the Men's Locker room for a 6-19.' And everyone would have to go judge."

She wrinkled her nose up in disgust. "That is the grossest thing I have *ever* heard. Who'd think of something like that?"

"I couldn't tell you," I said. "All I know is a guard named Tim won hands down with one that stood up out of the bowl. He called it Alpha-Mega-Turd and said they should make a movie about it attacking Tokyo."

She closed her eyes and stuck her tongue out between her teeth and shook her head from side to side.

"That's the same face that stupid cat makes," I said.

"Cottontail? After he cleans himself?"

"Well, if you mean after he licks his own butt, yeah."

She nodded and said, "Yeah, he looks like, 'Why'd I do *that*? Now I got poop tongue.'"

"Alpha-Mega-Turd's a true story," I said. "Shoveling horse hockey at the racetrack next door wasn't near as gross as that place."

"River Downs? You worked there too? It's called River Downs. Dad used to lose his paycheck there now and again." Then she shook her head like she'd had her bell rung and said, "What's wrong with guys?"

"I couldn't begin to tell you, but lifeguard Tim wore a T-shirt the rest of the summer that said 'Go Big or Go Home,' and we were the only ones that knew what it meant. You know what else? He's the only guy I ever met that used rubbing alcohol as cologne. Thought girls would think he was a doctor."

"I bet Misty smelled a lot of rubbing alcohol," she said, fiddling with her Publix bags. "Did she see a doctor?"

I told her a doctor came by, but I didn't bother to tell her it didn't matter because it was all already gone and done by then. He probably wouldn't be back. And even though I couldn't remember the last time I was in a hospital, I suddenly couldn't get that hospital smell out of my head.

"Come to think of it, we used to use 100 octane up at the airport in Lake City, to get grease off our hands. It worked great but it turned the top layer of your skin dead white."

Her eyes went big and she said, "You worked at an airport too? Parking big jets with those orange sticks and earphones? Driving those little tractors around with peoples' luggage going all around the world?"

I didn't want to tell her it was all a lot more low-rent than that—just small planes and a few business jets, a helicopter once in a while, that there were some old orange sticks so dirty we just used our hands and our boss was too ignorant to buy earphones and the trucks didn't even have ground clips until my best friend Lee and I raised a stink about it. But I didn't want to think about that, because that day was a lot like today, a hell of a lot more blood, but it meant less. And before last night, I wouldn't have thought that was possible.

12

MICHIGAN LIZARDS

We cut through the elementary schoolyard behind our street, and I stopped by the playground swings. Since Missy went away, I'd forgotten how much toilet paper a girl can go through.

I set my bags down. "Break time." When Tammy set hers down, I said, "I swear we just bought toilet paper."

"We couldn't have *just* bought some," she said. "That stack of McDonald's napkins has been sitting on the toilet tank for a week."

She eyeballed the swings and I said, "Free stack of toilet paper with every purchase. How do you girls go through so much toilet paper?"

She raised her eyebrows and said, "Jeez, Pere. I don't know. Do we have to talk about it?"

"Ask your mom," I said. "She could make a roll disappear like that." I snapped my fingers. "I swear, I think she sticks one end in the water and keeps flushing until the roll runs out just to watch it swirl around."

She smiled and said, "She wouldn't do that."

I thought about Lowell Correctional, and how many boxcars of toilet paper a women's prison must go through every week. But I didn't say anything. I sat down in a patch of shelly sand. "Want to swing for a minute?"

She looked back at the swings like the idea had never crossed her mind. She shrugged and said, "Yeah, I guess. For a minute."

While she arranged the plastic bags into a tidy group, I peeled off my T-shirt and threw it to her. I said, "Don't burn your legs like last time."

She held it by the shoulders and snapped it, just exactly the same way Missy always did. She folded it twice and then made a face. "I can't believe you put this on. Don't you smell that?"

I held out my hand and said, "Give it here. Burn your butt, see if I care."

Tammy laid it carefully across the black swing seat and kicked off Missy's flip-flops. "Put it in the hamper, that's all. I just did a load this morning."

She's not wild on the swings, just slow and steady as an old clock. One of those lightning-fast little lizards was clinging on to the plastic bag stuck to the sweating milk jug, probably trying to get cool. He almost looked like an *S* on the end of *Publix*.

"Look at that," I said. "One of those little lizards is hanging on here just like he belongs. I prob'ly hauled him all the way from Publix."

She asked, "He's not doing the throat thing is he?"

Tammy used to try and catch them, with a cup and string trap Clyde made her, until one day she saw one push its throat out like a red bubble about to pop. I cocked my middle finger behind my thumb and leaned forward to draw a bead on him.

Tammy yelled, "Don't do that!"

I sat back and crossed my arms across my knees. "Not like he won't hop down a long way from home either way," I said. "Why do you suppose they're always mouth-breathing?"

"Probably the heat," she said.

I looked up at the sun. "Then they prob'ly ought to load up their Lincolns and head back to Michigan."

Tammy asked, "You been to Michigan too?"

"Just to visit. Too damn cold in Michigan. All that lake-effect snow, like Cleveland and Buffalo."

She just nodded, and then there was one of those strange, still times when no cars went by on the beach road. The only sound was the creaking of the salt-corroded chain of Tammy's swing, but only at the top of her swing, in that frozen moment before she flew away.

I knew the answer, but I had to ask anyway. "Think your dad's coming after you?"

"Don't count on it."

"I mean, before school starts?"

"I wouldn't count on that either," she said. "School's already started back home."

"Hmm."

"He didn't know Mom wasn't meeting the bus," she said, but not like she believed it.

Seems like he could've waited to see how the sentencing went. But I only said, "Yeah."

She swung up and back half a dozen times before she said, "He's not coming back."

I reached into the bag with the milk and the lizard hopped off. I wiped the condensation on my face. "Then maybe we need to get you signed up for sixth grade or something"

She stopped pumping her legs. "Here?"

I asked, "What's wrong with here?"

She turned to look at the school and started twisting side to side. "I don't know, Pere. What if they ask stuff?"

"What kind of stuff?"

"Like who, exactly, you might be."

I thought about that, then said, "We'll have to get your mom to sign something."

"Grandma Sue signed everything back home," she said. "Dad wouldn't sign his real name to anything."

I asked, "What about eyeglasses?"

She looked at me and said, "What *about* eyeglasses?"

Doris was the one to say something, back when Tammy had only been here a couple of weeks. At first, I was having a hard time figuring out what Doris was getting at, I think because it was the first time she'd stood close to me for that long and she smelled really good. Then I started paying attention. She thought Tammy might need glasses, because Tammy tended to lean back to read the computer screen. I said she didn't have a problem watching the TV and Doris said she wouldn't, not unless she was right up on it. She told me sometimes the Recreation Center around the corner has free screenings and it was something I ought to think about. Once I knew to look for it, it was pretty clear. And even though she screws her eyebrows down, or holds things out at arm's length to read them, she won't even talk about glasses. She's vain as an old woman with rouged cheeks, as vain as Vera. One time I told her she didn't even know how ugly those cats were.

She finally twisted to a stop and asked, "Are there bombs?"

"Bombs?"

"The news said there were bombs under the school. Old bombs."

It took me a minute to shake some memory loose. On the TV—old ordnance, and mothers worried about their babies, just like mothers everywhere, except poorer. They were closing off the schoolyard with a chain-link fence and the TV reporter was pointing at a *Danger* sign with a skull and crossbones.

"No, Tammy. That's just one school. Up north of Orlando. From back in World War II. I think they just found the one. It wasn't even live." I didn't know if they found a hundred or whether they were live or not.

"Why would they do that?" she asked. "Why would they test bombs in a school?"

"It wasn't a school back then. They just built the school on the same piece of ground where they used to test them I guess."

She stopped twisting, and stared down at her toes touching the sand. "What if they're here? Under the sand? Just waiting."

A born worrier, just like her mom. "When they found those," I said, "they checked all the other schools." That's what they said anyway, but seems like we might've noticed armored-up guys with metal detectors. Clyde would've been all over that.

Tammy hopped off the swing and worked her feet into Missy's flip-flops. "We better get this milk in the fridge." She tossed me my T-shirt and as I put my arms through, she said, "Don't put that stinky thing back on, Pere! Just drape it over your shoulders till we get back. I can't remember the last time you used sunscreen."

I knew better than to argue so I draped it over my shoulders like an old woman's shawl and, for the first time, caught the rank smell of old sweat. We crossed the yellow dirt of the rundown baseball diamond. A Publix shopping cart was playing shortstop.

I looked at it. "Where the hell was that when we needed it? That wasn't here on our way down."

"It's stealing to take it out of the parking lot," Tammy said. "It says so on the sign."

"Even if you take it back next time you go?"

She said, "Stealing is stealing."

She stopped on the mound and looked in the trench where the pitching rubber used to be. Somebody, probably just out of meanness, had torn it out, pulled it up from the long hammer spikes that held it in the ground. And down in that small shallow grave, not as deep or dark as that one on a hilltop in the Blue Ridge Highlands, there was still one shining head of a spike sticking up.

She stared at it and said, "Chain-link won't save them."

I knew she was right. Chain-link won't save any of us.

13

WHAT TO WATCH OUT FOR

When we got to the sidewalk, I looked across the beach road to the picnic shelter. Tammy asked, "What are you looking at?"

"Nothing."

She motioned with her head back toward the school and said, "Mom'll have to sign something."

"Then we better find out. And we'll have to get you some shoes."

She considered her grubby feet in Missy's pink flip-flops. "I got the ones I came down in."

I shook my head. "No. The ocean took them. Remember?"

She smiled and said, "That's right. The ocean took them. That first day."

"You left them in the sand when we walked up to the jetty."

"Before I even knew what high tide was," she said.

"I guess I should have been paying more attention."

She looked down. "I don't guess these'll work...but I wish they would." She stopped again at the access lid painted pink and blue. She looked at it and said, "Where do you think it goes?"

I couldn't think of anywhere it might go but down in the ground so I said, "I don't know."

She switched the bags in her hands and said, "Someplace nice I bet."

I wondered what might be going on inside her head, and all I knew was there was a stuffed unicorn named Buddy, come to life.

"You better stop watching the news," I said.

"You've got to watch the news, Pere. That's how you know what's going on in the world."

"You don't need to know what's going on in the world," I said. "You're only ten."

"I'm eleven," she said. "And if you don't know what to watch out for, how are you ever going to watch out for it?"

She had a point, but I still said, "I'll watch. I'll watch out for stuff."

"They postponed the shuttle launch again," she said.

You can walk right out on the beach and watch the rockets go up from NASA, but nothing's gone up since she got here. They keep finding one problem after another—leaking hoses, faulty relays, and cracked foam. Missy liked to go out and watch the satellites go up, especially at night. The shuttles you can feel right through to your bones, like you might be inside it instead of miles away. But Missy didn't like watching the shuttles, like it hurt too much to think about all of those people being shot off into the nothingness.

A white and green Brevard County sheriff's cruiser came slowly down the beach road and rolled to a stop against the curb.

I held my hand up to Tammy and said, "Stay here."

She nodded. As I crossed the little strip of grass between the sidewalk and the street, the deputy cracked the passenger window a couple of inches, just enough to talk. I'd seen him around, a young guy with his hair still high and tight. He was a body builder or something, because his biceps made the cuffs of his short sleeves look like rubber bands, and his arms were waxed and cheese-curl orange from some kind of fake tan stuff.

He pulled his sunglasses down with one finger and said, "Get in."

"Where we going?" I asked.

"Nowhere," he said. "Just get in."

I slipped my T-shirt back on and tried the back door, but it was locked.

"What're you doing?" he asked, patting the front passenger seat.

Old habits. I opened the door and sat down. He said, "Could

you close the goddamn door? If I wanted to air-condition the great planet Earth, I wouldn't have asked you to get in."

I was going to point out that he didn't really ask, but instead I turned to Tammy and said, "We're not going anywhere."

She looked worried, but she set down her bags and gave me a little wave.

I shut the door and he turned down his police radio. "You live around here, right?" he asked.

"Pretty close."

"A crazy just stopped me down in Cocoa," the cop said. "Said someone ran him off with an ax up here." He jerked one thumb over at Cherie Down Park.

"An ax?"

"Yep. Told him he was going to chop off his dick and feed it to him."

I said, "No kidding?"

He looked at me for a long moment and then said, "Why do you suppose someone would make an offer like that? I mean, to chop a man's dick off and feed it to him?"

"I don't know." I didn't mean to, but I glanced at Tammy. She was talking on her broken cell phone with a worried expression on her face, scanning the tinted glass, trying to see past her own reflection to be sure I was still there. "Maybe he was doing something with it that he ought not to have been."

He said, "Sounds to me like a pretty goddamn reasonable guess." He leaned forward to look past me at Tammy. "Who's she talking to?"

I thought about that, and said, "God only knows."

He sat back. "Do me a favor, if you see him again, give me a call."

And I asked, "See who?"

He smiled to himself and said, "Either one. The crazy, or whoever wants to chop his dick off. Either one."

"You got it," I said, opening the door.

As I shut the door, he powered down the window a few inches. "The guy with the ax? He's got all his hair shaved off."

I rubbed the stubble on my scalp and said, "If I see him over there with an ax again, I'll let you know."

He pushed his sunglasses back up and said, "You have a good day, sir." Then he leaned forward to see Tammy better and said, "Sweetie, you better get inside before you melt away to nothing."

Tammy held onto my elbow and tried to smile. He rolled up his window and drove away.

"What did he want?" Tammy asked. "Did CPS send him? You didn't tell him my name, did you?"

"No, I didn't tell him your name."

"Was it CPS?"

"No, it's not child protection services. I told you, you got to get that out of your head."

She shook her head. "But you got no standing, Pere. If they come, you got no standing."

I leaned down to look her in the eyes. "They're not coming." I didn't want to tell her why they weren't coming, that the only person in the world that might call them was the useless son of a bitch who sent her down in the first place, and he was bunking in his Peterbilt one step ahead of the repo man.

She looked at her feet. "But up in Ohio—"

"It wasn't about you," I said.

She looked up and asked, "Was it about Mom?"

"No. They're just looking for somebody."

"Who? Who are they looking for?"

"Nobody," I said. "Some homeless guy talking crazy is all."

"Tampon John?" she asked. "Tampon John talks crazy."

"No, not Tampon John. And you shouldn't call him that. Don't you worry about Officer Orange."

She tried to smile, but she scanned the park and the picnic shelter before she said, "Okay."

14

FREE CHEESE

When we turned onto our street, we could see another section of palm trunk in the gutter. Duane had a pickaxe and was trying to cut a trench around the last few feet of stump.

I asked Tammy, "Who were you on the phone with back there?"

She scuffed her flip-flops along and said, "I was trying to call Mom. But that mean old guard, she wouldn't let her come to the phone no matter what."

I thought about that, and whether to say something, but then I figured life was already hard enough if you couldn't even get your mom on a pretend phone.

I looked up our walk and said, "Damn if the cheese elves didn't come again."

On our front stoop was another block of orange cheese, about the size of a brick, and behind it, something long and thin and wrapped in a Publix bag. Tammy pushed by me and set her bags down on the walk. She picked up the block of cheese and held it to her cheek.

"It's still cold," she said. "Maybe Officer Orange has ate too much of this surplus cheese." Then she held her forearm to the sunlight and examined it closely.

"What's in the bag?" I asked.

Tammy picked it up and held the handles apart to look inside. She raised her eyebrows and said, "Candles?" She pulled out a bundle of five cardboard tubes, each with "roman candle" printed up the side in red and black letters.

"Better than candles," I said. "Fireworks."

She asked, "What's a 'roman' candle?"

"They shoot out fireballs. Like glittery fireballs."

"Are they loud?"

She doesn't like loud noises, so I said, "No, just a little pop and bright balls of fire."

"What do you do with them?" she asked.

"Shoot them up in the air. We'll take them out to the beach tonight and I'll show you. You can stick one end down in the sand. Or just hold them if you want to."

She said, "That doesn't sound safe. Are you allowed to shoot fireworks off on the beach?"

Probably not, since they've got rules against everything now, but I said, "NASA does."

Tammy wrapped them carefully back up in the bag. "Who could it be?"

And I said, "Surplus cheese and cheap fireworks? Sounds like West Virginia elves to me."

She frowned. "Grandma was from West Virginia, you know."

I nudged her shoulder with my elbow. "Yeah. I know. Hell, I'm *almost* from West Virginia, from that dingleberry hanging off the west end of Virginia that no other state would take. If Tennessee, Kentucky, *and* West Virginia won't claim you, you are, by God, sucking hind tit. Just a half a dozen country miles north of the Greater Wytheville Metropolitan area proper. With the right wind, I could've kicked a cat over Big Walker Mountain into Bluefield."

She smiled and asked, "Why'd you want to kick a cat into West Virginia?"

"To see if I could," I said. "One less barn cat in Virginia."

"You wouldn't kick a cat. You *like* cats."

"What got *that* foolish notion in your head?" I asked. "Cats are a dime a dozen."

She rolled her eyes. "'Cause you took care of Flopsy, Mopsy, and Cottontail. When Miriam was in the hospital. Before I come down."

"Did Miriam tell you that?" I asked.

"No," she said. "Clyde."

"Clyde's got a big mouth to go with that big butt of his. I

was just helping the Cat Lady out." I can't say I like cats, but I like those three, probably just because she does.

She smiled down at the bag of roman candles in her small hands, then she asked, "Did you like it there? In Virginia?"

I thought about that. "Hard to say. There wasn't much *there* to like. It was way out in the boonies. A little wood house on some property that's been in my mom's family since before the Civil War. A cemetery and a little church with pews cut from a stand of poplar off the next hill. We didn't stay there long. Second or third grade maybe."

"What's *your* mom like?" she asked.

I just said, "Dead and gone."

And she said, "I'm sorry."

"It's okay," I said. "I don't remember much about her. But you know what I do remember? Her standing in front of the stove, cooking Sunday breakfast—biscuits and table syrup, bacon and eggs, and pan-fried potatoes with ketchup. And she had this little thing she did. After she fried the bacon and poured off most of the fat into that coffee can on the counter, she fried the eggs in that hot oil. And what she did was stand there with a little spoon, an old spoon, flicking bacon grease up on top of that frying egg." And I showed her, a quick, jerking little flip of the wrist. "That's what I remember, that gesture. And I don't think I've ever tasted an egg as good, and I can't smell bacon without it playing in my mind like a movie."

"Biscuits and table syrup?" she asked. "What's wrong with biscuits and white gravy?"

"My dad couldn't abide white gravy. Said it was wallpaper paste."

I didn't tell her about the football-sized tumor they found inside my mom, or the next two years in that furnished apartment near the hospital in Roanoke, or that cloudless summer day back at that little cemetery, or why, in my ten-year-old brain, I thought a tiny goldfinch roller-coastering up and down across her open grave meant something.

Tammy squeaked her fingertips along the plastic wrapping.

"I think it's WIC cheese. 'Women, Infants, and Children.' It seems like I remember a lot of cheese. From when I was small. Just me and mom." She scanned the street. "It's like they know when we're coming home. Do you think it's Clyde?"

And I said, "I don't think so. Clyde's prob'ly still fishing up at the jetty." I pointed across the street, "See, his garage door is shut."

She scanned the street again. "Hmmm."

We took all of the groceries into the kitchen, then she shooed me back outside so she could put them away. Me, I just shove crap anywhere, but Tammy's got a system.

On my way out, Tammy said, "Get you a clean shirt off the dryer. Take the top one 'cause I just folded all those."

I took the top shirt and snapped it open. I never knew anyone but Tammy and Missy that could fold a crease into a T-shirt liked it'd been ironed. Clyde's garage door was open, and he was standing in our driveway watching Duane. He just tipped his head at Duane and said, under his breath, "Who knew he could heft a pickaxe?"

Duane was wearing an old Molly Hatchet concert T-shirt with the sleeves torn off and the black-faded-to-grey was stained dark with sweat. He wasn't making much headway digging out the stump, because every time he pulled the flat end free, the sand filled back in behind it.

"Je-sus Key-rist," Duane yelled, "if this ain't shoveling shit against the tide." He glanced back at us over his shoulder, then took another swing.

"The shuttle launch is on hold again," Clyde said.

"I know," I said. "Tammy told me."

"What?" Clyde asked, "Is she working there now? They just called it this morning."

"When she has trouble sleeping she likes to watch the NASA-TV. I tell you what now, that place is falling apart without you."

"You know what they say," he said. "'Close enough for government work.'"

Duane finished cutting the circle around the stump, then

Clyde looked at me and shrugged. He clapped his hands together and called over to Duane, "Might as well do this."

Duane leaned his balls on the end of the pickaxe handle and said, "Ya think my truck'll yank it out now? If I tie off on the frame?"

Clyde considered the Chevy and snorted a little laugh. "That truck couldn't pull its own dick out of the mud."

Missy had a hillbilly expression to describe somebody so pissed off they can't even speak, about them not knowing whether to "shit or go blind." And as Duane looked from Clyde to his truck and back to Clyde again, it sprang to mind, because it seemed like he couldn't decide whether to do the one or the other, even though "shit" and "go blind" were the only two things on the menu.

"They's three of us," Clyde said. "Just put some back into it."

Clyde hitched up his belt under his belly and walked to the stump, rolling his thick shoulders. He pointed to the far side and said to Duane, "You get on that side and pull." Then he squatted down with the knuckles of one hand on the ground like a linebacker and dug the toes of his shoes into the trench. He brushed the palm's necktie of frayed clothesline out of the way and snugged the trunk between his neck and shoulder. I reached over his back and leaned my hands into the empty bark under Duane's locked fingers.

"On three," Clyde said. Duane started jerking on the stump, bouncing forward and back like a chimp. The back of Clyde's head shook slowly from side to side. "Don't hurt yourself," he said.

Duane stood up and said, "I thought we were doing it."

And Clyde said, "Might as well." His back flexed down, and I could feel the tension through the trunk. By the time I got my two cents in, it was already moving, and by the time Duane got a hold, he had to jump to get his feet clear. The root ball wasn't much wider than the trunk, and just a mass of finger-thin tendrils that looked like hair.

"That's it?" Duane asked, looking at the roots.

I slapped Clyde on the back. "What'd you need us for, Grandpa?"

And he said, "I didn't."

Duane said to himself, "Damn if I don't think I earned myself some cold beer and hot titties." He turned to the condo and yelled, "Hey, Pearl!"

Pearl opened the front door. "Hey, Clyde. Hey, Pere," she said. "You get it out for him?"

Duane glared at the ground and said, "Son of a... No, sweetheart, it just jumped out all on its own. I'm going down to Melbourne to look at a bumper for Ole Blue."

Pearl thought about that. "Well, tell Ole Blue to take you by the Wal-Mart and get me a new clothesline. And not that cheap plastic stuff either."

"Clothesline at Wally World. Check." He gave her a small salute and high-stepped over the pickaxe on his way to the Chevy.

"And tell Ole Blue if I see him parked up at that damn strip club, I'm having him towed to the junk yard," Pearl yelled.

Duane drove off and waved without ever looking back.

Pearl yelled after him, "Don't forget whose name is on the title." She turned to me and Clyde and said, "Would you believe I'm on a first name basis with the bouncer at Sassy Merlot's? I think he has me on speed dial." She held up one hand and looked at her fingernails, then went inside and shut the door.

The only bouncer I know up at Sassy's is Del Ron. I've met him a couple of times, over at Barry's place in the Whispering Palms Trailer Park, and he always smells like industrial-strength citrus degreaser. Tammy even mentioned it, that he "really" smelled like oranges. Barry and Del Ron used to work together at Sassy Merlot's, before it burnt down and they built the current Sassy Merlot's II. It was Barry's first job when he came to town, before he got the Neil Diamond gig on the gambling boat. One of the girls does a baby oil shower, which is a bone of contention with the OSHA inspector and a mess to clean up, but too wildly popular to cut.

The last time I saw Del Ron, he was sitting in Barry's breakfast nook, sloppy drunk on sloe gin and Diet 7 Up at ten in the morning. I thought you had to be queer or a high school girl to drink sloe gin and Diet 7 Up, but since he was crying over some woman, I guess you can be something else. He told me, "Stevie Nicks ruint every woman in California." It took me a minute to remember who Stevie Nicks was. At first, I didn't know what he meant, but the more I thought about it, I thought I might. I remember looking past him through the window of Barry's single-wide, at Tammy's narrow back as she played in the gravel drive with the hillbilly girls from the next trailer, wondering whose heart she would break.

Clyde watched as Ole Blue turned the corner at the end of the block. "No 'thank you,' or 'kiss my ass,' or nothing,."

And I said, "No invitation."

Clyde said, "Like you couldn't see that coming." Then he pointed to the pickaxe. "What kind of man leaves his tools laying out in the yard?"

"It's prob'ly not his."

Then we both heard Tammy say, "Thanks, Clyde."

We turned and saw her standing in the thin shade of the garage, staring at the uprooted palm stump.

She said, "Thanks, Clyde. Thanks for the fishes for the kitties." But she never took her eyes off the tangled web of newborn roots.

15

SOMEONE'S SLEEPING

Me and Clyde watched Tammy kneeling down in Pearl's mangy little front yard next to the stump, staring into the tangle of thin roots like something she lost might be there.

Clyde mopped his sweating face with a pink palm and said, "I got to get indoors for a while." Then he looked at Tammy for a long moment before he said quietly, "What do you think she's...?" But he didn't say anything else, and he gave the ground between his feet a sad smile before he turned away.

After he disappeared into the shadows of his garage, Pearl came out with her cigarettes and sat on the low step of their front stoop. She watched Tammy lost in the roots and scratched absently at the safety pin tattoo on her ankle. It was inked on to look like it was piercing her skin, with two little blood-red spots where it went in and came back out. It must have meant something, if not now then whenever she got it. And even though I'd seen it before and knew what it was, all I could see today was an old *Tom and Jerry* cartoon, the one when they're taking care of a baby mouse in a cloth diaper with a big safety pin in front holding it all together. All I could see today was a diaper-pin and I don't know why. Tammy and me, we watch a lot of cartoons. Bright TV hasn't shut off the cable yet, even though I quit paying a couple of months back.

Tammy has a tattoo, on her shoulder blade, like Missy's. She found a picture on the internet that looked just like it and Doris printed it up the right size and Tammy made me copy it on her back with a black pen. I knew I couldn't freehand it, so I held the paper against her shoulder blade and poked the pen through along the lines. After I connected the dots, I told her boys don't like tattoos on girls, and she just gave me a look that said, *Seems to me you liked it well enough.* Doris says it's a cherub but Tammy insists it's just a little angel. It gets faded and smeared so every couple of days I shake down the pen and trace back over the dim lines. The last thing I do is her name in the heart, and Tammy can feel the curling letters and whispers, "Misty!" It hurts. It hurts when somebody pries open your chest to write their name across your beating heart with a thousand tiny needles. But I know it's just temporary.

Pearl called to Tammy, "That's sure something, isn't it, honey? Don't look like they'd hold a thing up in the sand, much less a big ol' tree."

Tammy opened one hand out over the roots and held it there, not quite touching. She said, "It looks like someone sleeping."

Pearl pursed her lips at Tammy's back. "Does it?" Then she looked at me and said, "Yeah, I guess it does."

Tammy slipped her hands gently under the frayed clothesline. "I know what this was for."

Pearl flipped open her cigarette pack and pulled out one of those thin girlie cigarettes, long and thin as a soda straw. She held out the pack. "You want one?"

I did, and I didn't care if it made me look like a Puerto Rican drag queen in a Miami Beach gay pride parade. But instead I said, "I don't smoke," which is almost true. I smoke one unfiltered Chesterfield a night after Tammy goes to bed, hunkered down in Clyde's garage, my back up against Vera's Kenmore dryer and my feet under the Buick. They're stashed in Clyde's toolbox. And with money going the way it is, I'll probably be rolling my own Bugle Boys when this pack runs out. I used to think if you were so poor-ass you had to roll your own cigarettes, it's probably time to quit. Now I'm not so sure. I had two last night.

Pearl took a drag so deep I could feel the rush in my own lungs, then she smiled and said through the smoke, "Oh, that's right." She scratched at her tattoo again and said, "Can you believe this humidity? I feel like I'm living in Duane's ass crack." She stood up and tapped an inch of ash off her cigarette into her upturned palm and took it in the house.

I squatted down on my heels at the edge of Pearl's driveway and scooped up a little sand. I watched Tammy and poured it from one hand to the other, losing a little each time, until there was nothing left. "Lunch?"

Tammy closed her eyes tight and whispered, "Shhh! Someone's sleeping." Then she leaned forward, slow as smoke in the still air, and placed one ear gently against the trunk. After a long minute, she jerked upright so fast I jumped. "Doris," she said. "We have to go see Doris now."

16

FIND OUR WAY BACK

When Doris saw us come in, she stood up and smiled. Tammy hadn't said a word the whole way to the library, and I'd chased her dirty feet nine blocks south and three blocks over. I'd worked up a sweat, and I pulled my wet T-shirt away from my skin to let the air conditioning in.

I stretched the collar up to mop my face and said, "Good thing I just put a clean shirt on." But Tammy was already gone, padding across the carpet like one of the cats under the board-walk.

"Hey, Tammy!" Doris called. "Where do you...?" But Tammy brushed right past her and sat down at her favorite computer.

I made it as far as the counter and the little paper sign that read Check Out Here. Doris looked at me and cocked her head in Tammy's direction.

I shrugged. "Don't ask me. What the hell do I know about anything?"

Doris frowned, and then smiled again and said, "Hey, I saved something for you." She reached under the counter and pulled out a thick dog-eared paperback called *What to Expect When You're Expecting*, with a drawing of a pregnant lady in a rocking chair on the cover. "We got in the new edition and we're just getting rid of this one. I thought maybe...The information is all still good, it's just a little worn."

She held it out to me, her fingers slim and straight as flower stems, but I just couldn't take it. I looked at it, and her, but I couldn't seem to raise my arms up.

She sucked her upper lip in a little, then said, "Seems a shame for it to go to waste." Then she set it down on the countertop between us and said, "Well, I guess maybe we could sell it at the library sale. If you don't want it."

"Doris. Come on," Tammy called.

I watched Doris cross the few steps to the computers, the scent of her still with me. She was wearing nice jeans, not like you get at Wally World, and a white button-up shirt with the tails out. When she knelt beside Tammy's chair, I decided that maybe her hips aren't too wide after all, and if you were that goddamn lucky, in no time you wouldn't want her any other way than stoop-shouldered. She couldn't have been ten feet away, but I knew I could walk around the world in either direction and never get any closer.

Doris looked at Tammy and said, "Mom?"

"Mom?" Tammy shook her head. "Mom knows what I'm doing."

I said, "Mom doesn't know what Mom is doing," but not loud enough for anyone to hear.

Doris asked, "Do you want to look at her picture?"

"No. Not yet," Tammy said. "Do you remember the palm trees?"

Doris asked, "The palm trees?" She thought about it. "You wanted to know what was making them sick?"

Tammy nodded. "There's something I need to find again. About palm trees. In Hawaii, I think."

Doris put her arm across the back of Tammy's chair. "Okay, okay. It might take a few minutes, but I bet we can find our way back."

Tammy looked into Doris' face as unblinking as a dog, and said, "That's what I need to do. I need to find my way back."

I said, "Don't we all." But the words never really made it out of my mouth.

"She called last night," Tammy said.

Doris asked, "And how's she doing?"

I backed away, back toward the comfortable chairs and the magazines, but I still heard Tammy say, "Not so good. She talked to Pere." Then I was far enough away that whatever Doris said next was just the sound of bubbling water. I pulled a magazine off the shelf and sat down in my usual chair. It was called *The Atlantic* but it wasn't about the ocean on our side of the state. There were lots and lots of words but not many pictures, except for some weird little drawings and ads for books and big companies. I put it on the chair next to me and thought about Missy. She likes to read. At least she did when she wasn't wasted. Who knows about now? She never asks me to bring her any books, not that I get up to see her that often, but I can't imagine that prison library is stacked too deep in those romances she likes. I think she's worried that if she asks for one more thing, I might just disappear. I won't, but it seems easier for us both to pretend I might.

An old man two seats down kept nodding off, his chin on his chest and his dentures rattling like death. He reminded me of my dad before he passed away, except that I knew this guy still had a wife that dressed him because his khakis were ironed and the buttons on his plaid shirt matched up with the right holes. My dad was a mess. He had Parkinson's but was too stubborn to not live on his own, so there was always food on his face and clothes, the floor, tray table, and chair in front of the TV. He looked like he shaved with a chainsaw, and when he died the VA wanted his brain for a study because they thought the Parkinson's might have come on from that plane crash forty years earlier. I didn't let them, but I can't say why.

Doris whispered something to Tammy, then stood up and walked over. "She's sailing the South Seas—Tonga, Tahiti, and Samoa, Hawaii, New Zealand, and the Cook Islands, Maori mythology, and Marquesan art."

I asked, "And Lowell Correctional?"

"No. Not yet," she said. "She likes the tiki statues. She's smart as a whip, you know." She worried a spot of carpet with the toe of one shoe. "She said her mom called."

I looked past her, at a silver-haired woman talking to Tammy. Tammy looked down into her lap and slid her feet up under the desk.

I said, "Hold on a minute."

As I got closer, I heard the old lady say, shrill and mean, "Where's your mother?"

I put on my best don't-scare-the-old-people smile. "Can I help you with something, ma'am?"

She turned on me, all navy polyester and fake pearls, her mouth pinched by years of looking like she just smelled something she stepped in. She looked at my sweaty T-shirt and old fatigue shorts and snorted, "I hardly think so." She stepped around me and said to Doris, "Who's in charge here?"

"I am," Doris said. "I'm in charge."

Then the old lady said, "Then perhaps you'd be kind enough to come and read this sign on the door with me." When she passed by the sleeping old man, she yelled, "Lloyd! Go start the car. And don't forget to turn on the air conditioning this time."

Doris held up one flower stem finger and mouthed, *Wait.* Then she turned and followed the old lady to the door.

Tammy was staring at the computer screen, at Missy's picture. I knelt down and asked, "What did she want?"

And without looking at me, Tammy shrugged and said, "Nothing."

But I could tell just by looking at her that it wasn't nothing. "Hmmm," I said. "Did she like your pretty blonde hair?" Tammy stared at the screen and shook her head. "'Cause lots of ladies like your hair. They say it all the time. They say, 'I wish I had that pretty blonde hair!'"

"She didn't like my hair," Tammy said quietly.

"That surprises me."

Tammy scratched the back of the little plastic mouse and said, "She said I had to have shoes. That it was a rule."

I thought about that a minute, then said, "That's all she said?" Tammy shook her head but didn't say anything else. "What else did she say?"

She put her small fist up next to her face so I couldn't see her eyes, and said, "She said I was filthy. And un-hy-gien-ic. She wanted to know where Mom was."

I stood up and said, "I'll be right back."

Tammy touched my arm and said, "Don't, Pere. It don't matter."

"If she's so worried about your shoes, I expect she wants to buy you a new pair."

Doris was by the front door when I pushed through it and all I heard her say before it closed was, "Don't."

Old Lloyd was trying to back out their big Mercury, and I stood behind it and knocked on the trunk lid. When he looked into the rearview mirror, I turned an invisible key in the air and yelled, "Turn it off."

I heard the locks click down as I walked up the passenger side. The old woman put her window down an inch and said, "What do *you* want?"

"What do *I* want? I want to know what *your* problem is. You got nothing better to do with your life than make a little girl feel shabby about herself?"

She said, "You should take care of her."

I thought about punching out the window and snapping her scrawny neck, but instead I just said, "What do you know about a goddamn thing? I *do* take care of her."

She sneered and said, "Oh, I can see that."

I leaned down close to the slot and said, "You don't know shit. You don't know shit about her or her life. But I'll tell you something for nothing, she's smarter than both of us put together, and ten of you wouldn't make half of her. There's not a mean bone in her body, and mean's all you got left."

Her husband leaned forward and said, "Son, if I hadn't just had open heart surgery, I'd show you what for."

I poked at him through the glass and yelled, "Shut the fuck up, Lloyd! If you had any stones, you'd have this old bitch on a choke chain."

The old lady said, "We're calling the police."

"Why don't you do that." I tapped the parking decal on her side of the windshield. "Fleur de Merde. Nice place. And this is your unit number here, right? Hell, we're practically neighbors."

She told Lloyd to start the car, and when they backed out, I slapped the hood twice and waved like we were old friends. I pointed through the windshield with two fingers and yelled, "I'll see you around."

When I turned to go inside, I saw them watching me from behind the glass doors, from behind the little No Shoes-No Shirt-No Service sign, Tammy in front holding Doris's arm across her narrow chest.

17

BAD MEDICINE

Tammy was back on the computer and Doris was brushing things I couldn't see from the empty countertop. The book was gone but I couldn't think of when it might have disappeared.

Doris said, "Tammy said her mom called?"

"Yeah. Last night. Late."

Doris rubbed her hands together, like something wouldn't come off, and I checked my own. The only grease still left in the calluses is from Clyde's old outboard, and the black stains from all the 2-part flotation foam we use around the marina are worn away to almost nothing.

Doris looked up from her soft palms and said, "I just wanted to say how sorry I am."

"Yeah. That hepatitis C," I said. "She got a hold of the wrong medicine."

She said, "Well, that's not right! That's not right at all! You should get a lawyer. That's what you should do."

I smiled, but it never made it to my face. I don't know much about Doris, but I know her life, her friends and family, and everything she knows, doesn't have much to do with mine and Tammy's. Her mother wasn't turning yellow from mainlining meth, and in her world lawyers might actually do something besides seize a twelve-year-old Ford Escort with a cracked exhaust manifold when the check bounced.

"They didn't *give* her the wrong medicine," I said. "She got *a hold* of the wrong medicine."

I watched her turn that over before she said, "Oh."

"From another inmate that's sick. It starts with an R. I forget. It's for hep C too, but not if you're..." Then I drew a little circle in front of her stomach and I'm not sure why.

She looked down at that circle in the air and said, "Oh," again.

"She was just trying to get better. She didn't know."

And Doris looked over at Tammy and said, "No. How could she?"

I said, "I don't think Missy's thinking too clear on that other stuff." And I wasn't even sure which 'other stuff' I meant.

"If that color printer feels like working today, I'll make her a copy of that photo she looks at all the time," Doris said.

"Of Misty?" And I didn't know why I said that either.

"If that's okay," she said. "If you think she'll like it."

I tried to smile and said, "What's not to like?"

Doris grabbed my shoulders and gave me a quick hug, so quick it was over before I knew to enjoy it. She smelled like honeysuckle, not like I put my nose in the blossoms, but like a dim dream of honeysuckle, on the evening breeze in early summer when I was no bigger than Tammy. And she made me remember something I'd forgot. I'd forgot women don't smell like rotting teeth.

Doris knelt beside Tammy, and I stood there in the chill air rubbing hard at my eyes.

I heard Doris say, "Hit 'okay.'"

Tammy said, "'Okay.'" And something started whirring behind the counter.

And Doris said, "Okay!" Then, like Flopsy and Mopsy, they chased each other behind the counter like Cottontail might be hiding there. Doris helped the last of the paper out of the printer, then turned it over and frowned. "Oh, shoot! It's still on the fritz."

How can you not love a woman that says, "Oh, shoot!"?

She put it on the countertop to show Tammy. It was Missy's photograph, but the printer had made horizontal bars across it, every inch or so, each the colors of the rainbow.

Tammy held it up for me to see. "Look what Doris made me."

"I think it needs a new cartridge," Doris said. "But the cartridge costs more than the printer."

Tammy said, "I like it. The bars are really pretty."

"Those are some pretty bars," I said. "Maybe Altagracia's painted them that way."

Altagracia is Missy's cellmate, a little Dominican woman old enough to be her mother, who's always smiling and doesn't speak a word of English. Altagracia watches out for her inside and brushes her hair every night before lights out.

Tammy said, "Mom calls her Gracita. Or Mamita."

I brushed my hand in front of the paper and said, "But the bars go the other way, I think. Which has to be a change of scenery."

Doris said, "I'll make you a good one when the new cartridge comes in."

Tammy nodded without taking her eyes off Missy's picture. "I'll wear my flip-flops next time."

Doris shook her head and said, "Don't worry about that lady. I've dealt with her before. She's just not a nice person."

"C'mon, Pere," Tammy said, taking my hand. "Doris has work to do and so do we."

We stepped outside and stood in the withering heat off the asphalt.

"I'm not worried about that old lady," Tammy said. "I just don't want Doris to get in trouble."

I nodded and squinted up at the sun. "Fun in the sun."

"Don't look into the sun, Pere," Tammy said. "You can permanently damage your retinas."

I looked at her and said, "Yeah, no point being dumb *and* blind."

Tammy smiled and held up Missy to shade her eyes. "We ought to get out of this parking lot."

"Circle K?" I asked.

"Gee, I don't know, Pere. Didn't we just go yesterday?"

I fished the change from my pocket and rattled the coins in a closed fist next to my ear. "I got you covered."

18

JUNIOR COLLEGE

Circle K was a mile north, and we darted like lizards from one precious spot of shade to the next, palm tree to palm tree, store awning to gas station, and through the tilted carports of that old apartment building from the '70s where some woman got murdered last winter.

Tammy waved Missy back and forth like she might be trying to cool her down and said, "Doris is so smart."

"That's what she says about you," I said.

She grinned. "Really?"

"Yep," I said. "Not ten minutes ago."

She skipped ahead a few steps and walked backwards, saying, "She knows *everything* about manatees. And she works with a group trying to save them."

I thought they'd been sailing the South Seas looking at tiki statues, but I said, "Then they should stop serving 'Manatee-On-A-Stick.'"

She barked a little laugh. "'Manatee-On-A-Stick'! Max the Manatee!"

Max is a manatee sculpture in Manatee Park, due west of us across Astronaut Boulevard on the Banana River. He looks just like he's doing a push-up on three poles, but the pole at the back is where I came up with Manatee-On-A-Stick. That first time we walked over there, I pretended I was at a county fair and said, "Gimme two of them Manatee-On-A-Stick, one funnel cake, and a diet Co'Coler." Tammy laughed until she cried.

"Doris says they're nine feet long and weigh 1,200 pounds and they sleep half the day," she said. "They're Sea Cows."

I wasn't sure that was right because I didn't think anything could hold its breath that long, but I said, "Sea *cows*? They sound like sea *cats*."

"That's why they get hit by boats," she said, "'cause they come up for air every twenty minutes. That's why they've all got those white scars on their backs. From boat propellers."

A half-ton manatee might swim away from catching a four-teen-inch prop, because a lot of them have the scars on their backs to prove it, but I knew a 200-pound man didn't walk away from catching a ninety-inch propeller. I had the proof of that too, in the dark memories etched in blood.

I blinked that thought away. "Yeah, she seems like a smart lady." And smart ladies like her, with their heads on straight, were always smart enough to steer clear of me.

She said, "I wish I was smart like that."

"You're smart," I said. "You're *really* smart. Smarter than I'll ever be. I never met a kid knows so much stuff." I hadn't hung around any kids in a while, but I knew she was smarter than all of us in most any way that counted.

"Oh, I know some stuff," she said, "but Doris knows a lot. And if she doesn't, she knows how to find it. And that there, that's what's important."

"You're prob'ly right about that."

She took a quick glance at Missy and said, "Yeah, but like Grandma used to say, 'Wish in one hand and poop in the other and see which one fills up first.'"

I laughed. "My dad used to say that too, but he sure didn't say 'poop.'"

She looked sideways at me. "Neither did Grandma."

"I have to tell you, that one always made me stop and think, because I couldn't figure out why anyone'd want to shit in their own hand."

She raised her eyebrows like I might be even stupider than she thought. "No, I don't think it means anybody'd *want* to do that, but if you did, the wishing hand would lose."

I gave her the same look back and said, "Yeah, I got that."

"Grandma said a lot of stuff like that. When I was going

with Becky to her church youth group, not 'cause I believe in any of that stuff, 'cause I don't, or 'cause we went to that church, 'cause we didn't, but just 'cause it was something to do on Friday night. There was always some new boy Becky liked that changed every week and they showed Disney movies on an old TV and they had an eight-sided bumper pool table with sticks warped like you wouldn't believe from when the church basement flooded."

"I could never find a straight cue in a bar either," I said. "At least not one with cork on the tip." But God, I loved to shoot pool, and unlike most everyone else, I just got better the more I drank.

"Grandma didn't care that I went," Tammy said, "'cause she knew sitting around the trailer all the time with an old woman with arthritis wasn't that much fun, and I needed some time with kids my own age. Tommy Pafford came sometimes. But she always warned me off buying what they were selling. She said if God talked to me I should listen 'cause I'd be the first. She said it wouldn't do me a bit of good to kiss his behind—but she didn't say 'behind'—and ask for new Barbies, and I don't even *like* Barbies but Becky sure does, or a trip to Disney, or parents that weren't screw-ups. But she didn't say 'screw' ups, 'cause He didn't like people always asking for stuff and He'd give you the cancer and laugh."

"Yeah, I'm with her," I said. If He's up there, I don't know that I can take much more of His precious love.

Tammy said, "They even have a 'Holy Ghost Weinie Roast.'"

"I can't even guess what that might be." And I couldn't.

"It's what they do for Halloween," she said. "'A family-friendly alternative' to Satan worshipping trick-or-treaters."

"Did you go?" I asked.

"Just once," she said, "when Dad found Jesus for five minutes. I like a caramel apple as much as anyone, but a caramel apple and a Wally World hotdog on a day-old bun doesn't hold a candle to a pillowcase full of candy. And you had to put up with a whole bunch of Jesus jumping besides. Pixie Sticks,

Bottle Caps, Smarties, little boxes of Hot Tamales and Mike and Ikes—are you kidding? And Red Hots! Hell, even Becky was smarter than that, but her parents wouldn't let her dress up like anything scary. I'd trade her any little chocolate bar one-to-one for Nerds."

"Becky likes the chocolate, huh?" I asked.

"Yeah." Then she thought for a minute. "Mom always liked chocolate too, didn't she?"

I nodded, but I didn't really remember her liking it more or less than anything else. Toward the end, if she ate anything at all, it was just her wasted body begging for some calories.

We were closing in on Circle K, and we slowed down some to enjoy the shade of some overgrown bushes in front of a foreclosed house. Tammy stared at the picture of Missy and then held it up to her face like a mask.

Tammy whispered, "I wish I could be like Doris when I grow up."

"You can." And even though I knew it was bullshit, I said, "You can grow up to be whatever you want."

She shook her paper face slowly from side to side, a face that wasn't exactly hers, and said, "No. No, I won't. Doris, she probably went to junior college or something."

19

DEL RON'S TEARS

When we cleared the bushes at the corner of Circle K, I saw Barry's rusty white Corolla parked out front.

"It's the orange man," Tammy said.

I thought she meant Officer Orange, and I looked around and said, "Where?"

She pointed at Del Ron's huge arm hanging out the window of the little Corolla like he was wearing it. "Why's he always smell like oranges?"

She'd asked me this before, and I still couldn't think how to explain a bouncer at a strip club, or even just a bouncer or just a strip club, and even if I did, that wouldn't explain why he smelled like oranges unless I explained the baby oil shower and how hard it is to cut petroleum products. I said, "It must be his cologne."

She looked at me like I might have lost my mind. "*Cologne?* Do I *look* like I just fell off the turnip truck?" She looked exactly like she just fell off the turnip truck, but I didn't say so. She walked up to the passenger door of the Corolla and said, "Hi."

Del Ron was wearing a wife-beater and his good black pants, and he had an open bottle of Bailey's Irish Cream in his lap. When he turned his tearstained face toward Tammy, the bottle tipped over and spilled on his slacks. He turned the bottle up and dabbed at the damp and said, "Oh, no." Then he started crying.

I touched Tammy's shoulder. "Let's get inside."

"You go on," she said. "I'll stay here and keep Mister Ron company."

I've told her before that his first name is Del Ron, but she still doesn't believe me.

I asked, "Chocolate, vanilla, or swirly?"

She pulled on her chin. "Chocolate sounds good. But so does vanilla." She looked at Del Ron and said, "What would you get if it was you?"

He sniffled while he thought about it and said, "I'd get a swirl cone, 'cause then you get your chocolate, and you get your vanilla."

Tammy nodded. "He's right. Get me a swirly."

She always gets a swirly anyway, and even though I didn't have enough money, I said, "You want one, Del Ron?"

He shook his head and said, "No, I'd take no pleasure in it."

I palmed Tammy's head and said, "I'll be right back. You need me, just come inside."

Barry and Raj were bullshitting across the counter. Barry was holding up a short-sleeved white dress shirt on a wire hanger that was big enough for two of him. Raj keeps his Circle K cold enough to hang meat, and it smells like spices or scented oil or maybe incense and it's so strong I doubt anything short of a fire could get it out. He's Indian or Pakistani and he's told me a hundred times, always pissed off that I would mistake him for the other, and I still can't remember which.

I nodded to Raj and said, "Hey, Barry."

And Raj said, in his sing-songy voice, "Barry? Who is this Barry? Mr. Neil Diamond shops in my store." He started humming, and when he found his groove he bounced lightly on the balls of his feet. The lyrics escaped him until he sang something about an uncurling flag, then he threw both hands up like a football ref and shouted, "We're coming in America!"

Barry hung his head for a moment, then said, "It's 'unfurled,' not 'uncurled.' And you aren't coming 'in' America. Don't they teach you English over there?"

Raj has more teeth and speaks better English than most people in Florida, but he just said, "Nevertheless, a great song."

Barry asked, "If I stop singing it, will you all go home?"

Raj winked at me. "Somebody certainly fell off the wrong half of the bed."

"Something like that," Barry said. "Del Ron is driving me out of my mind. He comes blubbering around most every morning and that trailer's not big enough for him and anything else. And he's about to get fired or killed, one. He keeps making the DJ play that long Soft Cell version of 'Tainted Love/Where Did Our Love Go?', and I'm here to tell you, those strippers are in great shape, but they don't train for a marathon like that, if you know what I mean. I don't think you can bounce those fake titties around for nine minutes straight without doing some permanent damage. And it's bringing the clientele down. I'm glad I'm not working there anymore, so I don't have to take sides."

I looked under the paper American flag taped to the inside of the door to see outside. Tammy was holding the picture of Missy up for Del Ron to see.

Barry switched hands and held out Del Ron's huge shirt at arm's length like a little balding lawn jockey. I said, "That's got to be his."

And Barry said, "Duh. I can't leave it in the car or he'll try wiping his face and blowing his nose on it again. And it's his work shirt!"

"Do you know who it is yet?" I asked. "Is it one of the girls bringing him low?"

"No and no," Barry said. "You wouldn't think it to look at him, but he sure can keep a secret."

I said, "Raj, I need a small swirly cone."

Raj shrugged his shoulders, palms up. "No swirly cone," he said. "The machine is broken."

"Again?" I said. "I believe you're going to have to break down and buy a new one 'cause this one's broke as often as not."

He asked, "Is it for the little girl?" And after I nodded, he said, "I'll tell you what I am going to do. Today, one day only, Nutty Buddy, small swirly cone, same price."

And Barry said, "I'll take that deal!"

Raj chopped his hand in the air. "Not an advertised special," he said. "Just for the little girl."

I opened the chest freezer to get a Nutty Buddy and when I slid it shut, I saw the toy hanging over it that Tammy'd been talking about. It's called Pony In My Pocket, which isn't an easy name to forget, and was pink and sparkly with a picture of a happy little girl on the package. It was three fuzzy little ponies, each maybe an inch or so long, named Amira, Starlight, and Prancer, and a glittery bracelet you can stick them on and wear. I looked out the window and saw Tammy patting Del Ron's huge shoulder, like she was palming an Easter ham, and holding her broken cell phone up to his ear. He was talking to someone. Pony In My Pocket didn't have a price so I took it up to Raj with the Nutty Buddy.

I got a strip of beef jerky out of the big plastic jar on the counter and counted out my change.

Raj pointed to the sticker on the jerky jar and read it out loud, "'Two for one dollar.'"

I said, "Just the one, thanks." Then tapped the pink package and asked, "How much?"

"Ah, Pony In My Pocket!" Raj said. "Very collectible. Six ninety nine."

Barry picked up the package. "Six ninety nine? For a quarter's worth of petrochemicals? That's a little steep. I bet it's three ninety nine at Wally World."

"Wally World," Raj sniffed. "Wally World is not so good for business."

Barry laughed. "I guess not! If they start selling lottery tickets, I'd say you're back on a slow boat to Bombay."

Raj looked at Barry for a moment, then said, "It's Mumbai now. Where did your ancestors come from?"

Barry stopped grinning "Eastern Poland," he said. "And there's no way in hell we're going back either."

I shook the tiny horses and asked, "Do they have unicorns?"

"Unicorns In My Pocket?" Raj asked.

Barry put on a fake voice, like some old comic, and said, "Is that a unicorn in your pocket or are you just happy to see me?"

We both looked at Barry, then Raj said, "Neil Diamond is not such a comedian."

"That was just plain weird," I said.

Raj turned to me and said, "No. No unicorns."

Barry tapped the package and said, "Amira means 'princess' in Hebrew."

"We have a girl's name, Amita," Raj said. "It means 'limitless.'"

"At six ninety nine, I'll pass," I said.

Raj glanced out the door. "Are you certain?"

I was and I wasn't. I've taken to not leaving the house with any more than I can spend, not even to Publix. I know Tammy wants them because she's talked about them a couple of different times, just never while we're in the Circle K. But seven dollars is seven dollars, and seven dollars is a lot to spend on something you can't eat.

I tucked the jerky in one cheek and picked up the Nutty Buddy, and Barry said, "I'll walk out with you. I've got to get Boo Baby back up to work."

Raj picked the pink package up off the counter. "I'll put this back for you," he said.

I pushed open the door, and as we stepped out into the thick humidity, Barry said, "I'd give you a ride except Del Ron'd be late. I think I better hang out for a few and keep him away from the DJ."

"Hell, it's just a couple of blocks," I said. "We can do that in our sleep."

"Not me," Barry said. "I don't walk anywhere. And I don't drive anywhere without air conditioning. If gas wasn't so expensive, I'd leave it running twenty-four-seven so I could just run from the trailer and jump into sanctuary."

Tammy had her back to Del Ron and was looking over her shoulder at him with the sleeve of her shirt pulled to one side. She was saying, "It's a little angel. My mom has one just like it, but hers says, *Tammy* not *Misty*."

"She's got a tattoo," Del Ron said. "And it's pinned to my heart."

Tammy let her sleeve go and turned around. "That means somebody loves you," she said.

Del Ron mopped his eyes. "She does. But it doesn't matter," he said. "She's already bespoke."

"Hey, Tammy," Barry said, slapping the roof. "Tammy Wynette! When you get older you can come and work the boat with me. Be Tammy Wynette, The First Lady of Country Music. Fix you up in a big hair helmet. Then I can finally feed Reba to the alligators."

Tammy frowned. "Grandma said Tammy Wynette was a one-hit wonder, second-rate June Carter Cash. She couldn't stand 'Stand By Your Man.'"

"Those blue hairs don't care," Barry said, "just so long as it's a name they remember." He snapped the shirt once, then hung it on one of those wardrobe bars across the back seat, the kind you only see in salesmen's cars and old couples in Lincolns. Barry rolled his eyes at me before he climbed into the driver's seat. He looked past Del Ron at us and said, "Can you believe grown men crap their pants at the sight of this guy? When're you coming to visit, Tammy? I've got every flavor of Kool-Aid under the sun and those 'billies next door departed under cover of darkness to parts unknown." He patted Del Ron's shoulder. "C'mon, Killer. There's some naked ladies whose virtue is in need of protection."

Del Ron let his head drop back on the little headrest and closed his eyes. "She's a lady. In need of protection. But she's not naked."

Nobody knew what to say to that. Tammy gently folded Missy's picture so she could hold the edges together without creasing it, and it hung from her hand like a paper teardrop. She patted Del Ron's big arm and said, "You always smell so good."

20

TIKI MAN

By the time we got to our street, Tammy was suckling melted ice cream from the bottom of the Nutty Buddy cone, and I was still working the beef jerky in my cheek like a plug of tobacco. I was holding Missy because Tammy didn't want to get her sticky with ice cream fingers.

"I think Raj needs to spring for a new soft-serve machine." I said. "That one's broke about half the time."

"Nutty Buddies are good too," Tammy said.

"You got that right."

Down the street, Pearl was out with a broom and a dustpan sweeping up the sawdust and shreds of dried palm fronds from their front walk.

"Maybe we ought to head up to the marina tomorrow," I said. "See if somebody's got a boat needs washing."

She squinted at me and said, "Okay."

"If we both do it, we can knock it out quick. And we can split the money fifty fifty. Get you some walking around money."

"I don't need walking around money, Pere. Just put it in the kitty."

I thought about that, and then said, "Hell, everybody needs a little walking around money. You could buy yourself something."

She said, "I don't need anything."

"I didn't say you *needed* anything. Don't you just *want* something?" I could think of a million things she needed, and one or two things she wanted, but we walked a few squares of sidewalk without saying a word.

"Yeah, I do," she said. "But I don't think just the two of us can wash a boat that big."

We stopped at the palm stump and Pearl stopped sweeping. She rested her hands, one covering the other, on the end of the yellow broom. She asked "You see Duane?"

"Everybody but," I said.

Staring at the stump, Tammy said, "We saw Doris and Neil." Then she gave Pearl a look and added, "And Mr. Ron."

Pearl looked at Tammy and said, "I don't believe I know any of them."

"Doris. Doris is at the library," Tammy said. "She's a librarian. And she's in charge when that old one's not there."

Pearl said, "I've not spent enough time around books to know a librarian by name."

"You and me both," I said.

Tammy said, "Show her what Doris made us." And before I had a chance, she pushed at my elbow and said, "Go on. Show her."

I held up Missy behind her rainbow bars.

Pearl looked at it until she had two creases between her eyebrows. Then she smiled down at Tammy and said, "You'll grow up just like her."

Tammy frowned. "No. No, I don't think I will."

Pearl looked at Missy again. "You don't? You're her spitting image."

Then the little dark cloud passed from Tammy's face, and she smiled and said, "Oh yeah. I might *look* like her."

I'm not sure why, but all of the sudden, I felt like someone on the news, holding Missy's picture up in front of my heart like that. Like something terrible had happened, like mothers in China calling for the ghosts of their children, like all those people in New York City hoping photos might conjure their loves from the dust of those towers.

Then Tammy said, "And Neil and Mr. Ron were up at Circle K." She tilted her head in my direction. "What's Neil do again?"

I let Missy drift down by my side and said, "You mean Barry. He's a Neil Diamond impersonator. On the gambling boat."

Pearl pursed her lips. "I know Barry."

But I couldn't tell whether that was a good thing or a bad

thing, so I said, "He lives over in Whispering Pines." I'm not sure why.

Pearl snorted. "Whispering Pines. Screechin' 'Billies is more like it. You ever notice how trailer trash are the same no matter where you go? All disability checks and temporary tags."

Tammy knelt down by the stump. "He was taking Mr. Ron to work," she said.

"Del Ron, the bouncer up at Sassy's," I said.

Pearl looked up the street and lifted one foot up behind her to scratch at the safety pin tattooed on her ankle.

"You know, he always smells like oranges," Tammy said.

Pearl tapped the nylon broom straws on the sidewalk three times. "I'm done." Then she went inside and closed the door behind her.

I heard Tammy say, "Pere." But I didn't really hear it because I was still someplace far away, wondering if I had someone's soul captured in the stiff paper glued with sweat to my fingertips.

Then she said my name again, "Pere?"

"Yeah?"

"Can you make me a tiki man?"

I looked into her upturned face. "A tiki man?"

She stroked the sandy tendrils with an open palm, then she asked, "And the roots can be his hair?"

Then I saw that she was huddled in my shadow, and if I moved at all, she might turn to ash.

21

PORTRAITURE

I tried rocking the stump with one foot. "I don't know. Let's get it home and see what we got."

Tammy tucked the last inch of Nutty Buddy in the corner of her mouth like a stub of cigar, and said, "Let's do it."

"Hold on, Boss," I said. "You better run your mom in the house first."

I held Missy's picture up. Tammy wiped her hands on her shorts before she took it by two corners and quick-walked to the house. While she was in inside, I lifted one end of the stump to see what we were up against. The door opened, and I dropped it back in the bare patch of sand next to Pearl's driveway. It was so quiet I could hear the ocean and the slight sandpaper sound of Tammy's feet on the driveway.

She stood next to me and asked, "Now what?"

"Drag it over there," I said.

She took a hold of the frayed clothesline still tied around the trunk and pulled like it was tug-of-war, just bones and tendons working under the skin of her skinny arms. She leaned back and back until she finally sat down, her heels dug down in two little cups of dirty sand.

She said, "That's not going anywhere."

"No, you moved it."

"Really?"

I said, "Yeah, you moved it. But let me help."

I clasped my fingers together under the trunk, just up from the roots, and manhandled it across Pearl's driveway to ours. Tammy followed along beside me, holding the clothesline like a leash.

Before I dropped the stump, I said, "Watch your feet."

And she said, "I was just about to say that."

I looked at the stump and then at Tammy. "You could've got it over here all by yourself, you know. Would've took a little while. Might've only been an inch at a time, but you could've done it. You know that, don't you? I mean, you moved him, right?"

She shrugged her shoulders. "I guess."

"Then all you and me did was speed things up," I said.

She gave me that smile, not like she believed me, but like she didn't want to make me feel bad for trying to cheer her up. "Now what?" she asked.

"You tell me. What are we going for here? A mean guy with big teeth?"

She held up one finger and said, "Hold on." Then she ran back in to the condo.

There was a low cloud bank just south, out over the ocean, and it looked close enough to be over Cocoa Beach Pier but was probably way down off Melbourne. And for some reason I wondered if Missy could see it from Lowell Correctional, from some slim, barred window in the infirmary, and if she wondered whether it was hanging low over us. When Tammy came back out, she had her pad of paper, the ten-pack of colored markers in their clear plastic sleeve, Missy's picture, and a little stubby golf pencil with no eraser that I found in the tray under the waterheater. She looked just like she did that first day when I picked her up at the bus station in Titusville, just not so scared.

"That's just how you looked when you got off the bus," I said.

She looked down at herself for a moment, then said, "Except I had shoes."

"That's right. You had shoes. I bet some dolphin's wearing those shoes right now, and all of the other dolphins are like, 'Cool shoes.'"

She hooted and said, "'Cool shoes!'" Then she shook her head at the thought of that dolphin in pink gym shoes.

"And you weren't so tan," I said.

She considered the back of her hand and then her palm. "What's Clyde always say?" she asked. "Brown as a berry."

"He should know."

She put everything down in a careful pile and then got the nylon-webbed chair that was leaning against the garage. I found it out in somebody's trash, and besides being frayed and faded by the sun, there wasn't a damn thing wrong with it.

She opened the chair up on the other side of the stump and said, "You sit here."

I sat down and said, "But you had the paper and the markers when you got off the bus. That's what I meant."

She sat cross-legged on the driveway and fussed with the markers. "I was thinking I spent too much of my food money on them till we hit Georgia, then I thought they were a bargain at twice the price. I like to thought we'd never get out of Georgia."

"I'm with you there," I said. "What'd the Cookie Lady say? Give Sherman another whack at it? I'm with her, but you can't say that too loud down here."

Tammy said, "Sherman was an Ohio school teacher, you know."

"No shit? Guess you didn't want to smart off in his class."

She handed me Missy's picture and said, "Not unless you want your house burnt down. He was named after an Ohio Indian, a Shawnee chief. Hold it up."

I held the picture up so she could see it.

I said, "I didn't know William was an Indian name."

"Not William. Tecumseh." Then she got the joke and smiled. "A little lower," she said. "I need to see your face."

She chewed on the end of the black marker and stared at Missy, her nose wrinkled in concentration. Then she looked at me the same way. It's not easy being looked at that close. When I turned to look over my shoulder back up the street, she said, "Try not to move. Just look at me."

I said, "Okay. I'll try."

She made a few marks with the little pencil, and then stopped to look at Missy again. "She's not smiling."

"There's not much to smile about when you're getting processed into jail, I guess."

She made a few more marks. "Sometimes you see them smiling on the news."

God knows there's a few of me in the system looking like I just hit the lotto, but all I said was, "Those are usually mug shots. The ones they take right when they arrest somebody. When they're still drunk or high."

"I thought maybe it was 'cause of her teeth," Tammy said.

"Yeah. Her teeth was getting bad. But the state's working on them now. That's one good thing. Three hots and a cot and free dental." Toward the end there, she was covering her mouth like a Japanese schoolgirl every time she smiled. Except when she was so high she'd forget. "All that rot up along the gumline is bad. It lets that bacteria and stuff from your mouth get in your blood. You don't want that, especially when you're...Especially not when you're..."

"It doesn't matter, Pere," she whispered. "Don't hang your head."

I looked back up at her and said, "That's why you need to brush good. Those are the only teeth you get."

"I do," she said.

"I know you do."

She looked down at her work and worried one line over and over. Then she said, "Some of them are baby teeth."

22

BIG BOY

Tammy didn't even stop drawing when she asked, "Why'd you quit drinking?"

"So I guess we're going to be here awhile?"

She kept looking at her work. "You don't have to say if you don't want. It's just of everyone I know, you're the only one that's stopped. Daddy can't quit. That's prob'ly why I'm here."

"Well, maybe in five years that won't be true anymore." I don't know why I said that and I don't know why I picked five years.

She stopped drawing but she still didn't look up. "Don't say that, Pere. Please don't."

"Your mom's clean. She's been clean three months."

"But that's only 'cause she's in jail, Pere," she said. "You know that."

"Maybe not. Maybe she'll quit this time."

She looked up at me. "Pere, you don't have to say that. Not for me. We'll drive up to Ocala when she gets out, and it'll be all hugs and kisses and popcorn shrimp. And maybe we'll stay in a motel with a pool and a free breakfast bar. But you and me, we know she won't make the breakfast bar, and when you find her three days later, she'll look like an old whore with death on her breath." She stared at Clyde's garage door for a moment, and when she turned back to me she said, "Where do you think I been my whole life?"

I knew she didn't really want an answer, because we both knew the truth of it.

"The funny thing is," I said, "when you look back on it, what surprises you isn't what made you quit, even though that's usually pretty surprising. No, what you can't believe is all the shit that *didn't* make you quit." I took in a deep breath. "I buried my dad, but there wasn't much to do about that, drunk or sober. Maybe I would have done it better if I'd been sober. Maybe I would have taken better care of him. Known what to say at the end. When you think about it, 'Mom's waiting on you,' ain't much of a send off. But it's all I could think to say in that sorry little nursing home that always smelt of piss and Pine-Sol. The hospice nurse told me if I wanted to say anything, this'd be my last chance. And that's all I could think to say, 'Mom's waiting on you.' Like she'd been sitting out in the car for all these years, fishing through her purse for a stick of Wrigley's gum."

Tammy was quiet for a minute, then she said, "You couldn't help that, Pere. You did your best."

"No, I don't know that I did. I suspect not."

"Who'd know what to say?" she asked. "At a time like that?"

"There were other times. I had a friend, Lee."

"That worked with you in Mt. Vernon?" Tammy asked.

I gave a little laugh. "Monticello. But, yeah. And when he got a better job…"

She jumped in and said, "When he got a better job at the airport in Lake City, you come down to Florida. 'Cause you always wanted to fly."

I nodded. "Yep. He got a better job. And two dollars more an hour to hang out with your best drinking buddy around airplanes in Florida seemed like a no-brainer."

She said, "I'd take a job to hang out with Becky, two dollars or not."

I knew she would. I said, "But we…we were a bad combination. We brought out the worst in each other. Not meanness, but the drinking and stuff. It helps if one says, 'Hey, let's go get drunk at lunch!' and the other says, 'No, maybe we ought to wait till after work.' But with me and Lee, it was like we both just said, 'Hell, yeah!'"

I wasn't saying what I wanted to, so I tried to work out the beginning to the awful end. "We worked the line, fueling airplanes and jets, helicopters, some military, even a blimp one time on its way over to Jacksonville for a pro football game. And it started out small, sneaking a joint in between the 100 octane Avgas truck and the Jet A truck, which was its own kind of stupid since the nozzle on that Avgas truck dripped like the sink upstairs. Then we started slamming Tall Boys for breakfast to take the edge off last night's hangover, and then when it got really hot, we started doing Slush Puppy runs like we did in Georgia."

"Slush Puppies?" Tammy asked. "Like Icees?"

"Yeah, but we'd drink down an inch or two and top it off with 115 proof vodka. A 22 ounce cup could last all afternoon, but it was mostly just thinly colored vodka by the end."

She shook her head and asked, "You got drunk on *Slush Puppies?*"

I nodded. "Cherry. Lee liked Polar Purple."

"Purple's not a flavor," she said.

"That's what I always said! He said it tasted like grape." And I could see him there that day, grinning like he always did, like he knew your zipper was open but wasn't going to tell you until after you got shot down by the cutest girl in the bar. The heat was shimmering off the tarmac, and the sun glared off every wing and windshield. "I was just sitting in the truck. It was his turn and he was parking a King Air C90, one of those little six seat turboprops where the engines sit just that much further forward than you think they ought."

Tammy nodded, not like she knew the difference between a Beechcraft King Air and a C5A Galaxy, because she didn't, but like she knew I needed a minute.

"And I can't say why, and I can't say how I knew, how I knew what was coming but couldn't do a thing to stop it. He crossed his arms in an *X* for the pilot to cut engines, and then he started that slow John Wayne pimp-walk of his toward the cockpit window." Before those props even thought about slowing down.

"And then?" Tammy asked. "What happened then?"

I repeated, "What happened?" I dropped my Slush Puppy and slammed the inside of the windshield, trying to scream over the noise of those feathered props.

Tammy asked quietly, "He walked into a propeller?"

"He walked into a propeller." Then I looked at her. "How'd you know that?"

She glanced down and said, "'Cause I saw the piece of newspaper in your wallet."

"You shouldn't look in other peoples' wallets," I said, but not like I was mad.

"It was one day after Publix. You were talking to Clyde and you had me run inside to put your change away."

I just said, "Oh."

"Was it bad?"

I only nodded, because a little girl didn't need to know about that, or why I tried to tie off that short stump of arm with my belt when I could see the inside of his head. Or why I thought it was so important to find his shoe thrown by the prop wash and take it to that ambulance swimming in blood.

She looked so sad, sad and small and skinny, sitting there cross-legged on the concrete, like she didn't even have it in her to cry. "Is that why you quit?"

I laughed, but not like it was funny. "Hell, no! I went out and got drunk. That shit'll sober you up right quick. It was...what? Close on another two years before I met your mom."

"So why'd you quit? Why'd you quit then?" she asked.

"I quit 'cause I didn't like me anymore. Seems like I remember being a nice person, back when I was a kid, in high school, before I started drinking. I didn't hurt them, screw them over, betray them, disappoint them. Get them killed. I wasn't perfect, but I cared about people, was careful of their feelings."

She said, "You're a nice person, Pere."

"No," I said, shaking my head, "but I'm trying. But it seems like sometimes there's people that don't understand nice. They only understand mean." I took a deep breath, trying to get some oxygen out of the Florida air. And I wanted a cigarette. "I got a natural talent for drink. It's the only thing I was ever any good at. I used to drink a fifth...you know what a fifth is? It doesn't matter. It's a lot. That's what I drank *before* I went out to the bars. And for a while there, I was funnier, more charming, and good-looking than anybody ever born on God's green earth. I was hotter than a three-balled tomcat and everybody wanted some of me. You know how good that feels?" She shook her head. "Guys wanted to be my buddy. Girls wanted to…well, girls wanted to be my girlfriend, and they didn't care if I had other girlfriends. At least not at first." I turned Missy's picture around to look in those green eyes. "And that, *that's* the addiction, that feeling. Because it doesn't last. Because it lets you down. Because it makes you turn into an asshole. Get in fights. Treat people like shit. Blackout and not know what you did, or who you woke up next to, or who you made cry."

"But that…that's Mom," Tammy said, shaking her head.

I shook my head too. "I can't explain it too good. But I haven't drawn sober breath near long enough to explain it any better. I just know that night on the gambling ship, looking at all the lights on the water with your mother, I had a…a change of heart. That's all." I held out one hand, and turned it slowly palm up. "A change of heart. It was a little big thing. Like you. And it doesn't have a damn thing to do with your mother. That prob'ly doesn't sound right to you. Or maybe it does. But it started with her. That's important. It's important now. To me."

I don't know why. "I was just sick to death of who I was, and I'm trying to find my way back to who I used to be, and I'm not even sure he's still in here." I tapped one finger against my chest, and I could hear it inside my head like a small heart beating.

She scratched the end of her pencil against the concrete. "So now, even after last night, you're still going to wait on her?"

I nodded.

She said, "And you're not going to start drinking again?"

I'd thought about it, but not really any more than any other day, so I shook my head.

She said, "And you're not going to stick me on a bus to nowhere?"

"No," I said. "I'd never stick you on a bus."

I could see her thinking about that. She stopped worrying

the paint off her pencil and touched up the drawing in her lap. A few cars passed by, and in the quiet in between, there was faint music from an open window somewhere up the street.

"But Pere…" Tammy began.

Then she went quiet and I asked, "What?"

She started drawing again. "I'm just worried."

"About what?"

"About you," she said. "She'll get you lost. You know she will."

I smiled at her and said, "Don't worry about me. I'm a big boy."

"I know you are, Pere. I know you're a big boy."

23

FULL HERPES SUIT

Tammy tore the sketch from the pad and said, "Give me Mom."

She looked at them side-by-side for a second, then handed me what she'd drawn. It didn't look like any tiki man I'd ever seen. No fangs or flared nostrils, no fierce eyes or spikey hair. It looked more like something African, with a bald head and big eyes, a swollen belly and an open O for a mouth, hands up like it was pushing against something. Or holding something back.

"Wow. I thought you wanted hair? I thought you wanted the roots to be hair?"

Tammy looked at the drawing. "He doesn't have hair yet."

"How do you know it's a him?"

I was just joking, but she pointed and said, "'Cause there's his tallywhacker."

I'd thought it was a loin cloth like Indians wear, but once I took a good look there wasn't any mistaking it. "Yep, that's a package all right. Are you sure you don't want a mean guy? With big teeth?"

She said, "No. No, I don't." Then she poked the paper with the stub of pencil. "I want this right here."

I shrugged my shoulders. "I'll do my best."

"I know you can. If you put your mind to it." Tammy tucked Missy between the white sheets of her pad, then set the markers gently on top, tucking her in with a rainbow bedspread.

"Okay," I said. "Well, I guess we'll need a chainsaw."

Tammy looked across the street at the sun-yellowed fiberglass panels of Clyde's closed garage door.

I said, "No, I'm pretty sure he lent his to his boy down in Pahokee."

She pulled her mouth to one side, then looked back over her shoulder at Pearl and Duane's condo.

I sighed. "Yeah, guess I'll have to."

"Now that we got more tea bags, I'll fix you an iced tea," Tammy said. She walked barefoot up the front walk, slow and steady, holding the pad flat across her upturned palms like the ring bearer at a hillbilly wedding. After she closed the door with her heel, I went and knocked on Pearl's front door.

After a long moment, one of the upstairs vinyl sliders opened and Pearl yelled out, "Where's the truck *this* time, Duane?"

I stepped back off the porch so she could see me. "No, it's me."

She tucked one elbow in the corner of the sill and rested her chin in her hand. Her bare shoulders were striped with two thin tan lines. "Hey, Pere," she said. "What can I do you for?" Then she looked past me to the hole in her yard and said, "You take our stump?"

I checked the hole too, then said, "You want it back?"

She shook her head. "Oh no, you're welcome to it. Just curious."

I squinted up at her. "That's what I come to ask you about. She wants a tiki man and I was hoping to borrow your chainsaw."

Pearl wrinkled her nose up. "I just now got the sand out of it." She considered me for a long moment, like she was trying to figure out where, exactly, on the Duane scale of dumb I might fall. Then she said, "She wants a tiki man, does she?"

I held up the drawing like she might be able to see it.

When she said, "Let me put some clothes on. I'll be right down," I bit the inside of my cheek.

She opened the door, in a white tube top and denim cutoffs, and took the drawing from my hands. After she turned it right way around, she raised her eyebrows up and said, "Wow."

I nodded and said, "That's it."

"Guess you got your work cut out for you."

I took the drawing back. "I'm not figuring I'll get too close to this."

Pearl said, "You never know." Then she chewed her lip for a minute before she said, "Duane's up at the Wal-Mart buying me a new clothesline. Least ways he better be. God knows why I bother, you can't hang a thing out down here unless you want to steam the wrinkles out. And if it rains and there's no breeze, the whole state smells like old pee. I used to love the way clothes smelled off the line back home, didn't you?" She looked off, lost in the memory of some spring morning in Bakersfield. And I tried not to look at her tube top and the two triangles of untanned skin peeking out above it.

"I hate the smell of fabric softener," I said. And I don't know why I said that, even though it's true.

When Pearl came back from California, her eyes shifted slightly to look up the street. She said, "Then he's heading down to Melbourne to look at a bumper for his truck." I thought I was going to have to wait on Drunk Duane or Dumbass Duane, one, but then she said, "Well, if she wants a tiki man. Hold on." She disappeared into the condo and when she came back out, she had the chainsaw and a gas can, and a little greasy red shop-rag wrapped around a screwdriver and a bent wrench. She set the gas can down and turned the chainsaw for me to see. "Prime it five times before you even think about trying to start it, but you don't need the choke in all this heat. Half choke, maybe not even that. Hit this button every time you think of it to keep that chain oiled up and watch yourself when you go to set it down 'cause it don't brake fast as it should and it'll bite you."

"Got it," I said.

Pearl handed me the rag wrapped around the tools and said, "When the chain gets loose, and it will 'cause that palm is green and wet and wet and green, run that screw up down there until you take out the slack. If the whole bar gets loose, and it likes to, get the wrench on that bolt at the back. I got tired of watching Duane take the housing off every five minutes so I put a little bend in it so you don't have to." She handed me the chainsaw and tapped the gas can with the side of her foot. "That's the pre-mix. It's all there is so you better work fast unless you want to hoof it back up to the Circle K again."

I nodded and said, "Work fast."

I stared at the little white ends of her pants pockets, sticking out from the fray of her cutoffs, waiting on more instructions, but she tapped her bare wrist like there was a watch there and said, "Clock's ticking."

"Yeah, I appreciate it."

She took a step back, but before I turned to go she said, "I bet you wouldn't think I'd need to store a chainsaw and a can of gas inside next to the hot water heater, would you? Not when I've got a perfectly good single car garage for just such things. But you also probably wouldn't believe there's a Kenmore washer and dryer setting in my breakfast nook and a hole knocked through my wall for the hoses. I'd show you but I swear-to-God I would good goddamn well die of embarrassment, I surely would.

"And why? *Why*? Because Duane told my goddamn useless brother-in-law he could store all of his particle board and smoked glass crap here for the next six months while he makes 'big money' setting up light boards in Russian strip clubs. Big money! More like Big Moron. He'll come back with a little potato wife or a full herpes suit, or both. Either way, him and his shit are out of here."

I let my arm swing with the weight of the chainsaw. "You ought to have a garage sale."

"What I *ought* to have is a fire."

I thought about that. "Well, let me know on that so we can be out of the house."

She smiled for the first time. She has a pretty smile, but you can't help but think she might use it to chew your ass off. She cocked her head over toward our place and said, "She's pretty as a sweet pea, you know."

24

SWEET TEA

I was standing in the driveway still staring at the stump when Clyde piloted the Buick down the street, slow as a sand-filled barge. Vera waved without smiling just before they slipped under the opening garage door. I didn't have any idea how to turn a stub of palm wood into a tiki man, except it seemed like one of those things you could screw up in a heartbeat. One cut too deep and there wouldn't be anything left to fix. I held the bar of the dead chainsaw over the stump, but nothing came to me.

"Don't you have to start it up?" I heard Tammy say.

And I shook my head and said, "Shit! That's what I'm doing wrong."

She was just behind me, and when I looked over my shoulder, she held up a plastic Circle K cup filled to the top with ice and sweet tea. "Get some fluids in you before you get started."

I took a long drink.

"You better cut the cord." She pointed to the frayed length of clothesline still tied around the trunk. "You better cut the cord now."

"Yeah," I said, "we don't want that getting caught up in Pearl's chainsaw." I flipped open my pocket knife and cut just behind the knot, then I pulled it out from under the stump.

"Can you save me some?" Tammy asked. "Just a little?"

"Some what?"

She pointed to the clothesline. "Of that. Just like that much." She held her thumb and index finger a few inches apart.

I cut her a length and tossed the rest behind me. When I picked the chainsaw back up, Clyde came out of his garage, palming a bottled water, and crossed the street to join us.

He said, "I come over to tell you those work better if you yank that string on the side there."

"Tammy said that same thing not ten seconds ago." Then I looked at Tammy and said, "I believe Clyde's a bad influence on you."

Tammy smiled at Clyde. "Pere's making me a tiki man," she said. "Look." She pulled her sketch from under the faded webbing of the chair and handed it to him.

Clyde asked, "A tiki man?" He considered the sketch for a moment before he looked at me. "He's got your hair."

Tammy nodded and said, "Yes. Yes, he does."

I waved the chainsaw over the stump like a greasy wand. "If you was me, how would you go about getting started?"

Clyde scratched his chin and said, "If I was you, I'd run down to Beal's and buy one and save yourself the heartache. They got 'em. We were just there. And I mean *just* there. Vera can't go twenty-four hours without buying some knick-knack crap at Beal's. It won't be long before we have a full-size cigar store Indian. There's one she has her eye on. That'll piss off my boy's in-laws. And I got to take her 'cause she's scared to back the Buick out of the garage."

Tammy gently took the paper from his hand. "But that wouldn't be him," she said, then tucked him back into the lawn chair, at the cross of two blue bands.

Clyde nodded and then considered the stump. "If I was you, I'd be careful. Maybe we ought to think on this a minute. What're you drinking?"

"Tammy just made sweet tea," I said.

"Oh, you angel!" Clyde said. "Now look behind me...Don't *look* like you're looking! That's better. Now tell me if the storm shutters on the upstairs window are all the way closed or if they're open just a little tiny bit."

Tammy squinted across the street. "All the way closed."

Clyde asked, "Are you sure?"

Tammy checked again. "Positive."

Clyde smiled and said, "You are an angel. She's taking her

beauty rest. Now take this…" He handed her his bottled water, "And pour this poison down the sink. Fill it up with sweet iced tea."

Tammy rolled the bottle between her palms. "Are you sure you don't want it in a cup? With ice? It's not too cold yet."

Clyde frowned and said, "That sounds better, but I might have a fighting chance if she looks out and sees me with the bottle." Tammy shrugged her narrow shoulders. "This isn't that colored water they call 'iced tea' up North, is it?"

"No," Tammy said, "it's that so-sweet-it-makes-your-teeth-hurt stuff y'all drink down here. Just the way Pere likes it."

"That's my girl! A little syrupy?"

"Uh-huh," Tammy said. "I thought you were diabetic?"

Clyde considered her a moment before he said, "Borderline. Only borderline. You don't miss a thing, do you? Now get in there and get me my tea. And if Vera catches wind of this, you'll be waking up with a flounder in your bed. And you *know* I've got one."

Tammy smiled and shook her head before she turned to go.

Clyde watched her pad up the walk. "You know, back before I retired, Vera wasn't in my business all the damn time. The worst mistake a man can make, the second worst, is to let a woman go to the doctor with you. They're just waiting to suck the fun out of your life anyway, and when a doctor in a white coat tells them they're supposed to, well, it's all over for you. Salt, sugar, bonded whiskey, fried food, and fornication—that's the top of the pyramid right there, buddy. And I'm here to tell you, that last one ain't near as much fun without all the others. Then your kids get together and decide the old man needs a cell phone 'for emergencies,' and when you call the operators to help you program it, they're some little foreigners that can't hardly speak English shouting at you 'cause they think you must have the Oldtimers disease already."

'Oldtimers' is what Clyde calls Alzheimer's, and he's been doing it so long now I don't know if he remembers the difference.

"Bottled water," he snorted. "Shee-it. I can hear my daddy

spinning in his grave every time Vera makes me take the cap off a bottled water."

"I always thought water was what you pissed in," I said.

"You got that right," Clyde said. "It's what you drink when you're dragging your ass through the desert and you've done sucked the blood out of the camel. "

In the silence, we both stared at the palm stump.

I asked, "What are the chances he's going to jump out of there all by himself?"

"I'd say between slim and none," Clyde said, shaking his head.

I finished it for him and said, "And Slim was just seen leaving town. Any ideas?"

Clyde curled his top lip up and said, "I'd start at the feet and work up. That way, you might halfway know what the hell you're doing by the time you get to the detail in the face."

I nodded and said, "That makes sense."

Clyde slapped me on the shoulder with a big hand. "Hell," he said, "that's why you need a supervisor."

You've got to have a supervisor.

Clyde slipped Tammy's sketch out from the lawn chair and eased himself gently down into it.

"What's the matter there, big guy? Think you might be one big ass too many for that old chair?"

He shifted uncomfortably and said, "No, the piles are flared up."

I pointed my chin at the stump and said, "By the time I'm done with this, I'll be good enough with this chainsaw to fix you right up."

He made a silent scream and then looked down at the sketch. Tammy came back out of the condo and handed him his water bottle, filled with sweet tea. "Thanks Tammy,."

And she bobbed her head and said, "You're welcome."

Clyde took a sip and smiled. "Maybe you should come and live with Vera and me. You know, just for a while."

She blushed under her tan. "It's just tea," she said.

Clyde shook the sketch. "I see you signed it."

Tammy looked at the sketch and said, "I had an art teacher in Ohio—Miss Patterson. She said if you make something, you should put your name to it. That if you're too embarrassed to put your name to it, you didn't do your best work."

"I don't even know Miss Patterson," he said, "but I like her already."

"I liked her too. She was my favorite."

I pumped the little black bulb under the saw's handle five times, then pulled the choke knob out halfway. Before I yanked on the pull rope, I said, "Stand back."

It started on the third pull, and as I stood there revving it I heard Clyde yell, "Hold on there, Pere. Let me get you some safety glasses."

I shut the chainsaw off and Tammy tapped one foot while we waited. He quick-stepped back across the road, and as he handed me the clear plastic glasses, he said, "Damn if those didn't fall in my lunch box one day over at NASA."

I fired the chainsaw back up again, but just stood there for a minute getting my courage up. I finally made a long cut at one end, the start of what I hoped would be his legs. I heard Clyde yell something, and when I turned to look, Tammy turned away from him with a quivering lip and ran in to the condo.

I shut the saw down and Clyde shook his head and said, "I'm sorry."

"What happened?"

He rubbed at his chin and stared at the ground before he said, "I was making a joke. About you being slow." He looked off down the street and said, "About babies."

I tried to look in the window and said, "About babies?"

All the air rushed out of him at once. "I said 'I don't believe a real baby takes as long as this.' Dumb joke. I wasn't thinking. Should I go talk to her?"

I ripped at the starter cord and said, "No, stay put." The engine caught and I over-revved it, yelling, "Hell, where would I be without a supervisor?"

I attacked the stump, the shower of sawdust and fine splinters stinging my sweat-soaked skin.

25

LABOR

When it was all over, I was covered with sweat and sawdust, fine splinters and a thin glaze of bar lube. I was gasping like a dying fish, trying to find some oxygen in the thick air. There was a dried line of blood from my right wrist to my elbow, because, like Pearl told me, the saw wasn't too fast to brake, and the chain unzipped an inch of my forearm when I brushed against it setting it down. It probably needed stitches if someone else was paying, but as it was, I'd just try to remember to wash it out good later and Super Glue it. A Pakistani doctor up at the Urgent Care showed me how, back when I was still working at the marina. We didn't have insurance there either, but the boss had some kind of cash deal with Urgent Care. The trick is to get everything as dry as you can, then hold the edges together tight while you glue it.

Like every job I've ever done in my life, the tiki man took four times longer than I thought it would. And like every job I've ever done in my life, it took more tools than I own. I borrowed some from Clyde. And Pearl. And I could've bought some, and rented some, and stole some without having everything I needed at hand. They were all laid out on a stained white towel. There was my sheetrock hammer and mismatched screwdrivers, an old chisel Clyde had touched up on his bench grinder, our best kitchen knife, the back edge now hammered into waves, and a half dozen of Clyde's files, in different shapes and each with a different colored plastic handle. The tiki man had some detail.

I brushed some sawdust gently from the dome of his bald head and Pearl said, "I'm going to run and get the camera."

And Tammy said, "I'm going to get you more tea."

When they were gone, Clyde stood up and started yelling across the street at his condo, "Vera! Vera! Come to the window! Hey, woman!" He turned to me briefly and said, "She ain't foolin' me." I didn't know what she was trying to fool him about, except that it probably had its roots back in the dim dawn of their marriage. Or maybe just since his retirement. He muttered to himself, "I'll be goddamned and dipped in shit if I walk across this street."

And just when it was looking like he might end up damned and dipped after all, one of the upstairs storm shutters opened just a crack. He motioned with both of his hands for her to raise the shutter higher and yelled, "You got to see this." He turned to me and said, "Do you mind?" I shrugged my shoulders and he picked the tiki man up and cradled him in his arms like he didn't weigh anything, like he wasn't thirty inches of rock-heavy, green palm wood. He smiled at me and said, "I know, support his head."

Vera had her chin resting on the window sill, and when she smiled you could see the gap between her two front teeth.

Pearl returned with her camera. "Now Clyde, give him back to Pere. Where's Tammy? Tammy!"

Tammy came out with my iced tea, and Pearl said, "We're taking pictures, honey. Now set that down and get over here." She fluttered her hand at Clyde. "Get out of there, these first ones are just family. Good Lord, Pere. Are you that big or is Tammy that small? You better kneel down."

I knelt down on one knee, with the tiki man's butt resting against my other thigh. Tammy hooked her arm around his neck and leaned her head against his. "He's wet," she whispered.

Pearl yelled, "Say, 'Cheese!'"

And we did. Then we took another with all three of us, then just him, then just him and Tammy, then just him and me, then him and Tammy and me and Clyde. Tammy took one of him and Pearl. Then we all crowded into the shade of the garage and looked at the pictures on that tiny screen, each shielding our spirits from the sun with our own hands.

Tammy laid her head to one side, her blonde hair hanging like a gold curtain. Then she smiled at me, her dark eyes faded in the sun, and said, "It's a boy."

Clyde snorted a little laugh, and Pearl said, "So he is."

"I got to get indoors for a while," Clyde said.

And Pearl said, "You and me, both."

Pearl walked away still smiling at the back of her camera. Clyde gathered up his files and crossed the street. All those plastic handles sticking up from his fist looked like he was taking Vera a bouquet of flowers.

Tammy came close to me and worked a small fist into the palm of my hand, and as I closed my rough fingers around it, she whispered, "Name him Lonnie. Please."

"He's yours," I said. "Call him whatever you want."

She looked worried, and said, "No. No, he's not mine. But I'll take care of him just like he is. I promise."

I squeezed the ball of her hand as gently as I could, like it might be a bird's egg the color of sky, and whispered, "Lonnie."

26

SALT WATER EYES

We decided to go down to the ocean for a swim, to wash off the sweat and sawdust. I wrapped Lonnie in the dirty towel and carried him into the cool of the garage.

When I laid him down flat, Tammy looked at him and said, "That's not right." She pulled the towel out from under him and folded it into a rough triangle, then she worked it back underneath him and wrapped him up tight as a burrito, with just his head sticking out. "You got to swaddle him, Pere. Snug as a bug in a rug. Babies like to be swaddled. Warm and tight, like inside his mommy's tummy."

I emptied out an old blue plastic storage box, filled with mildewed bedclothes. Missy's queer for bedclothes, always has been—quilts, comforters, sheets, shams, bed-skirts, and throw pillows. She'd go to Beal's or Big Lots and buy Bed-in-a-Bags, shiny polyesters in pink and red and gold, or brown and blue, with fringe and tassels and ribbons that pull to shreds if you look at them. The one time she came home and said she'd bought a duvet, I honest-to-God thought it was a French toilet women use to freshen-up down there. My only problem with duvets is they slide off the bed for nothing, which kind of defeats the purpose of having covers in the first place. I packed all the bedding up when Missy went away and got out my old cotton blankets.

I let Tammy pick one, a king-sized blue satin pillow sham, and she fixed Lonnie up a little bed in that box. She'd flipped it over to the plain side, and with tufts of pale blue satin all around him, I couldn't decide if it looked more like a crib or a little coffin. Tammy made me lock the garage door and I can't remember the last time I did that during the day.

As we walked down our street toward the ocean, Tammy pointed and said, "Isn't that Mr. Ron?"

It was, standing down at the corner where our street meets the beach road, looking up our way but trying not to look like it.

Tammy said, "I thought he was supposed to be at work?"

"He is."

When Del Ron realized it was us, he looked up the beach road and pointed, like he'd just found what he was looking for, and quick-stepped until he disappeared behind the line of condos.

"Grandma Sue's egg-sucking dog Jasper didn't look *that* guilty," Tammy said. Then she looked back over her shoulder for a moment before she frowned at me. "Where's Neil? I thought Neil was with him?"

"You mean Barry? 'Bout now Barry's serenading a bunch of old biddies with 'Song Sung Blue.' I bet we can see the boat when we get to the beach."

"Mr. Ron doesn't need to be out roaming around by himself," she said, shaking her head. "Especially not now. Barry should know better."

I shrugged my shoulders. "Del Ron's a big boy." Then I laughed and said, "Big as a Winnebago with Michigan plates."

She looked at me like I couldn't have said anything dumber. "You know that's got nothing to do with it, Pere. Sometimes you need taking care of. Everybody does."

I knew she was right. Everybody needs taking care of. Maybe not all the time, but most of it. Because it's a goddamn hard row to hoe the other way. I may not know much, but I know that. Clyde's got Vera and Vera's got Clyde. Duane's got Pearl, even though she's got a mouth that might make him wish he didn't. Del Ron's got Barry, even though he might not appreciate it. Missy has Gracita, and Tammy's got me, and even Flopsy, Mopsy, and Cottontail have Miriam the Cat Lady. I think that's what finally goes wrong with the homeless guys on the beach, like Tampon John and Crap Pants from this morning. They've got no one to take care of, and no one to take care of them, so they just don't give a shit about any of it. How else could you end up squatting in the bushes, staring at some little girl's ass and playing with your dick? How else could you fall in a hole so deep?

When we got to the beach road, Tammy looked up after Del Ron but he was long gone. We passed by Fleur de Merde and between the palms into the parking lot. The cats were huddled down in the shade under the boardwalk, and not even Tammy's calling and clapping was enough to bring them out in the afternoon heat. This time I didn't pause at the leaping dolphin carved into the sidewalk, but she slowed a half a step before she caught up. We walked up the steps of the crossover, but the breeze was almost nothing, the air as still and hot as the waves coming off the cars in the lot.

I said, "Race you!" and took off running for the ocean.

I heard her behind me, yelling, "This hot sand don't bother me no more. You're in trouble now!"

I let her catch up, then pulled ahead again and listened to her squeal. I pulled up before the sand got damp and let her beat me to the sea. She jumped up over the little shore lap and came down with both feet, splashing and yelling, "I told you! I told you!"

I left her at the water's edge and high-stepped out through the surf, far enough to dive without scraping my belly on the sand. I pulled for the dark water out beyond the sand bar. There's something about swimming that I like. I like the weightlessness of it, I like the quiet when your head is under, I like not being nailed to the ground. But what I really like about it, what keeps me struggling along out there in the deep water, is knowing that the only thing keeping me alive is me, that if I quit I die, and that's about as simple as it gets. It's all I need to know, and swimming out in the ocean makes me remember that. And that's a good thing.

When I turned back, away from the cape and catching my breath on the beach side, I saw someone sitting next to Tammy in the sand, someone I couldn't place right off. So I swam in on an angle, the waves lifting me up. Whoever he was, he was old, and he and Tammy were sitting side-by-side, both digging into the sand between their knees. When I could stand up, and was slogging lead-legged through the surf, I saw it was the old man from the library. When he saw me he stood up and threw his hands up in surrender, like a dog exposing its belly. His shirt was unbuttoned and there was a pink line of scar disappearing under his food-stained wife-beater. He was bleary-eyed and his thin white hair was sticking out on one side, like maybe he'd been drinking or napping. Then he turned and wobbled back up the beach toward Fleur de Merde.

When I made it to where Tammy was, she looked up at me with one eye squinted shut against the sun. "Don't bother him, Pere. He come to say he was sorry."

I stood there and thought about that while the water-filled pockets of my fatigue shorts leached out down my legs. I couldn't remember whether his name was Floyd or Lloyd, but either way, he was less of a sorry son of a bitch than I thought, apologizing like that, even if he had to be drunk to do it.

Tammy pointed and said, "You're bleeding again."

The cut on my arm had opened back up, and the blood and salt water were dripping off my ring finger and making small dark saucers in the sand near her feet. I can't say why, but I've always found the sight of my own blood oddly reassuring. Before that thing with Lee, and even after. Like it reminds me that I'm just skin and bones, muscles and blood. I guess it reminds me I'm still alive when I might have forgot.

"You'll have to help me glue it up when we get back," I said.

She nodded, then held her palm up and showed me two white shells the size of silver dollars. She asked, "Can you make him eyes? We each found one."

It took me a second to figure out who she was talking about, but then I said, "Yeah, Lonnie can open his eyes. I can notch them in."

She smiled. "And we can paint little black spots on them?"

I nodded. "Yep, dollars to doughnuts Clyde's got some black paint somewhere in that garage of his."

We headed home, and when we came down off the dune

crossover, we stopped to consider the leaping dolphin in the sidewalk.

Tammy held one sun-warmed shell to each cheek. "He said she didn't used to be so mean. Not back before the doctors took her breasts."

27

SURGERY

Lonnie and I looked at each other across the breakfast nook. He was standing on the other bench, the swaddling towel tied around him like a diaper. I shifted in my wet shorts and they made a sound like rolling paint. We could hear Tammy upstairs in the bathroom, going through drawers and opening the medicine cabinet behind the mirror. I flicked the little tube of Super Glue again and watched it spin between the two shells like a broken compass.

"If she's going to do it, she's going to do it right," I said.

Lonnie didn't say anything. I looked at the postcard on the refrigerator of those two license plate oranges right above Swampy the World's Largest Alligator. There was drawing on the oranges. One had sunglasses and a cop hat and a mean face, and underneath, it said, *Officer Orange*, and the other was sad and crying and said, *Mr. Ron*. And while I couldn't quite make it out from across the kitchen, it looked like Del Ron orange had cartoon stink lines hovering over him and a safety pin through the leaf on his head. Maybe it was his earring. I tried to figure out when Tammy'd had time to make a postcard about today. The drawers stopped closing over my head, and I heard her talking upstairs. I couldn't make out most of it, until she said, "Super Glue!...I know! It's crazy! Get it? Like Crazy Glue.... I'll call you back."

Tammy came down with all of her supplies bundled up in a yellow hand towel faded almost white. She set it all on the table and said, "There isn't any hydrogen peroxide. All we got is rubbing alcohol." Then she frowned and said, "Are you s'posed to have alcohol in the house?"

"That's not the kind of alcohol you can drink," I said.

"Unless you want to end up dead right quick." As opposed to the other kind, that just kills you slow.

"Is this what that poop king lifeguard thought was after-shave?"

"Tim?" I asked. "Yeah, same stuff, but it seems like it used to smell more medicine-y."

She smelled it and frowned. "And he thought it smelled like aftershave?"

"No," I said, "he thought it made him smell like a doctor."

She thought about that and then said, "Oh."

She'd found some cotton balls Missy used to use for her make-up, a roll of paper surgical tape, a plastic bottle of Publix brand 70% isopropyl alcohol, and a couple of bottles of nail polish.

I said, "I don't want my nails done."

She giggled and held up a bottle of black nail polish. "It's to make his eyes. When we're done. We don't have to bother Clyde." I took the little bottle from her and turned it slowly to make sure it wasn't dried out. "I didn't know Mom wore black fingernail polish."

"I believe it was for Halloween one year," I said. What I didn't tell her was that near the end there, I couldn't tell Halloween from any other day. Even with her Florida tan, her skin had that fish-belly paleness, and there wasn't enough make-up or cotton balls in the world to hide the dark circles under her eyes. And the more she tried to cover it all up, the more she looked like something dead that had just forgot to lie down.

Tammy snapped the towel once and smoothed it out on the table, then she splashed some rubbing alcohol into a cupped palm and washed her hands like a surgeon. "Put your arm there and let me take a look." She got in so close I could feel the breath from her nose on the hairs of my arm. She put a thumb on either side of the cut and worked it open as gently as she could. "I don't know, Pere," she said. "You sure you don't want to get some stitches up at the Urgent Care? I can see meat."

I shook my head. "No, that doctor up there says Super Glue

works every bit as good as stitches. He did my knee with glue."
I put my foot up on the bench to show her the white scar under my kneecap. "An edge of unfinished fiberglass up at the marina."

She put her skinny leg up on the bench to show me her knee. "I got one in almost the exact same place. I knocked Grandma Sue's old safety razor into the bathtub with me and then knelt on it. *That* was a mess."

"I bet it looked like you butchered a hog in that tub."

"I still don't know why they call 'em 'safety' razors," she said.

We've had these scar comparisons before. Sometimes we start with the oldest and work our way forward and sometimes we go backwards. The beach does funny things to scars. Old ones you'd forgot show up like pale ghosts, and some only show up in the water. We cover all the cuts and the burns and the scrapes that were big enough to leave a mark. But we never seem to get to the big one hiding in her hair across the back of her scalp, when her dad pushed her through a storm door after a three day meth fest and Grandma Sue showed him the business end of that snub-nosed .38 hand-cannon she called her "pocketbook pistol."

Tammy turned to Lonnie and said, "Now, don't you worry. It's just part of growing up." She pressed my arm down gently on to the towel and picked up the bottle of alcohol. She eyed me. "Are you sure about this?"

I smiled at her and said, "Oh, it'll hurt like hell, but just for a minute." And it did.

It's funny how when you're Tammy's age, physical pain seems like the worst, most scary thing in the world, but the older you get, it's all the other kind of hurt that haunts your dreams.

She asked, "What now?"

I caught my breath and said, "Now? Now we got to get it dried real good before we glue it."

I started blowing on the cut and Tammy yelled, "Stop that! You're blowing your nasty old germs in there and we just this second killed them all off." She dabbed at the cut with a cotton ball that was probably as old as her, and every few dabs she'd peek under it. When she was finished, she turned up the pale pink cotton ball and smiled. She showed it to Lonnie and said, "Grandma Sue had an old rose bush with flowers just this color."

"Okay," I said, "now hold the ends together and pull it tight."

She knelt down close and pinched the open edges together while I unscrewed the cap of the Super Glue with my back teeth. She knotted her eyebrows together and pulled the ends apart like she was stretching a short piece of thread. "Like that?" she whispered.

"Just like that."

I ran a thin bead of clear glue along the cut, and through the burn I said, "Now you've got to blow your nasty old germs on it. It's the moisture what makes it set up."

She pursed her lips and ran a little warm jet of breath back and forth over the cut. After three breaths' worth, she stopped and asked, "Will there be a scar?"

I considered the thin line, already glazing over, and said, "I guess. There's not much that doesn't leave a scar."

28

SECOND SIGHT

Lonnie and I watched her work. At least I think he was watching, even though he didn't have real eyes yet. She had the two shells laid out on one of the door hanger ads from House of Tan that we get about every other day. I thought it was a Chinese restaurant for the longest time because I couldn't believe anybody would pay good money to use a tanning bed in Florida when you can get all the skin cancer you want for free just walking around. She'd painted black circles on the two shells with the black nail polish. After she almost passed out from blowing them dry, she still waited another ten minutes just to be sure, and the whole time she snapped the little bottle of clear polish like she was shaking down a thermometer. Every woman I've ever known does it the same way, and I don't know whether they all take a secret class or if it's in their blood. She painted a clear layer over each shell, following the fine grooves with the tiny brush.

While she was waiting for the first coat to dry, she said, "How are you going to...do it?"

"Do it?"

She shifted her eyes toward Lonnie without moving her head, like she didn't want him to know we were talking about him.

I nodded. "Oh. That *it*. I'll make a couple of notches. Like a *V*, but not that meets all the way." I held up my hands to show her what I meant. "Then I'll wedge the shells in until they're tight."

She pointed to the high, narrow end of one shell and said, "Can this be this end?" Then she touched a fingertip to the corner of her eye against her nose. "It looks like where the tears come out."

I couldn't think of what to say to that, so I just nodded.

When she was painting the second coat of clear, she said, "I was Io once. In a school play. Last year. First I was pretty, but then I had to dress up like a cow."

I remembered her saying something about this before, but I just said, "Who's Io?"

She kept her head down and said, "A beautiful river goddess, much beloved by Jupiter." After another dip in the bottle, she said, "But his wife, Juno, she was real jealous. And when she came around, Jupiter changed Io into a cow. That's why I was pretty at first, then I had to be a cow."

I asked, "What made you think of that?"

"These eyes. Juno had a monster with a hundred eyes, and she set it to watching Io so Jupiter couldn't change her back from a cow, back into a beautiful river goddess. It was Jimmy Belcher with eyes we'd cut out of magazines taped all over him."

"Was Jimmy your boyfriend?"

She wrinkled her nose up. "First off, Pere, I've not had a proper boyfriend yet. Second off, Jimmy's the short-bus kid who squeezed his wiener. He didn't have to do anything but stand there with paper eyes taped all over him until Mercury killed him."

"Mercury *killed* him? What kind of plays do you guys put on up there in Ohio?"

She rolled her eyes. "It's mythology. It's famous."

All that stuck with me about mythology was that the gods were forever turning themselves into some kind of animal, like a swan or a bull or something, so they could have sex with the humans that they thought were hot, and I never understood that. It seems like they'd have got more play as gods. It seems like if you were a hot chick in ancient Greece or Rome or wherever, and you had your choice of doing it with a god or a barnyard animal, you probably pick the god, but I don't recall that they ever did.

I watched her paint the shells for a minute, and then said, "Was Mercury your boyfriend?"

"No," she said. "Not Mercury either." She dipped the brush in the bottle, but before she took it out, she smiled a small smile and said, "I liked Prometheus."

That Tommy kid. I thought she was going to say more, but when she didn't, I said, "Who's Prometheus again?"

"Tommy Pafford," she said. "I got to visit him in the cow suit. He was chained to a cardboard rock and an eagle ate his liver everyday and it grew back every night."

My favorite vodka had an eagle on it, but *my* liver grew back during the day. "Jesus!" I said. "What'd he do to get chained to that rock?"

She stopped her little brush in mid-stroke and said, "He gave man fire. He stole it from the gods and gave it to us. Because he made us from clay and was proud of us and thought we were special."

I thought about that. "Hmmm. Well, if he did all that, I like him too."

She started painting again and said, "He had nine fingers, but that didn't bother me none."

I couldn't remember if that was Prometheus or Tommy Pafford, but I didn't guess it mattered.

When she'd put on so many layers that the shells looked like they'd been dipped in molten glass, I found my yellow box knife and flipped over the blade to the sharper end.

"How do I know they're dry?" she asked.

I held up one pinky and said, "Touch one, light as you can, and see if it leaves a fingerprint. It's a trick I used up at the marina."

She set her chin on the table, touched her pinky to the clear lacquer and smiled. When she tried to lift one up, the smiling orange woman from the House of Tan came with it. She looked up at me on the edge of tears and said "Pere?"

I waved the box knife and said, "No worries."

I pared the shells away from the paper and held them up to the wide ovals I'd thought were Lonnie's eyes. "Where do you want them?"

She looked at Lonnie, then at me, then back at Lonnie. "Just a little, tiny bit closer together." When I'd shifted them, she looked at each of us again and said, "That's right."

I notched in the first one and pushed it in tight, and when I was cutting the notches for the second one, she said, "Wait." She leaned down, her smiling face right in front of his, and said, "I want me to be the first thing he sees."

29

SAFETY SEAT

Tammy and Lonnie and me were standing in the driveway, and Lonnie's new shell eyes were the only ones not squinting against the glare off the concrete. Tammy had one arm around his shoulders, and she drug her toes through the sawdust and palm wood scraps.

Without looking up, she said, "He wants to go to the library."

I looked at Lonnie and said "You want to go to the library?"

She sniffed the top of his head and nodded.

I asked, "He can read already?"

"No," she said. "But you know it's never too young to start. The earlier the better."

"Who told you that?"

She looked up at me and said, "Doris."

I said, "That sounds like Doris." And it did. I rubbed the stubble on my head and said, "Well, I guess she'd know. Wish somebody'd told me that when I was his age. Or your age. Hell, I can barely write my own name now. Sometimes I just make an X when I'm s'posed to sign something."

She smiled and shook her head. "Besides, he can look at pictures and stuff."

I asked, "How are we going to get him over there?"

She wrapped her arms around him and struggled to lift him up. "I'll carry him. See." She took a half a dozen wide, wobbling steps, like a drunk at closing time, before she set him down. She looked up at me and raised her eyebrows.

"Don't look at me," I said. "I won't make it much further."

She looked across the street. "Has Clyde got something?"

"He's got the Buick, but it can only leave the garage once a day and it's already been out."

I thought about it for a minute. Vera has one of those folding shopping baskets with the little wheels on it, probably a Lillian Vernon purchase, and it's been hanging on a hook in their garage for longer than I've been sneaking cigarettes in there but it doesn't look strong enough to haul a jug of milk around the block. Clyde has a cooler with a pull-out handle and wheels, but Lonnie wouldn't fit in that, and even if he did he'd fall out as soon as you tilted the handle up far enough to use the wheels. I shook my head.

"What about Pearl?" she asked.

I shook my head again. "We've hit up Pearl enough for one day. She's probably still getting that chainsaw back good as new."

Tammy rubbed the top of Lonnie's head absently while she stared off up the street. She said, "What about...?" But she shook her head before she finished.

We stood there with our hands in our pockets, looking up and down the street like we were waiting on a bus. "How 'bout that Publix cart?" I said. "Over on the ball field. At the school."

Her eyes widened. "Yeah!" she said. "And we can put him in the safety seat and buckle him in"

"That wouldn't be stealing would it? Not if we put it back where we found it."

"No. No," she said, shaking her head, "not if we put it back where we found it. You think it's still there?"

I hefted Lonnie up on my shoulder and said, "Only one way to find out."

The cart was still there, but Lonnie wouldn't fit in the safety seat without falling over, and pushing that cart through the sandy crabgrass of that rundown ball field with him in it was like it didn't even have wheels.

When I finally wrestled it out to the sidewalk, Tammy said, "We got to go back by the house." She pointed to Lonnie lying flat on the wire grid and said, "He can't ride like that."

I knew it wouldn't do any good to argue and it was only a half a block back in the wrong direction. When we got to the condo, she said, "Get him up out of there and then go change your shirt."

"Change my shirt? I already changed my damn shirt once today already."

She put her little fists against her hips and said, "I don't care if you already changed your darn shirt twenty times today, Mister Poopy Mouth. We're taking him out in public for the first time. We're going to see Doris, and that one's got blood on it."

It did. I must have wiped my arm off with it after we went swimming in the ocean. I headed in the house and she yelled, "You know, there's some shirts with collars hanging in that closet up there. And a little deodorant wouldn't kill you either."

I came back out smelling like Aqua Velva because I guess what Tammy thought was deodorant was an old bottle of after-shave but I splashed some under my pits anyway. I was wearing the orange golf shirt I bought at Beal's when I interviewed up at the marina and she'd fixed up the cart with the blue satin pillow sham for Lonnie to lay on.

I lifted him in and she said, "No. Turn him around the other way. With his head up at the front. So he can see me."

After I flipped him around, she draped another blue sham over the front of the cart so he didn't "get too much sun." When we finally started off to go see Doris, she wouldn't let me push, so I stayed up near the front to help her make the corner where our street meets the beach road.

I waited with Lonnie in the cart under the shade of a palm tree on the far side of the library parking lot. I pulled the sweat-stained polyester golf shirt away from my skin, and when I let it go, I got a blast of Aqua Velva.

When Tammy came out the front doors with Doris, I heard her say, "It's a pram."

"A pram?" Doris asked.

"It's what they call a baby carriage when the baby's facing you instead of the front," Tammy told her.

Doris smiled like she'd just learned something she didn't already know, even though you could tell she did. Then there was another one of those strange moments of quiet, and Doris's shoes clicked across the asphalt like somebody throwing pebbles against a window. She smiled at me, and as much as I liked that, I'd have liked it more if there wasn't something too much like pity in it.

Tammy pulled back the sham and said, "It's a boy."

Doris leaned in the cart and put an open palm on Lonnie's belly. "He's beautiful," she said. "Just perfect."

Tammy gazed at him and said, "Isn't he though?"

I tried not to look down the gap of Doris's shirt when she was bent over like that, but when I finally did, when I just couldn't help myself, I clenched my jaw so hard I thought my back teeth might shatter.

"His eyes look real," Doris said. "Like they follow you around."

Tammy smiled at Doris. "Don't they though? I made them, but Pere did everything else."

They both looked up at me and Doris said, "Did he?"

Tammy said, "Go on, tell her."

I shrugged my shoulders and looked at the asphalt. Then I pointed a thumb back over my shoulder like someone might be standing there, and said, "Our neighbor had this stump..." I thought I had more to say but it didn't seem to be making it all the way to my mouth.

Tammy said, "Tell her about the chainsaw." But before I could begin, she said, "He did it with a chainsaw mostly. And a chisel. And some screwdrivers. And a little axe." She turned to me and said, "What's that called? That little axe?"

"A sheetrock hammer. It's got a hatchet on the back—"

Tammy interrupted and said, "A sheetrock hammer! You wouldn't believe what he can do with a sheetrock hammer. Wood chips were flying, I tell you what." Tammy tugged at the fold of loose skin over my elbow and said, "Get him up, Pere. He slept the whole way down."

I picked Lonnie up like he was nothing and held him in front of me like he was standing on my forearm. Doris traced his face gently with her slender fingers like she might be blind. Then she sucked in her bottom lip and ran her palm over his bald head. She was close enough to count her dark lashes, and when she breathed out, I could smell the faint sweetness of it.

Doris looked me dead in the eyes. "Who knew?" she said quietly. "Who knew you could do such a thing? It's art you know. It really is."

"Doesn't he smell good?" Tammy said.

Doris smiled at me. "Yes," she said, "he smells very nice."

I was pretty sure I knew who Tammy was talking about, and while I didn't know who Doris was talking about, it made me feel better to pretend I did.

Tammy leaned her head over slowly until it just touched Doris's arm. "He's my baby brother," she said. "His name's Lonnie."

30

CHUPACABRA KITTEN

Tammy and Lonnie were inside and me and Clyde were sitting in the shade of the garage. He turned to me and said, "You smell like a French whore's ass."

I laughed. "I bet you say that to all the girls. Besides, ten bucks says you've never been within sniffing distance of a whore. French or otherwise."

He looked across the street to check the storm shutters on their upstairs window, then he lowered his voice and said, "First off, you don't have ten bucks. Second off, I went to New Orleans once when I was in the service."

I asked, "And she smelled like BO and Aqua Velva?"

Clyde thought about it for a minute before he said, "Just her ass."

"Maybe she was a he."

Clyde stroked his chin. "Well, that prob'ly explains it," he said.

And I said, like I was supposed to, "Explains what?"

He dropped his voice even lower than it already was and said, "'Turn the lights down, soldier boy.'" I laughed and Clyde grinned, and after I quieted down, he said, "What are you all dressed up for?"

I tugged at the front of my sweat-soaked shirt and said, "Hell if I know. She made me change before we took the tiki man to see Doris."

He looked at me wide-eyed. "You carried that all the way to the library?"

I pointed over my shoulder at the Publix cart parked in our garage. "No, we used that. It was sitting in the ball field." I convinced her we'd just take it back on our next trip since Lonnie'd probably want to go along with us.

He shook his head and said, "And she made you put on the smell-good?"

I nodded and he frowned at his condo for a long moment before he said, "She's starting young, but there's no point in fighting it. You know that, right? Six curtains on every window, five hundred throw pillows, long-tailed cats, and polyester church pants the color of Easter eggs that grab your leg hairs."

I thought there was going to be more, but he just shrugged his big shoulders and shook his head like he'd explained everything there was to explain. We sat quiet for awhile. There wasn't a cloud in the sky and no breeze, no traffic, no noise at all. And except for the dark flashes through the sawdust and palm wood scraps of those little lightning-fast lizards, it seemed like the world might have stopped.

Clyde cocked his head and held up one hand like a Saint Francis lawn jockey. He looked up the street and said, "Ole Blue."

And just then Duane's truck cleared the end condo and turned on our street.

I said, "Damn, you're good."

He shook his head. "No, I'd know the sound of that shitbox anywhere. I'm about ready to buy him a new muffler my own self." We watched Duane lurch Ole Blue down the street. "Shit, that's why they got no kids, he can't even find second gear."

Duane pulled up over the curb and into their yard until Ole Blue's right front tire dropped down into the hole left by the palm stump. He honked the horn, and as he swung out with the opening door, he yelled, "Pearl! You ain't gonna goddamn-well-believe what I got!" He saw me and Clyde for the first time and said, "What're you all dressed up for?" But before I could answer, he smiled and said, "You gotta see this!"

Clyde said under his breath, "Didn't know I was getting dinner and a show."

Duane looked into the truck bed and yelled, "You little goat-sucking sonofabitch! That's a brand new bungee cord you just chewed through. Pearl, c'mon!" He drug something metal across the corrugated floor of Ole Blue, and watched the front door. When Pearl opened it, Duane lifted out an animal trap, careful to hold it at arm's length. There was something almost black and hairless curled in one corner, the size of a small dog but definitely not a dog. It had a black hairless tail like a rat and loose gathers of skin at the joints.

Pearl asked, "What in God's name is that?"

Duane swayed gently in a bleary-eyed beer fog and said, "You'll never believe it!"

Pearl pulled her mouth to one side and sighed. "No, I don't guess I will." Then she glanced over at us. "Hey, Clyde. What're you all dolled up for, Pere?"

Duane set the cage down on the hood of Ole Blue and stared at the thing inside. He said, "It's the only one in captivity anywhere. It's a chupacabra kitten."

Pearl checked her nails and said, "A what?"

"A baby chupacabra," Duane said. "A kitten. They suck the blood out of the goats down in…Cuba?"

Pearl waved her hand at the cage. "Well get the poor thing off there before you cook it to death. You know that engine runs hot." She looked into the cage again. "What are you going to do with it?"

"Do with it?" Duane asked. "Well, first off we're going to take some pictures with your digit camera and sell them to the internet. This little fucker's going to pay for himself about a gazillion times over."

Pearl straightened up and said, "*Pay* for himself? Duane, do not tell me you paid good money for that thing."

Duane held out his hands, palm up. "The guy said it killed all his chickens."

Pearl screwed one foot hard down into the dirty sand. "What guy?"

Duane pointed back over his shoulder like the guy might be standing behind him and said, "At the junkyard. Down in Melbourne."

Pearl asked, "How much?"

Duane looked off up the street and mumbled, "Hundred and a quarter."

"A hundred and twenty-five *dollars*?"

"Yeah," Duane said. "But twenty-five of that was the cage."

Pearl considered Duane and snapped her nails together. "So this guy, in a junkyard in Melbourne, he sells you the one-and-only-ever-in-captivity chupacabra kitten, for only a hundred bucks?"

The hairless thing stood up, revealing a double row of teats like so many spoiled blackberries.

Duane said, "And twenty-five for the cage."

Pearl asked, "He was out of Big Foots?"

Duane kicked the corner of the cage lightly with his flip-flop. "It killed his German Shepherd." But it didn't even sound like he believed it.

Pearl took a step closer and peered into the cage. It yawned, a pink tongue curling out of it narrow jaws. There were small sharp teeth set in black gums. She said, "That German Shepherd must have been ailing."

Clyde leaned over to me and whispered, "The chickens too."

Pearl quick-walked up to the stoop and jerked open the front door, and before she slammed it, she said, "Take it back."

Duane said, to no one in particular, "I can't just take it back. It was a cash kind of deal." He wandered the few steps over to our driveway, and drug one flip-flop through the carpet of sawdust and wood chips. "What're you making?" he asked.

"A tiki man, for the girl," I said. "Out of your old palm."

"That's cool." Then he looked around and asked, "Where?"

"They're inside," I said. Duane looked at our condo and nodded slowly. I pointed my chin at the cage. "It looks like a big rat fucked a little dog."

And Clyde said, "I always wondered what that would look like."

"Tammy!" I yelled. "Get out here and take a look at this."

Tammy came out and as she walked down the short sidewalk, she said, "This better be good."

I asked, "Are you reading him that book Doris gave you?" It's called *Pat the Bunny* and Doris said it was a good first book for babies. I don't know whether the bunny's name is Pat or whether it's about patting a bunny. On the way home I called it *Smack the Cat*, but Tammy didn't think that was funny.

"No," she said, "we already read that a bunch of times. Now we're watching *Tom and Jerry*. The one where that big Black lady in house slippers keeps whacking Tom with the broom."

Clyde snorted a laugh. "I know just the one she's talking about. Lord knows I'm not supposed to, but that's funny stuff."

I pointed to the cage in front of Duane's truck and asked her, "What do you make of that?"

She knelt down at a distance and said, "What is it? Is it a baby? What's his name?"

"It's *supposed* to be a chupacabra kitten," Duane said. "That's what the guy told me."

Tammy shook her head slowly. "No, I don't believe so," she said. "They think chupacabra's a canid. So it'd be a pup, not a kitten."

I was thinking it, but Duane asked, "What's a canid?"

"Like a dog," she said. "Or a wolf. Or a fox. But this looks almost like a baby aardvark, except around the mouth. But they're only in Africa."

Duane stooped to peer into the cage over Tammy's shoulder. "Where do you suppose a junk man in Melbourne got hisself a African hard vark?"

"Oh, it's not an aardvark," she said. "It just favors one, except around the mouth. I don't know what it is, but it's ugly enough to scare Christ down off the cross."

We all laughed until one of the vinyl sliders opened upstairs and Pearl yelled out, "Congratulations, honey! The governor just called and you're officially the stupidest man in Florida." The window slammed shut and Duane kicked the cage again.

Clyde said, "It's a hairless raccoon."

And Tammy and I both said, "Really?"

He nodded. "Yeah, my boy's father-in-law down in Pahokee

has one they keep as a pet. Mean as a…well, mean as my you-know-who when she was still getting her monthly visitor. Don't tell me there's no upside to menopause. The pause that refreshes, I say. They're pretty rare, and they don't usually make it in the wild. Look at the paws."

Duane stared at the black paws.

Tammy tilted her head to one side. "They look like little hands," she said. "Hard to believe they're so cute with the fur on."

Then Duane spun around, stamped the sand, and yelled, "Goddamn sonofabitch garbage eating 'coon."

"I wouldn't be so quick there, Duane," Clyde said. "Hairless 'coon's a rare thing. Got to be worth something. To somebody. The right somebody."

Duane scratched his chin. "You think?"

Clyde nodded and said, "Like one of the alligator farms for the tourists. They got other animals. One up outside of Christmas has an albino."

That was the place Missy and I went, where we got the Swampy the World's Largest Alligator postcard. Swampy wasn't even a real alligator, just the long concrete storefront made to look like one. The boardwalks were spongy with rot, and you couldn't hardly see any alligators from all the duckweed. Kids were pelting baby gators in a pen with hot dog pieces you could buy in the gift shop.

Duane asked, "An albino what?"

"An albino raccoon," Clyde said.

There was an albino raccoon, as yellowed as old underwear, and a man in a safari shirt with a .357 magnum strapped on his hip was telling a new guy never to go in the big Florida panther cage by himself because they'd just as soon kill you as look at you and were fast as lightning. What he'd actually said was, "Once they got your guts on the ground, no point shooting 'em then."

Duane smiled. "An albino raccoon? No shit? Bet that's weird looking." He rubbed his chin. "I'd paid to see that."

Clyde said, "There you go."

Duane thought about it a minute. "Not much, but something."

"We had raccoons once, at Grandma's," Tammy said. "A momma had her babies in the flue. You could hear the kits through the wall squeaking to be fed. Grandma and me thought it was the cutest thing ever till the house filled up with fleas. Dad smoked the 'coons out and then we had to bomb the place."

Duane looked over his shoulder at the cage. "I'm figuring this one don't get fleas," he said.

"Bet you're right," Clyde said.

Tammy worked the toes of one foot under a pile of sawdust, then she said, "I better get back inside. Before Lonnie starts bawling." And she was gone.

Duane watched her go. "Who's Lonnie?"

I shrugged my shoulders, watching his chupacabra kitten curl itself inside the cold comfort of its bare tail, its black eyes flashing green before they closed. But I knew, I knew on the inside who Lonnie was. Whether he's slipping from Missy's warm center, or cowering in a junkyard cage, waiting patiently inside layers of palm wood, or stepping off a bus in Titusville, things need a name.

And like he read my mind, Duane kicked the cage and said, "Pere's right. I think I'll call you Rat Fuck."

The upstairs vinyl slider opened again, and Pearl yelled out, "And don't forget my clothesline."

Duane picked up the cage and slung it into Ole Blue's bed, saying, "C'mon, Rat Fuck. I believe you and me, we could use a drink."

31

CHASING PINK

I finally got Tammy to put Lonnie down for a nap so we could take a walk on the beach, but only after she made Clyde promise he'd sit in front of our garage and listen for him. We stepped off the dune crossover into the warm sand, and I pointed up the beach with one hand and down the beach with the other. The sun was getting low on our side of the state, but the old geezers over in Clearwater were probably still working on their skin cancers. The beach was empty except for a huge family of Mexicans, huddled close together, sharing a half-gallon jug of blue fruit drink and swimming in their clothes. A boy about Tammy's age, with boobs bigger than Missy's plastered with a wet T-shirt, smiled and waved at Tammy. She acted like she didn't see him and motioned with her head so I followed her south toward Cocoa Beach Pier. We walked along in silence at the damp edge of the sand, and every once in a while, she'd glance up at the one tiny cloud in the sky, painted pink by the low sun.

She pointed to the wet sand just ahead of us and said, "How come we can't ever catch it?"

I asked, "Catch what?"

She kept pointing and said, "The pink. That splash of pink light there. It always looks like it's just right ahead of us, like it's just right there, but when we get there, it's that much further ahead. We never catch up to it."

"Your mom asked me almost that exactly same thing. Just almost exactly. About those lights on the ocean. How come they followed us around on the gambling boat that night."

"The shimmering on the golden sea?"

I smiled at the memory.

"Yeah, the shimmering on the golden sea."

She looked up at me. "What'd you tell her?"

"Same thing I'll tell you. I have *no* idea. I know the pink's reflected off that little cloud there, but I don't know why we never get to it."

"Okay," she said. "Let's chase that pink to the pier!" Then she took off running, scooting up the beach like one of those little birds when the low shore lap came too far up the sand.

When I caught up to her, she'd stopped to look at what was left of one of the big sea turtles that nest this time of the year. It was rolling at the edge of the surf and looked like the sharks had gotten to it. Some gulls were picking at what was left.

Tammy said, "That's too bad."

"Some tourist will get a stinky surprise tomorrow."

She thought for a second about how that might play out and then laughed. "I saw two box turtles doing it once. Behind Grandma's house. I looked out the kitchen window and it looked like one was floating in the air, but when I got out there, it was just the male up on top of the female. Then he stretched his neck way out and made a little groan. I ran in to tell Grandma and she tried to find the camera 'cause she'd never seen such a thing."

"Me neither," I said. "And I've seen plenty of box turtles, back in Virginia. We even had one as a pet for a while. My dad drilled a little hole at the edge of his shell and tied on a piece of string so he could wander around the yard when he wasn't in his set tub."

She asked, "What was his name?"

I couldn't remember that we'd ever given him a name, but I said, "Speedy."

She giggled. "That's funny." My mom would have made us give him a name if she'd still been around. "What happened to him?"

That was a good question, because one day we put him out in the yard and when we went out to get him, all that was left was a bloody end of string. My dad thought probably a fox. But I said, "We let him go."

She nodded. "They can move fast when they want to. By the time Grandma and me got back out there with the camera, which was like a minute, it was just the female looking sad with her head half in and we couldn't find the male anywhere. Dad said he was already off in the woods smoking a cigarette and calling his buddies on a little turtle phone."

We walked side by side to the pier, and even though the ocean was almost dead calm, there were still a few surfers out in the deep water, sitting on their boards and looking hopefully out to sea. Before we got to the rows of pilings, Tammy looked over into the dunes and said, "Jesus, he's one big Indian."

I looked over and saw Standing Bear and Oxana, huddled between two low dunes covered with sea oats, blowing blue smoke. Standing Bear waved us over.

I turned to Tammy and asked, "You want to go talk to them?"

She shrugged her shoulders. "You go on. I'll just kick around the water a little bit."

"You sure?"

She looked sideways at them. "I like Mr. Bear, but she creeps me out. I'll come over when they're done smoking that skanky ditch weed."

I asked, "What do you know about ditch weed?"

She rolled her eyes. "What *don't* I know? You can smell it all the way over here and the wind's not even blowing this way. Dad used to plant it out in Grandma Sue's stand of corn. That's a cash crop up in Ohio, buddy."

I said, "Can't see Grandma Sue putting up with that."

"You wouldn't think, would you? But she didn't care. She said everybody grew it up that way during the war for rope. She smoked it when she was just a little girl on the farm, but back then they called it 'Life Everlasting.'"

I laughed. "Life Everlasting!"

I headed up toward the dunes and she headed for the sea, and when I turned back she was already looking at me and she yelled, "I know, I know. Not past my knees."

When I got to where they were sitting, Oxana pinched off the end of the joint with her fake purple nails and flicked the ember into the sand.

Standing Bear stood up and shook my hand. "Hey, Pere," he said. His eyes were bloodshot and heavy-lidded, but Oxana looked like she always did, like some second-string Russian porn star, snapping her gum and looking bored in too much make-up.

Standing Bear said, "Say 'Congratulations!'"

I asked, "Why?"

"Just say it," he said. "Just say 'Congratulations!' You'll be the first."

"The first what?"

Oxana threw her hands out palm up and whined, "For fuck's sake, man. How hard is this?"

"Okay," I said. "Congratulations!"

She rolled her eyes and said, "Thank you!"

Standing Bear grinned. "You're the first!" he said. "We're getting married!"

I looked up at Standing Bear, then down at Oxana, then back at Standing Bear. I didn't even know they knew each other. They both just worked on the pier. "Is this some kind of immigration deal?" I asked. "So she can stay in the country?"

Standing Bear looked hurt, and Oxana pointed a long fake nail at me and said, "You are such a fucking asshole. *That's* why I never gave you a new necklace." Then she looked at Standing Bear and said, "I told you. I told you that's what people would think."

Standing Bear rolled his shoulders and grimaced down at me before he said, "No, it's love."

I smiled and said, "Well, if it's love, congratulations!"

He smiled big and said, "Thanks! We're going to get married out on the pier."

Oxana made a face. "Maybe. *Maybe.* All that wind and my hair. I don't know."

I turned and yelled to Tammy and waved her over. "They're getting married!" I called.

Tammy ran up through the sand double-time, and when she got to us, she got right down in Oxana's face and panted, "You're getting *married?*"

And for the very first time, Oxana's face opened up and she smiled, smiled like a girl in love about to be married, not like some bored Russian porn star in too much make-up.

Tammy said, "Mr. and Mrs. Bear! Did you get a ring?" Oxana nodded and held out her pale hand to show Tammy the thin gold band with the clear purple stone. "It's beautiful."

Oxana said, "It's amethyst."

"It goes with your nails," Tammy said.

Oxana wiggled her fingers and long fake nails. "I love purple."

Standing Bear shrugged and said, "I figured she'd want a diamond, but no."

Oxana gazed down at the ring. "I don't need a diamond. This is what I wanted."

Tammy asked, "Are you going to have babies?" And I elbowed her in the shoulder.

But Oxana smiled and blushed, and said, "Yeah, maybe."

Tammy danced in place, digging her feet down into the sand. "Can we come?" she asked. "Will you send us an invitation in the mail? With silver writing?"

There was a moment of quiet while Standing Bear and Oxana looked at each other, then Standing Bear said, "I don't know—"

Oxana interrupted him, "We've not even made a date yet. And we don't know who can come. My family, his family, who knows?"

It got real quiet and nobody knew where to look, then Tammy said, "We should probably be getting back, Pere. Who knows how long it's been since Clyde changed a diaper?"

Standing Bear sat back down and wrapped his big arm around Oxana, pulling her close.

Tammy looked at Standing Bear and said, "We'll be grilling baloney later if you and the Mrs. want to stop by." Then she giggled and ran back down to the water, shouting, "You can see what Pere made me."

Oxana watched her go and said, "Come by tomorrow. I'll get her a new necklace."

I was going to tell her we were making our own, of shells we found ourselves no bigger than the nail on my ring finger, that Clyde gave us silver swivel-snaps out of his tackle box and Vera had found us a length of black cord. But I didn't. Tammy could use an extra of something.

On our way back up the beach, Tammy asked me why her mom and me hadn't gotten married. And I couldn't tell from the way she asked whether she thought it would be a good idea or a bad idea. I told her it was because she was pregnant and didn't want to be pregnant in her wedding gown. I told her that me and Missy wanted her and her baby brother to be part of the wedding, part of the celebration. I told her that Missy was going to take her shopping for a shiny pink dress with matching shoes and she was going to be the flower girl and toss rose petals for her mom to walk on. I told her there was going to be a three-layer cake with a bride and groom on top and a chocolate fountain.

She asked me how long her dress was going to be and all I could think to say was, "All the way to the floor."

"Then how will anybody see my shoes?" she asked.

But before I could think of anything to say, she asked if she could keep the bride and groom on top of the cake, and if we were going to save the top layer in the freezer for a year because it was good luck, and if there were going to be fresh strawberries and cubes of buttery pound-cake for the chocolate fountain. I said yes to everything. I said yes to everything because it was all bullshit anyway. Missy and me never talked about getting married. We never talked about Tammy or rose petals or anything else. A pregnant meth addict doesn't mean anything, you might as well say sun-burnt meth addict. Or a blonde meth addict. Because the only part of that that means a goddamn thing is the meth. It's about that and nothing else.

It's about that and no one else. Nobody on the outside. Nobody on the inside.

She stopped and looked back down the beach, toward the pier pilings now so far away they looked like little cocktail straws stuck in the sand, leading a drunk out to drown. She squinted like she might be able to make out the specks of Standing Bear and Oxana and said, "You know, first off, I thought it was one of those immigration deals. But I guess not."

She galloped ahead a few steps and skipped along the edge of each incoming wave. When she took out her cell phone and started talking, the only words the breeze carried back to me were "flower girl."

When we made it back up to the crossover at Cherie Down, the Mexican family was still there, and the little boy with the big boobs was sitting near the ocean digging in the sand. When we walked by, he looked up at Tammy and said, "Sandcastle?"

Tammy gave him a half-smile and threw her arms out to the side real fast. She said, "I don't know. We probably have to get home and feed my baby brother."

He nodded seriously and said, "I have a baby brother."

She looked at me and raised up her eyebrows. I said, "I think we got some time, yet. I'm going to sit up by the dunes. I'll holler when it's time to go."

She bounced once and smiled at me. Then she ran a quick half-circle and dropped to her knees in the damp sand beside her new friend.

32

CAT LADY

It wasn't too long before the Mexican family packed up, shaking the sand out of an old green bedspread and policing their little patch of beach of every speck of trash. I'd been watching Tammy and the boy take turns talking on her broken cell phone. He was laughing and serious, covering the mouthpiece with his palm to tell her the latest from some dusty border town. Tammy walked up from the water's edge with her new friend, and they each did a little finger wave when they went their separate ways. She flopped down next to me and folded her arms across the tops of her knees. We watched them load up. The mom was doing six things at once, and the whole time she held the baby brother against the crook of her neck, jiggling him and speaking Spanish softly into his ear. When they all headed for the crossover, they grinned at us and bobbed their heads, which down this way usually means they don't speak much English, and I smiled back to let them know they were okay with me, that I didn't care if they spoke English, and that I wasn't going to chase them off or call them names, even if I might look like I would.

"He's a dribbler," Tammy said.

I thought she was talking about the baby, but then she starting talking about the sandcastle. Tammy's decided there are only two kinds of sandcastle makers, builders and dribblers, and there's no mixing the two. Builders use cups and buckets and shovels, do lots of molding and patting and carving. Dribblers just dribble. They dribble wet sand into bigger and bigger piles, into higher and ever more delicate towers. And while she thinks the builders end up making castles that actually look like castles, she likes dribble castles better because they look like something nature made.

I asked, "Any good?"

She nodded at me wide-eyed. "Real good," she said. "I just made the moat."

"Maybe they'll come back tomorrow."

She shook her head. "No. No, they're headed up to northern Ohio to pick cucumbers."

"That's too bad."

She snorted a little fake laugh and said, "Not if you like pickles!" Then she put her head down on her folded arms so I couldn't see her face.

After a while I said, "What should we do now?" She shrugged her shoulders but didn't look up. "Dinner? Is it getting baloney grilling time?" She shook her head. "Okay, I can wait." I tried to think of something else, and when I did, I said, "What about those roman candles?"

She turned her head enough to peek at me from behind her arm with one eye. "It doesn't have to be *dark* dark?"

It wasn't near dark enough for fireworks, but I know she doesn't like the dark, especially not out on the beach with all of the sand crabs. She doesn't like the dark, period. That first week she came down, we had to go to Beal's and buy a nightlight. It's a real shell, just like the old Shell gas station signs, with a little four watt bulb behind it, and in the wee hours when I'm not sleeping and filled with worry, I check on her and she's curled inside herself, bathed in the pinky-orange of that shell, dim and blurry around the edges like a memory I'm having trouble getting a hold of.

"No," I said, "it's dark enough for roman candles."

When we came down off the dune crossover on the parking lot side, Miriam the Cat Lady was getting her milk jug of cat food out of the hatchback of her old Honda.

"See?" Tammy said. "Shorts and long-sleeves."

Miriam shook her jug and called, "Maidel! Dreidel! Knaidel!"

Flopsy, Mopsy, and Cottontail raced out from under the boardwalk.

"Kitties!" Tammy yelled.

Miriam turned to her and smiled. Tammy skipped and

Miriam limped, and they met at the pile of cats turning each inside the other like they were braiding invisible rope.

Miriam bent stiffly and the calico with the missing tail stood with his front paws on her knee to get petted. She cooed, "Meine kaetzele."

Tammy petted the mostly white one, the one she calls Mopsy, along the length of her back until she arched her butt up in the air, and the mostly black one meowed for attention. Tammy scooped up Mopsy and looked up at Miriam. "What do you call this one?"

"Dat one? Same vat I vould call you, *Maidel*. Little girl, like you."

Tammy smiled and pointed to the black one she calls Flopsy. "What about him?"

Miriam puffed her cheeks out and said, "*Knaidel*. A dumpling. I must hold him back, or he vould eat everyone's share." She scratched at her forearm, then wagged a crooked finger at Flopsy and said, "Shvartz goniff."

Tammy pointed to Cottontail, still standing up against Miriam's knee, and Miriam said, "Him?" She stopped petting him and held her palm over his head until he looked up at it, then she made small circles in the air, getting just a little bigger at each pass. Cottontail stood taller as he watched her hand, then he stood on his hind legs and hopped in a circle. It was no mean feat for a cat with no tail.

Tammy clapped her hands and said, "He does tricks!"

And Miriam said, "Meine *Dreidel*. Spinning like a top."

"I call him Cottontail," Tammy said, "on account of his tail. And how it looks like a rabbit's. And there's three of them."

Miriam looked down at her and shook her head and smiled.

"We best go get those fireworks," I said.

"You go on, Pere. I'll help Miriam feed this mess of cats till you get back."

I could be back inside of five minutes, but I still didn't like the idea of leaving her alone. I smiled and said, "I don't think Miriam wants to hang around waiting on me."

Miriam waved me away and said, "Go. Go. She can get the vasser."

The parking lot was empty except for a yellow jacked-up Jeep with oversized tires and Miriam's Honda, and no one was in the picnic shelter. I scanned the bushes along the boardwalk and by the bathrooms for shopping carts loaded down like pack mules.

I asked Tammy, "You sure?"

"Go, now," Miriam said. "Go. Ich bin a shtarkeh." She held up a fist like old boot leather stretched over sinew and bone, and said, "I am strong."

I jogged across the parking lot and before I disappeared through the palms, Tammy yelled, "Bring Lonnie!"

I rounded the corner to our street and saw Clyde still sitting in front of our garage. When I got there, sweating and out of breath, he said, "Where's Tammy?"

I pointed back toward the beach. "With...the Cat Lady." Then I bent over to catch my wind.

"The Cat Lady?" Clyde asked. "I don't know much about the Cat Lady."

"Shit. Get me that shopping cart out of the garage." I ran in to the condo and hefted Lonnie up out of his blue plastic crib and grabbed the Publix bag of roman candles off the kitchen counter. Clyde had the shopping cart waiting for me at the end of the sidewalk. I set Lonnie down in the basket and dropped the bag on the safety seat. "You didn't have to stay."

He said, "The hell I didn't."

I turned to wheel off down the street, then I stopped and asked, "You got matches?"

He looked across the street to his house, then back over his shoulder before he said, "They's some in the bag."

It took me a second to add up that column, but when I did, I just said, "Thanks, Clyde."

When I got back to Cherie Down, Miriam was sitting in her old Honda with the door open and Tammy was hanging through the driver's window like a ragdoll. I could see they were talking and the cats were all huddled under the car. I bulldogged the cart through the sand between the palm trees and on to the pavement. Miriam pointed at me and Tammy turned and waved with both arms like I might not be able to spot them in a parking lot with two cars. Tammy met me halfway and hopped on the front of the cart.

She looked down at Lonnie. "Was he still sleeping? Was Clyde there? Was he wet? Where's his blanket, Pere? He can't ride on that old wire."

"He was still napping and Clyde was still there, but I didn't check to see if he was wet 'cause that's Vera's job."

It took her a second but then she hung her head and laughed. When we got to the Honda, Miriam looked too tired to get up. She peered at Lonnie through the small bars and Tammy said, "Here he is."

Miriam smiled as sad a smile as I've ever seen. "Eine kleine pisher. He's hungry."

Tammy leaned in and rubbed Lonnie's belly. "Pere made him."

Miriam stared off into the distance, and in that moment of quiet, one of the cats cried just like a baby.

I showed Miriam the Publix bag. "We're lighting off some fireworks. Want to come and watch?"

She made a face and shook her head. "So much like the shooting." Then she pulled her mouth to one side and made noises like a little boy playing army.

"They're roman candles," Tammy said. "Pere says they're not loud."

Miriam shook her head again and when she turned the key, the Honda started with a sharp whine and the cats bolted from underneath for the safety of the bushes.

"Sounds like you might need a new belt," I yelled. "Or maybe your tensioner needs adjusting."

She waved absently as she backed up and called something we couldn't make out over the engine. We watched her until she turned south on the beach road, but we could still hear that shrieking long after she disappeared.

I wheeled Tammy and Lonnie up to the crossover steps. I asked, "How are we going to do this?"

"You get Lonnie," Tammy said, "and I'll get the bag."

"I figured it might be something like that."

I lifted Lonnie up on to my shoulder, and Tammy said, "That's no way to carry a baby."

"It's a way to carry *this* baby," I said.

She frowned at the cart and then scanned the parking lot and picnic shelter. "Would anybody steal a baby carriage?"

I didn't tell her most people wouldn't know it was a baby carriage. I didn't tell her that most everybody will steal just a little something, even if it's just a stack of McDonald's napkins for the top of the toilet tank when times are tight. And I didn't tell her some people, addicts and alcoholics and just plain trash, will steal anything they can. They'll steal the food from a baby's mouth, the pennies off a dead man's eyes, and the peanuts from a turd. They steal the hours and days of their own lives and don't even know it.

But all I said was, "No."

We found a nice clean spot of sand at the edge of the dunes, and I stood Lonnie up to watch the show. I pointed to the bag and said, "Give 'em to me one at a time."

Tammy handed me a roman candle, and as I peeled the fuse free and straightened it out, she said, "What's an SS?"

"Chevy Super Sports! Muscle cars. From back in the late '60s and early '70s. Big four barrel V-8s that'll snap your head back."

She handed me another one and said, "I don't think so. Like the ones Grandma Sue's dad fought. This one lives at Miriam's retirement home."

I rolled the cardboard tube between my fingers like a small baton and said, "She said a fucking Nazi SS lives at her retirement home?"

Tammy nodded. "She prays for God to kill him every night, and she doesn't know why He hasn't."

"How does she know? How does she know he's SS?"

She touched a spot on the inside of her upper arm. "She saw a tattoo. Right here. When he was swimming in the pool. He'd had it removed but something about the sunlight through the water, she could see it plain as day."

I asked, "And it said SS?"

She shook her head. "No. It said his blood type."

I didn't know why she told Tammy such awfulness, but I know sometimes there's things you can only tell certain people. I don't know why that is.

Tammy looked me in the eyes. "They're bad?"

"They were. Back in World War II. Bad as they come. They killed a whole bunch of people. A bunch of Miriam's people."

Tammy touched Lonnie's head. "Yeah," she whispered. "She told me she had a baby brother."

We watched the gentle surf for a few minutes without really watching it, then I said, "There's some things you never get away from. And it's like all the years don't matter at all."

It wasn't what I was trying to say, but she nodded like she knew what I meant. I was thinking about my dad, and how he didn't seem to hold a grudge against the Vietnamese for what happened. Well, not most of them. He thought they were "elegant," which was not a word that fell easily from my father's mouth, and he liked the food. Or he liked the memory of the food, since you couldn't get pho anywhere in Dingleberry, Virginia. But he hated the VC, in the way that all soldiers hate snipers and sappers, and whenever he mentioned them, which wasn't often, "tough little fuckers" and "bat-shit crazy" always went together.

I picked at the glue that held the fuse down, and Tammy said, "Funny thing is, she's got a tattoo on her arm too. Numbers. Right here." She drew a finger along the inside of her left forearm, just the same way you'd use a razor if you meant to do it right.

33

ROMAN CANDLES

I tried to get her to hold the first roman candle but she wouldn't, so I had to hold it and the matchbook with one hand, and tear off a paper match with the other. For some reason, the matchbook had a drawing of Herbert Hoover and read, "Thirty-first President of the United States 1874-1964." Only Clyde would have Presidents of the United States matchbooks. Vera probably bought them out of a catalogue. When I flipped it over to strike the match, I read the back, and said, "Did you know Herbert Hoover was born in West Branch, Iowa?"

"No," Tammy said. "But I know he was the thirty-first president. And I know the state capital of Iowa is Des Moines."

I struck the match, and as it flared in the breeze I said, "Learn something new every day." I got the fuse lit and held it up at arm's length and she covered her ears. The little balls of sparkle popped up one at a time, and she smiled as they arced over the ocean. After nine little pops, I dropped the tube. "See?" I said. "They're not loud at all."

She shook her head. "No. They're pretty," she said. "They look like Tinker Bell."

I remembered who Tinker Bell was—that little fairy that flies around at the beginning of all of those Disney movies. Hard to believe I could forget that this close to Orlando, not with the giant Mickey Mouse cruise ship docked right up at the port. Missy bought all those movies, on VHS, at garage sales. She was getting them for when Tammy came down, but she liked watching them too, especially when she was crashing. Then one day the VHS player disappeared, probably the down payment on an injection between her toes. Then not long after that the basket full of tapes disappeared, because I guess she figured there wasn't much point in keeping a box full of Disney tapes with no VHS player. Not when she could get a few bucks for them anyway.

"That's right," I said. "You like that little Stinker Bell, don't you? You want to do one?"

I held one out to her but she scrunched one eye shut and shook her head. "You do another."

I said, "We only got four more."

"Maybe the next one."

I lit it and held it up high and Tammy watched the stars shoot away to nothing without covering her ears. When the last ball fired off, I threw the smoking tube down so it stuck into the sand.

Tammy turned to Lonnie and said, "What do you think about *that?*"

"I bet he's thinking, 'Gimme one of those!'" I said.

She looked at me like I couldn't have said anything dumber. "Pere, you can't give a baby fireworks. Not even roman candles. Not even little sparklers."

"No, I guess not," I said. "But you know that's what he's thinking."

Tammy looked back over the dunes toward the condo for a long moment, then she said, "Can Mom see these from where she is?"

Missy is a hundred and forty miles away, but since the whole damn state's only about two feet above sea level, maybe it wasn't such a stretch. I said, "Yeah, maybe. If she knew where to look."

Tammy smiled. "I bet she knows where to look. What's she doing, right now? What do you think she's doing right now?"

I thought about it. Right now she was probably still in the infirmary, trying to scam the nurse out of some pain meds or Xanax to take the edge off, and depending how new the nurse was and how sorry she felt for her that she lost her baby, she probably scored. But I said, "Right now? I bet right now Altagracia's brushing her hair. A hundred strokes. A hundred strokes until her brown hair shines like an antique table buffed with bee's wax." Tammy sat down next to Lonnie and I looked out to the ocean. "I don't know about your mom," I said, "but dollars to donuts there's a dolphin with pink shoes out there watching the show."

She looked out to sea, then rocked Lonnie back in the sand, easing him down across her lap. "What does it mean that her 'water broke'?"

I thought about how to explain it, and I said, "The water, it's around the baby."

"So it's not like breaking waves?"

"No, it's what protects the baby. When it leaks out."

She asked, "The water protects the baby?"

"It's not water exactly," I said. "It's some kind of fluid, that starts with an *A*."

"Amniotic fluid? Is that it?"

I nodded, but it didn't seem to matter if she saw me or not. "Yeah, that's it. Amniotic fluid."

She watched the breaking waves and said, "I bet it tastes salty like the ocean. Or tears."

It probably did, but it hurt too much to answer.

Behind us a voice said, "You can't shoot fireworks off on the beach." He was a young guy with short hair, ripped and waxed and bronzed with one of those muscle T-shirts cut down the sides. He was talking too loud and his pupils were as big and black as a shark's. I wasn't sure what he was on, not that I guess it mattered.

I said, "What are you? A fucking cop?" I took a step toward him and he stepped back into a T-stance. Just because he was tweaked didn't mean he wasn't ready for some fun.

Tammy whispered, "Pere!"

I held an open hand in front of her without out taking my eyes off Tweaky, but she whispered, "Pere!" again.

Tweaky smiled a crazy smile and said, "You don't remember me? Hell, it was just this morning. Right across the street."

And I remembered right when Tammy whispered, "The deputy."

Officer Orange said, "That's right, honey. It's the deputy." Then he looked at me and made a motion in the air like he had a little tomahawk and said, "Chop, chop."

I couldn't think of anything to say except, "What's up?"

"What's up?" he sneered. "*What's up*? I tell you you can't shoot fireworks off on the beach and you step to the line. *That's* what up."

All I could think to say was, "You're out of uniform."

He laughed and clapped his hands. "You got me there. I don't care. Fuck, I like a man that's ready to get to it." Then he looked at Tammy and said, "Pardon my French."

I brushed my palms together and held them up like a blackjack dealer getting off shift, and said, "No problem. We're done anyhow."

And like tweaks and drunks everywhere, his emotions flipped on a dime. "No, I'm sorry. I'm just messing with you. I don't care if you shoot fireworks off on the beach. I wouldn't say anything even if I *was* in uniform. I love fireworks. Matter of fact, I came over to see if you'd sell me a couple. Ten bucks. Ten bucks for two of those candles. And matches. That's a good deal. What'd you say?"

He took out a thin fold of cash and fished out a ten. Ten bucks was ten bucks, especially for ten cents worth of black powder and cardboard we didn't even buy. But I couldn't help thinking it was too good of a deal to make with a tweaky cop that might wake up tomorrow and wonder what the hell happened to that ten. Which wouldn't be a problem until he remembered what happened to that ten when he saw us walking down the street. I was trying to figure a way out of it when Tammy hit my leg and said, "Take it!"

Officer Orange said, "All right!"

I handed over two of our last three roman candles and the book of Herbert Hoover. I figured he would just take them and walk without paying, but he only pretended to snatch the bill back once before he handed it over. He bent over to talk to Tammy and said, "Can you wait right here? Just for a minute? I have to talk to your dad about something over on the crossover.

You'll be able to see us and we'll be able to see you. Okay? It's not but a hundred feet away."

Tammy looked up at me and I nodded.

He said, "Come on!" I followed him to the dune crossover and kept looking back to wave to Tammy. As we got closer, he said, "You're gonna love this!"

He held a finger to his lips, then hopped up on the flat hand-rail like a chimp. He walked along it, scanning the dense bushes, then he stopped and handed me down the matches. He held the two roman candles out to the side and whispered, "Light me up."

After I lit the fuses, he stood up and aimed the candles down into the bushes. When the first one popped, he screamed, "INCOMING! INCOMING! THERE'S GOOKS IN THE WIRE!"

Tampon John jumped up out of the bum nest he'd hollowed out of the sand under the bushes and scrabbled through the underbrush to the beach. Officer Orange drew a bead and tracked him, shooting fireballs off the back of his faded army jacket, screaming, "GET SOME! GET SOME! GET SOME!" Tampon John zigzagged through the sand along the edge of the dunes like a flushed rabbit, the bright white tampons woven into his dreads bouncing against his black cheeks. He cut back into the dunes down the beach as the last fireball flew past his shoulder.

The cop yelled, "Keep running, motherfucker! Keep on keepin' on!" He jumped down into the bushes and waded through to Tampon John's shallow sanctuary. He unzipped his shorts and started pissing on the piles of meager belongings. He pissed on his sleeping bag and an old dirty comforter. He pissed in an open trash bag of clothes, and he shook off on a bag of day-old Sunbeam bread.

He shouted at me, "My old man did two tours in 'Nam and he didn't come back home and go crazy. No, he didn't. He drove a bakery truck for thirty years and did brake jobs on the cars and coached Knothole."

I wanted to tell him so did mine, but that he didn't raise an

orange asshole that'd piss on a starving man's food just for a
laugh.

It seemed like he wanted to say something else, but he didn't.
He waded back through the brush and as he climbed over the
railing, he looked behind me and said, "Hey, sweetie."

Tammy was at the end of the crossover with Lonnie, watching us, and the long trench from where she'd drug him through
the sand looked like one of those big sea turtles had struggled
up from the surf to lay her eggs. She glared at Officer Orange.
She said, "That's mean."

He narrowed his eyes at her, and after a moment he looked
at me and said, "She's yours. You explain it to her."

"You didn't have to...you didn't have to pee on his stuff,"
Tammy said. "He's hardly got nothing."

He barked a laugh. "Hell, you ever *smell* Tampon John? He
won't even notice." Then his face changed, like whatever crazy
light was on behind his eyes went out. He rubbed his face like
he just woke up and said, to no one in particular, "I'm going
for a swim." He peeled off his muscle shirt and threw it in the
sand as he walked by Tammy and Lonnie, headed for the ocean.

I hefted Lonnie up on my shoulder and took Tammy by the
hand, and as we crossed back over the weathered planks, she
tried to look down into Tampon John's nest. When we came
down off the other side, the shopping cart was gone.

I said, "Son of a bitch!"

Tammy squeezed my hand but didn't look up from the
dolphin carved into the concrete between her feet. "It doesn't
matter, Pere. Let's go home."

I looked across to the yellow jacked-up Jeep sitting all alone
in the parking lot and said, "Yeah, just one more thing."

We walked to the far side of the Jeep and I set Lonnie down.
I found the little sheriff's star decal in the corner of the windshield and squatted down on my heels next to the front driver's
tire. I said, "Is he coming?"

Tammy squinted at the crossover. "You're good."

I grabbed the over-sized valve stem and twisted it back and

forth until the rubber tore through and the air rushed out. We watched the tire go flat, and then I picked Lonnie up and said, "Let's go."

Mean never set well on Tammy's face, but she looked as mean as I'd ever seen her. She was still watching the crossover and she hissed, "Do 'em all. And the spare too."

34

BALONEY BAR-B-Q

Lonnie and me fired up the little grill on the driveway. I scavenged it from somebody's trash and Tammy says it's called a hibachi and it's Japanese. I think the only difference is it's a rectangle instead of round. It's really small so you don't have to use a shitload of charcoal and lighter fluid just to grill some slices of pre-packaged baloney and toast a few marshmallows. I started using it before Tammy even came down because the microwave disappeared up Missy's veins, along with all of the other small appliances, and once the air conditioning finally crapped out, I didn't really feel like firing up the range and heating up the whole condo just for a can of Dinty Moore stew. But it tastes a lot less like dog food when it's hot, so that's why I started with the grill. Now we grill as often as not, but the menu doesn't really change that much, usually baloney and surplus cheese on white bread or hotdogs on white bread folded like a bun, baked beans or corn or applesauce on the side, a few cheese curls.

We usually wait until the sun goes down and things start to cool off, but tonight, even though it was pitch dark, there was hardly any breeze and the heat was leeching out of the concrete like an overheated engine. The dark doesn't get in the way of grilling baloney because between the light over our garage and the light over Pearl's garage and the industrial arclight Clyde has over his, it's easy to see. Hell, with the one over Clyde's garage you can see the bones through your hand. And the lights give the bugs something else to go after. I'm not positive, but I think Clyde's might have fallen into his lunchbox over at NASA too, if his lunchbox was the size of, say, a Buick trunk, because what it really looks like is one of those big ones they put up in parking lots but without the pole.

Tammy yelled at me from the front door, "Beans, beanie weenie, corn, or corn and beans?" She was holding the little stamped stainless pot we use on the grill. Missy got it from her mom when she moved down this way, and the knob on the lid is an old porcelain drawer pull I put on there when the wire-nut Grandma Sue was using finally split.

I shook the grill to even out the coals and said, "You know me, I like corn and beans."

She shook her head. "I don't know why I even bother to ask." Before she disappeared back into the house, she pointed and said, "Get him back away from that grill before he burns himself. He doesn't know that's hot."

I rocked Lonnie back a little ways. I like corn and baked beans mixed together. I don't know why, but I always have. It's probably something my mom fixed. Tammy calls it an "acquired" taste, but she's acquired it since she's been here, and while she likes to pretend she doesn't, she likes it as much as me.

Tammy came back out and set the pot down on the little front porch. "Come and get this. I'll be right out with the tray."

By the time I got the pot on the grill and turned the handle backwards out of the way, Tammy came out with the tray. It's big and blue with yellow sunflowers. Missy and I bought them one Monday morning at Beal's. There used to be three of them, all matching, but the medium one split, and I don't know what happened to the small one. She put it down on the seat of the lawn chair and then sat down cross-legged on the concrete next to Lonnie. The tray was snowed over with plates and forks, McDonald's napkins, Sunbeam bread, Publix brand baloney still in the package, thick squares of surplus cheese, yellow mustard in a squirt bottle, a bag of cheese curls and a bag of marshmallows, and the special tool Clyde made us just for toasting them—two feet of thin stainless rod. The last six inches are pressure set in a piece of wooden broom handle that doesn't transfer the heat, and it's in a whole other league from the coat hanger we were using.

I asked, "How do you want your steak?"

She made a face. "I wish you'd stop asking me that. I don't even like steak." Then she sighed and said, "Like always."

"One not-too-dry, mustard smiley face, grilled baloney on white bread coming right up."

I flopped two slices of baloney hissing onto the grill and Tammy said, "Did you wash your hands?"

"Did you wash *your* hands?" I asked.

"As a matter of fact I did, to get that stinky cheese smell off them."

"I think you're supposed to wash them *before* you mess with all the food."

She looked at my hands and said, "Yeah. I'll keep that in mind."

I flipped the baloney over with my fingers, and Tammy got up to fix the plates. She asked, "You want cheese?"

I said, "Sure."

She shook her head. "Not me," she said. "I'm a little pooty myself. I'm grateful to whoever's leaving it, but you can only eat that surplus cheese so many meals before you explode. 'Specially with beans and corn. And if they leave anymore, we can build a tornado shelter. That whole bottom shelf of the fridge is filled."

I said, "Hurricane shelter." I glanced over at Clyde's. "It makes good grilled cheese."

She glanced over at Clyde's too, then she said, "We had tornadoes in Ohio. But you're right. It makes the best grilled cheese."

And just like we'd conjured him up, Clyde came rambling out of his garage and crossed the street to join us.

He waved to me, shouting, "Leonardo! Or is it Michelangelo?" Then he rubbed Lonnie's head and said, "Which one carved the statue of David?"

"Is that the big one with his tallywhacker hanging out?" Tammy asked.

Clyde looked embarrassed. "Yeah, I guess. The Bible David?"

"That's Michelangelo," Tammy said. "It's in Florence. He's thinking about having to fight the giant."

Clyde asked, "Goliath?" Tammy nodded. "How would you come to know that?'

"Doris told me, when we were looking at big art books."

He slapped me on the back and said, "Doesn't matter. You, sir, are an artist. Which I can honestly say I never knew. I knew you were handy with tools and could tear down an outboard like nobody's business, but who knew you could do that with a chainsaw?"

"It just goes to show you," Tammy said, "that you don't know what you can do till you try."

I peeled the baloney off the grill and put it on the bread on Tammy's plate. I shook the mustard and squirted a smiley face on the circle of baloney and left the other piece of bread for her to put together.

"I swear I never saw the like," Clyde said. "I told Vera over supper, 'I never saw the like.' As soon as she gets done sanitizing the kitchen, she might come out and take a closer look. Ever since she bought that steam cleaner off the QVC, she's turned into Howard Hughes in there, slaughtering germs wholesale. I can get my next heart bypass done on my own kitchen table. I'm sure a trip to the Burns Unit at Orlando Regional is in our not-too-distant future 'cause I can't seem to convince her how fast steam'll peel your hide off, even though between the two of us, I'm the only one's seen it kill somebody. Go figure."

I pointed at his old johnboat, bottom up and spotted with the flaking colors of years of hopeful paint jobs. "Hard to believe she lets you keep that scabby thing out in the yard."

"Even Vera knows better than to mess with my fishing," Clyde said.

"Want a baloney sandwich?"

Clyde looked back over his shoulder at their condo and said, "Well, I'm not saying that flounder was bad…"

Tammy stopped chewing. "Hey! I'm eating here."

Clyde smiled at her and said, "There just wasn't much of

him. And what little there was of him wasn't *fried.* It was *poached* in a microwave-safe dish, which is surely an abomination before the Lord. Brown rice and broccoli and not a hushpuppy in sight. No cornbread, no biscuits, no muffins. Hell, I'd settle for one of those sorry dinner rolls that looks like a butt for Christ's sake. Or a slice of bread. But do I even get a slice of bread?"

I looked at Tammy and said, "Move that tray so Clyde can set down." I flopped a couple of more slices hissing onto the grill. "She'll be decontaminating in there for hours, big guy. Get you some slices of bread and we'll even stick a couple slabs of grilled pig lips in between them. You want cheese?"

"Do I want cheese?" Clyde asked. "Didn't I just tell you… *brown* rice and *broccoli?* Hell, yes, I want cheese."

Tammy jumped up and said, "I forgot the Kool-Aid!"

While Tammy was in the house, Pearl came out and joined us. She palmed Lonnie's head for a long moment and said, "Hey, Clyde."

Clyde said, "Hey, Pearl."

"Where's your better half?" Pearl asked.

"She might be out later," Clyde said. "We dirtied up some utensils at dinner so she's returning the condo to hermetic conditions. Like the 'clean' rooms over at NASA, I swear. I'll be wearing a hairnet and little blue booties over my shoes before too long. Where's your ball and chain?"

Pearl frowned up the street. "Probably slotting quarters in some whore's ass over at Sassy Merlot's. Maybe doing the cruiser cam two-step for one of Brevard County's finest. Like I give a shit."

"Thanks for sharpening that chainsaw," I said.

Pearl snorted. "Yeah, I guess. If I hadn't, you'd have done about as well finishing up with a spoon."

Tammy came back out with a jug of red Kool-Aid and a stack of plastic cups we've saved from Icee purchases up at the Circle K. She looked at Clyde eating his sandwich and said, "I don't know what you think we're saving these plates for."

Clyde brushed a few crumbs from his shirt. "I don't need a plate."

"You're fighting a losing battle, honey," Pearl told Tammy. "If you can keep them from pissing in a sink full of dirty dishes, you're doing pretty good."

Tammy smiled at her. "You want a baloney sandwich, Pearl? They're good off the grill."

Pearl shook her head. "Thanks anyway, honey. I just had me a little something."

"We're having marshmallows after a while," Tammy said. "After the baloney cooks off."

Pearl said, "Well, that might be nice." She squatted down next to Lonnie and Tammy squatted right beside her. Pearl said, "I can't believe how much he looks like your drawing."

Tammy said, "Doesn't he though? Just exactly?" Then she smiled a shy smile and said, "You saw my drawing?"

Pearl nodded. "Yeah, it was something else. Pere showed it to me when he come to borrow the chainsaw."

Tammy whispered, "His name's Lonnie."

"I like Lonnie," Pearl whispered back.

"Oh, shit. Vera," Clyde said, stuffing the rest of his sandwich into his mouth.

And sure enough, Vera came out of the darkness of their garage into the noon sun of that parking lot lamp. She and their youngest daughter looked just alike, with the same gap between their front teeth, except Vera is three shades darker. I've only met the daughter once and I never remember her name because Clyde always just calls her "our youngest." She lives up in Jacksonville and does something in medical records.

Vera limped across the street and nodded to each of us in turn. "Pearl. Tammy. Pere." Then she turned to Clyde, still choking down the last of his sandwich and trying not to look like it, and said, "Are you eating again?"

He shook his head, eyes wide and innocent, and Vera said, "You lie worse than the grandbabies."

He grimaced when he finally got his bread choked down and said, "I was just being polite."

Vera pointed at us and said, "No, *they* were just being polite. You're just a hog long at the trough." Then she bent to touch the tiki man. "This must be Lonnie."

Tammy smiled like a June bride. "Yes. Yes, this is Lonnie."

"Pere did an awfully good job, didn't he?" Vera said.

"He did!" Tammy said. "And your husband supervised."

"Oh, he's good at that," Vera said. "You know, the thought just come to me, but maybe if you was to come to church with us on Sunday, we might could stop by Corky Bell's for a Little Mate platter."

Clyde eyeballed me behind her back and sliced his fingertips back and forth across his throat.

Corky Bell's is where we stopped for lunch the day we picked Tammy up from the bus. It was Clyde's treat. They serve hubcap-size platters of fried seafood for a good price and it's snowed over with locals on the weekend. Tammy may not be a fan of flounder, but she'll eat as much fried shrimp with cocktail sauce as you put in front of her, and that did Clyde's heart good.

"Let me check the calendar and talk to Pere," Tammy said.

We didn't have a calendar or anything to put on it, but it was as polite a way as I'd ever heard to put off a straight "yes" or "no."

Vera smiled. "You do that and get back with me by Saturday."

"That Little Mate's platter has scallops and oysters, doesn't it?" Tammy asked. "Maybe just a basket of shrimp."

"Whatever you want," Vera said.

"I can't remember the last time Duane took *me* out for a nice dinner," Pearl said.

A car crept slowly down our street, and when it got close enough, I saw it was Barry's old Corolla, settled down on the passenger side like the springs were shot because Del Ron was in there with him. Barry pulled up onto the edge of the curb.

He leaned forward to see around Del Ron and called, "Baloney BBQ?"

And Tammy yelled, "You bet! The grill's still hot."

"You smell that all the way over at Whispering Pines?" I asked.

Barry said, "If I jumped in the car every time I smelled fried baloney in the Whispering Pines trailer park, I'd never get *out* of the car." He climbed out of the driver's side and came around to open the door for Del Ron. He turned and said, "We're not dating or anything. The inside handle's broke and Del Ron can't get his tiny arms around far enough to reach the outside."

Del Ron unfolded himself out of the car like one of those guys at the circus in a glass box. He nodded to everyone except Pearl and stood behind Barry like a bear trying to hide behind a fireplug. He looked like he was still drunk, or drunk again, because even though his feet were big as cinder blocks and wide apart, he swayed gently like all those Atlanta assholes up at the marina trying to get their land legs back after a day charter fishing.

Clyde said, "Hey, Del Ron."

"I can't remember the last time we saw you at Sunday service," Vera added.

Del Ron hung his head. "No, ma'am. I work awful late on Saturday night. It's our busiest night, and by the time I get done taking out the trash and mopping up baby oil, it's usually near on four a.m."

When he said "taking out the trash," I didn't know if he meant bouncing drunks like Duane or really taking out the trash, not that I guess it mattered.

Vera didn't seem inclined to consider the particulars of Del Ron's line of work, so she said, "Well, keep the Lord in your heart, and we'll be happy when we see you back."

He said, "Yes, ma'am."

Then Vera clapped her hands lightly and looked at Clyde. "It's time for my show. You coming?"

"I'll be along directly," Clyde said. After she'd limped out of earshot, he whispered, "Like I want to watch a bunch of fat people exercising and getting yelled at for an hour. I'm living that."

Barry said, "You wouldn't believe the size of the Seminole

we saw coming up the beach road. He had a little blonde tucked under his arm like a ventriloquist's dummy." He turned his head around to look at Del Ron. "Was he big as a house or what?" Del Ron nodded solemnly and Barry said, "Not as big as Biggun' here." Then he flexed his scrawny arms and said, "But tall as a telephone pole."

Tammy said, "That's Standing Bear!"

"Standing Bear?" Barry said. "I was thinking him and Del Ron ought to wrestle on the TV, and damn if he doesn't already have a wrestler's name. There's money there somewhere."

Tammy said, "That's Standing Bear and Oxana! They're getting married!"

Barry frowned. "Married? No, he should wrestle."

"I bet they're coming up here," Tammy said. "We invited them. And they might invite us to the wedding. I bet they will."

The whole time Barry'd been talking I watched Del Ron and Pearl. He'd look at her, and when she caught him he'd look away. Then she'd look at him and when he caught her, she'd look away. It was like they were pretending they didn't know each other but you could tell they did.

Tammy turned to Pearl and said, "I might be the flower girl. And I'll wear a shiny pink dress and matching shoes and I'll toss rose petals down the aisle for her to walk on. And they're going to have a three-layer cake with a bride and groom on top, and they might let me keep it, and they're going to save the top layer in the freezer for a year because it's good luck. And there's going to be a chocolate fountain with fresh strawberries and cubes of buttery pound-cake."

Pearl smiled down at her. "That'll be nice." But not like she didn't know the truth of it.

Then Clyde stood up to go and said, "Sounds like a fancy affair." He crossed the street and everyone called after him and he waved over his shoulder without looking back before he disappeared into the garage.

Del Ron tried to swallow a burp. "I like Clyde," he said.

"Me too," Tammy said. "He give us a bag of oranges last

night." Then she snapped her fingers and said, "I should go get some. That's just what I'll do. They're really good."

She skipped up the sidewalk and into the house, and then we all turned to watch the Brevard County sheriff's cruiser creeping down our street with the side searchlight checking out between the condos.

Pearl said, "Here comes Duane's taxi."

The cruiser pulled up ahead of Barry's Corolla and angled in against the curb. The passenger window hummed down, and it was Officer Orange, his short hair matted into spikes from the ocean. The deputy driving was in uniform and looked like he was Italian or maybe Spanish, with thick black hair greased back like it was still the '80s. He wore mirrored aviator sunglasses even though it was nighttime.

Officer Orange looked at me and said, "Hey! Buddy. You seen Tampon John? That fucking…" He looked at Del Ron and thought twice about whatever he was going to say. "That fucker tore up my Jeep. Ripped all my valve stems off. Even the spare."

The other cop leaned forward and smiled. "Hey, Del Ron."

Del Ron bobbed his head, and Tammy came out with a blue plastic bowl full of oranges. And for some reason, two thoughts came into my head at exactly the same moment. The first one was that cops don't like to get out of their cars if they don't have to. Not down here in the heat or up North in the cold. I had one tell me, "I don't get out of the car unless I get to shoot something." But that was back when I was a loudmouth drunk, so maybe he was just trying to make a point. The other thought was that oranges aren't that much of a novelty down here in Florida, not after you've lived here a while, but they're still special to Tammy, special enough that she'll eat so many she gets sores on her tongue if she's not careful. Well, oranges aren't much of a novelty unless they're wearing a cop uniform.

Tammy stopped behind me and didn't move, like she was playing freeze tag.

Officer Orange said, "I'm sitting on four flats and our tow driver's out on a run. When I catch him, I'm gonna taze him right in the nutsack. We'll see how those tampons dance around then."

Tammy put her forehead against the small of my back and I heard the hitch in her breath she makes when she's crying. I looked at him and said, "Sounds to me like you got off lucky."

He looked at me with one eye closed and said, "How do you figure?"

"Valve stems are, what, couple bucks a piece?" I said. "Hell, you probably get 'em free down at the city garage, and they'll even mount 'em up for you." Then I spit on the ground between me and the cruiser and said, "If you'd lit *me* up with fireworks and pissed all over *my* stuff, I'd have sliced open your sidewalls." I pointed at him and said, "Then you'd be looking at some real money."

The other cop turned to him and said, "You *pissed* on his stuff?" Then he cuffed Officer Orange in the ear so hard his head bounced off the window frame. "What in the fuck is wrong with you? Seriously, man. That 'roid juice is making you fucking retarded."

Barry looked at Officer Orange and said, "You urinated on a *homeless* guy's stuff? Couldn't you find any puppies to stomp on?"

The other cop barked a laugh, and Officer Orange checked the corner of his bleeding mouth and mumbled something I couldn't make out. The other cop cuffed him again and said, "Yeah, you don't think he's got enough problems without some asshole pissing on his stuff? If we catch him, I'm going to let *him* taze *your* nuts. If we can find any." Then he leaned across the front seat and said, "Sorry to bother you folks. You have a good evening now."

The window went up, and the cruiser ran up over the edge of the curb before it drove off.

"I hope that one pulls over my husband some night," Pearl said. But I didn't know which one she meant.

Del Ron sniffled and wiped his nose on the back of his hand, then he said, "Them two don't know how to play good cop-bad cop."

Nothing breaks up a party faster than cops, and it was just seconds before Pearl went in the house and Barry and Del Ron hit the road.

Tammy still had her face pressed against the small of my back, and when she spoke I could feel the warmth of her breath through the thin fabric of my worn T-shirt. She said, "Nobody stayed for marshmallows."

35

HAPPY FAMILY

We kept the coals stoked for Standing Bear and Oxana because Tammy was sure they were going to show up. I toasted her a "test" marshmallow while we waited.

I asked, "Is there anything better in this world than a toasted marshmallow?"

She blew on it for a few seconds before she said, "No. No, I don't think there is."

After she ate it, she stared down the street toward the beach road for a long time, then she clapped her palms on her knees before she stood up and said, "I guess they got lost. I'm going to get this stuff back in the fridge before it goes off."

I thought you could probably leave that Publix baloney in Clyde's tackle box out in the sun for a few weeks and it wouldn't be any worse for wear, but I just said, "Leave the marshmallows."

She glanced at me like I might be stupid and said, "Well, yeah."

Me, I hadn't really expected to see Standing Bear and Oxana because I figured they'd have something better to do on the night they got engaged than come to a baloney BBQ with a little girl and a wooden baby and a guy who, just this morning, was giving the finger to the bride-to-be. She didn't seem to hold a grudge though, but that might change when the first blush wears off and I'm back to shouting, "Oxana, you're number one!" every time we go to the pier.

I was sitting in the lawn chair, staring off at nothing when I saw a woman, walking, make the turn at the beach road and head up our street. In the dim, dark distance, something about her was familiar and out of place at the same time. She wasn't tall, but she was too tall to be Missy, and she wasn't pregnant, but then I remembered that Missy wasn't pregnant anymore either. She had nice legs but she wasn't shifting her ass back and forth into different zip codes like Oxana does. She was wearing khaki shorts and a white tank top and her hair was down loose. It was Doris. And even after I realized it was Doris, I couldn't really believe it because I'd only ever seen her at the library and it was like I couldn't let myself think about the fact that she might exist outside of that place. She was carrying something but I couldn't make it out.

I hadn't heard the screen door, but Tammy was right behind me when she said, "Doris?"

Tammy padded off down the sidewalk and led Doris back, holding her by the forearm with both hands. Doris had one of those yellow envelopes held closed with two red circles and a figure eight of string. It had a bunch of holes punched out of it and I wasn't sure why, like maybe something in that flat envelope needed to breathe.

I stood up and Tammy smiled and said, "It's Doris."

And I smiled back at them both and nodded. "So it is."

Doris handed the envelope to Tammy and said, "This is for you." Then she touched the top of Lonnie's head and asked, "Can I hold him?"

Tammy worked on unwrapping that little string and said, "Sure. Just support his head."

And I bent to Lonnie. "Let me help," I said. "He's heavier than he looks."

I hefted him up and placed him gently in her arms, feeling the warmth of her skin against mine as I let her take his weight. And that faint smell of honeysuckle, like something lost and forgotten, found its way inside me, passed all of the dark things that should have kept it out.

Tammy pulled out the photo of Missy from the prison website, and said, "It's Mom. With no bars."

It was Mom, without bars.

Doris gently jiggled Lonnie, his face buried in her neck, and said, "A new cartridge...I got one...We got one. One came in. For the printer."

Tammy cocked her head to consider the photocopy of her mother without the rainbow bars going in the wrong direction. "Thank you."

And Doris said, "You're welcome."

I turned to Tammy and said, "You better run that inside, before we get marshmallow goo on it."

Tammy looked at Doris and said, "I'll be right back. Okay?" Then she ran halfway up to the house and stopped to say, "Don't leave. I'll be right out."

Doris smiled and said, "Okay."

After Tammy disappeared into the house, I said, "I can take him now."

"Thanks!" Doris said. "I guess I'm not as strong as I think I am."

I leaned into that honeysuckle and gentle brush of warmth and thought that she was probably stronger than she thought. Most people are. But only when they have to be.

She smiled. "Whew! Lonnie's some dead weight!" That hung in the air between us for a minute before her smile fell away and she hung her head. "I'm sorry. I didn't mean..."

I wanted to take her in my arms, press her to me with my rough hands and never smell anything else inside my head ever again. But I didn't. I just said, "Don't hang your head." I turned my palms up. "I'm sure you got your own hurt."

She looked me dead in the eyes, like it was important that I understand, and said, "No, I don't think I do. I don't think I ever have. And that scares me." She turned to look at the condo just as Tammy came bounding out and said quietly, "What she has to carry around...it's not fair."

Tammy ran up to us. "Safe and sound!" she said. "In the drawer with Mom's papers. It's marshmallow time!"

I can honestly say it never crossed my mind whether it's "fair" or not. I know it's not "right," but I'm not sure that's the same thing. Fair doesn't seem to enter into most of the bad shit in life. Or maybe some people call it "fair" and a different kind of people call it "right." Maybe that's what makes Doris, Doris.

Doris said, "I can't stay."

I asked, "For a marshmallow?"

Tammy took Doris by the arm and led her to the lawn chair. "Sit down," she said. "Right here. Pere'll fix you the best toasted marshmallow you ever tasted. Nobody toasts a marshmallow like Pere."

Doris sat down and said, "Just for a minute. Just for the world's best toasted marshmallow."

Tammy sat down right in front of her and leaned back against Doris's legs. She said, "How did you find us?"

"I'm a librarian. We know everything."

"Really?" Tammy asked.

Doris smiled. "Your library card."

Tammy smacked her forehead and said, "Duh."

I toasted the best marshmallow I've ever toasted, slow and steady and not too close to the coals, blistered and brown but without a speck of burnt. I held Clyde's patented tool over in front of Doris and said, "Be careful. The inside's really hot." She squeezed it lightly with her slender fingers, but then leaned forward to pull it off with so many perfect white teeth.

Something inside me broke. It was broken before, since last night, but I'd been holding all the pieces of it together in place, until just that moment. I looked away, into the glow of the coals, and Doris said, "That is the best toasted marshmallow I have *ever* tasted!"

"Make me one, Pere," Tammy said. Then Doris started stroking her hair and Tammy closed her eyes.

I tried to toast another perfect marshmallow, but I was having a hard time seeing it. I held it up high enough and kept turning and turning it so it didn't burst into flames, and while I wasn't sure that it was as perfect as Doris's, it was perfect as I could make it right then.

When I held it out for Tammy, Doris had to stop stroking her hair to get her to open her eyes. Tammy said, "No, don't stop."

Tammy took the marshmallow and Doris started stroking

her hair again before she said, "Just a minute more. Then I have to go."

Tammy sighed. "No, don't go. It's early."

I said, "It's almost bedtime."

Doris laughed and said, "No, it's late! I left my boyfriend down at the beach watching the dolphins go by, and he'll be wondering what happened to me." She stood up, supporting Tammy's head until the last moment. I stood up too, and Tammy just sat there hugging her knees.

"Well, thanks for the picture," I said. "Thanks for bringing it by. You didn't have to do that."

Doris shrugged and looked at the top of Tammy's head. She said, "No, but I wanted to. Thanks for the marshmallow."

I looked down the dark street and said, "Want us to walk you down?"

Doris shook her head. "No, that's okay. If I know him, he's probably waiting right around the corner anyway."

Then I said, "I would be." But I didn't even mean to. I didn't even mean to say it out loud, but I was thinking it and it just slipped out. I looked up at the thin, fast moving clouds, and when I looked back down, she was watching me.

She whispered, "I know." Then, a little louder, "See you tomorrow, Tammy. Bye, Lonnie."

Tammy flipped her hand up in a little wave but didn't say anything. I watched Doris get smaller and darker and more blurry, until she was just a little shadow ghost disappearing down the beach road. I sat in the lawn chair, the webbing still warm, and Tammy leaned back against my legs with her face buried in the folds of her arms.

I heard the hitch in her breath before she said, "That was too good to be true."

I cradled her head with my hands and said, "She said the dolphins are back. You want to go down and watch the dolphins?"

"*Doris* is down there," she said. "With her *boy*friend. *They're* watching the dolphins."

"We could go further up. By the jetty."

She ignored me and said, "Her *boy*friend? She left her *boy*-friend watching the dolphins?"

I thought about it for a minute. "She's pretty. And smart." And while I didn't want to, I said, "She'd have a boyfriend."

Tammy smacked at my legs a couple of times with one hand while she wiped at her eyes with the other. "I know that. I *know* that," she said. "I'm not an idiot, Pere. I just thought…" Then she buried her face in her arms again.

She never said what it was she thought, but I was pretty sure I knew anyway. I tried to stroke her hair like Doris, but we both knew it wasn't anything like the same.

We sat quiet for a few minutes before I said, "It's time to go up the wooden hill."

36

UP THE WOODEN HILL

Tammy was so tired I followed her up the stairs with my palm in the center of her back to help her along. I call it the wooden hill because that's what my dad called it when I was small, even though ours are covered with cheap carpeting and there's no wood showing. I promised her I'd bring Lonnie up while she was brushing her teeth, and I had to promise to let her swaddle him before I set him down in his blue plastic crib. The room was hot, like it always is, even with the window open and the little desk fan going on the sill trying to suck some heat out. The condo seemed to get hotter as the night got cooler, and even though there's a thin cotton blanket the color of mint chocolate chip ice cream across the foot of the bed, all she ever uses is the sheet. I don't sleep in the bed Missy and I used to share, I usually just fall asleep for a few hours in front of the TV downstairs. I'm not sure why.

By the time I hauled Lonnie upstairs, Tammy was sitting on her bed wearing the oversized sleep-shirt she brought with her from Grandma Sue's in that black plastic trash bag. It's supposed to have a sparkly cartoon unicorn on it but all of the sparkles have come off in the wash and now it looks like a swayback nag with the mange.

I pointed at her sleep-shirt and asked, "Is that Buddy?"

"What?" She pinched at the fabric to look at her sleep-shirt. "No, that's not Buddy. But it's why Grandma Sue bought it, 'cause it looks like him."

She had a clean, folded towel ready, faded to baby blue, and she blew minty fresh breath in my face to prove she'd brushed her teeth. I don't even remember how that got started, but now she does it every night whether I ask or not. I flopped Lonnie on the foot of the bed, and she bounced up at the head of the bed.

"You got to be gentle, Pere. Lift up his butt while I get this under there."

I lifted up his chubby, squatting legs, and Tammy swaddled him in that blue towel.

She said, "Give kisses." That caught me off guard until I realized she was talking to Lonnie. I'd kiss her goodnight if she wanted me to, and sometimes I think she does, but since I'm not her mom, or her no-count, sorry-ass excuse for a dad, it's one of those things that's hard to work around. It's not like I can bring it up, and it's not like she can bring it up, and even if it did come up, it would probably just be awkward for both of us because it's one of those things you shouldn't have to talk about. She kissed Lonnie's rough check and settled back against her pillow, too tired to move. "Put him on his back, Pere," she said, "not his stomach. I read something about that."

I picked him up, careful not to mess up her swaddling job, and eased him down onto the satin sham in that plastic box, then I pushed it up right against her bed, up by her head. She was pulling on the lock of hair on the right side of her forehead that she only pulls on when she's dog tired. I remember when Missy told me about that, that when she's tired she worries her forelock, and has since she was a baby. It was a Monday morning, the only day Missy and I both had off, and we were still lazing in bed long after the sun was up, and she was telling me something that made her smile. That was back before the sentencing, back before the arrest, back when she still smiled without thinking about how her teeth looked.

Tammy asked, "What about Vera?"

"I like Vera," I said. "She puts up with Clyde and makes a mean biscuit when she has a mind to."

She shook her head. "No, I mean about Sunday. And church. Two hours of Jesus jumpers is a mighty high price for one basket of shrimp."

"It's an awful big basket of shrimp," I said. "With french

fries and hushpuppies and free refills on your pop. And it was nice of her to ask."

"That's true," she said. "I could bring half home for you, 'cause Lord knows I can't eat that much."

"I'd eat a piece of shrimp or two."

She widened her eyes like she'd just thought of it and said, "You could come with us!"

"No, I believe that invite was just for you."

"Oh," she said. "Well, maybe you could go up to the marina. See if your old boss has any boats need washing."

I smiled. "That's true. Long as your butt's going to be parked on that church pew, I can wash a whole mess of boats. Retire in style." I thought about those poplar pews back in that little church in Virginia, polished to honey-colored glass by generations of squirming, little raw-boned hillbilly butts, and how the last time I was back there was to see the government-issue headstone next to my mom's.

We sat quiet for a moment before she said, "What about shoes?"

"What *about* shoes?"

"I don't know much about church, but I don't think I can wear Mom's old flip-flops."

I didn't have any idea where that money would come from, but I just said, "Sounds like a trip to Beal's."

She said, "We'll get some I can wear to school."

I nodded. "Good thinking."

She picked at a scab on her knee and said, "Now shoes for a wedding, like Oxana's, *those* are church-going shoes."

"Vera won't mind if they're not church-going shoes," I said. "Just as long as they're clean."

"She's a lot like Grandma Sue that way," Tammy said. "Except Grandma Sue never would have married Clyde, 'cause he's Black and all." Then she stared down into Lonnie's crib and said, "You think she's going to be okay?"

And I knew "she" wasn't Grandma Sue or Vera, or Oxana or Pearl, or Doris or anybody but who it was. I tried to smile and said, "Yeah. She'll be okay."

"Do you think she's asleep?"

"Oh, yeah. It's way past lights-out."

It was quiet for a minute before she said, "I hope she doesn't dream. Not tonight."

I thought about that and it made me mad and sad at the very same time, that Missy had somebody that cared about her enough to even think such a thing, and she didn't even know or care. And even if somebody told her, she'd only care until the next time she scored.

"Who are *you* going to dream about?" I asked. "That Timmy Pilford chained to a rock?"

She smiled a tired smile. "Tommy Pafford."

"That's right. Tommy Pafford. Maybe he won't be chained to a rock, and you'll be the princess and not the cow."

She was blinking real slow, like she does before she falls asleep, and said, "A goddess. Not a princess. A river goddess, much beloved by Jupiter."

"That's right," I said. "A goddess."

"Maybe he won't be chained to that rock," she said. "And he'll have all his fingers. In a dream."

"I suppose he would, in a dream."

She shook her head and said, "No use dreaming about Tommy Pafford. I'll never see him again."

"You never know." But we both knew it was just one of those stupid things people say that doesn't mean anything. The short piece of frayed clothesline I'd cut from Lonnie before he was even Lonnie was on her pressboard nightstand. I asked, "What are you saving that for?"

She looked and said, "It's a length of his cord. For the baby book." She rolled on her stomach and pulled her sleeve to one side. "Can you fix my tattoo? It must be a mess."

It was. Smeared and faded from the ocean and sweat and her shirt rubbing against it, but I said, "It's not too bad."

"Can you do it over?"

"Tonight? How 'bout in the morning after your shower? Before we go see Doris."

She buried her face in the pillow at the mention of Doris. "No, Pere," she said. "I think I need it tonight."

I padded down the stairs to get the pen off the kitchen counter and on my way back up, I shook it down like a thermometer. I used to flick it until I realized that was what Missy did with her syringes before she jacked up, to get the air bubbles out, and all I was trying to do was get the last drop of ink out of a pen going dry. I could hear her crying before I got to the top of the stairs, not loud crying the way some kids do, but a soft sound, like maybe a lamb on the next hill back home, like you had to know what it was to even recognize it.

I sat on the edge of the bed and Tammy whispered, "Do your best job, Pere."

"I will," I said.

She sniffled and said, "He's going to hurt Tampon John, isn't he? Because of what *we* did."

"I don't think Officer Orange's going to do a damn thing, 'cause that other cop'll hand a chicken-shit like him his ass." Those steroids make your balls shrink away to nothing, but I didn't tell her that.

"And we forgot!" she cried.

"Forgot what?"

"We forgot to get a shell," she said. "For the necklace."

"We'll just get two tomorrow."

She shook her head and said, "That's not the same."

"No, it's not." But it'd have to do.

I held her sleeve to the side and started on the angel on her shoulder blade. I traced the fat legs and the edge of butt, the chubby arms and the head of curly hair, the little wings, the arched eyes, and the mouth puckered up like someone was about to get a kiss.

She whispered, "I don't want to go back to that library."

I knew she didn't mean it, so I didn't say anything.

I traced the heart the angel was holding, and before I started in on MISTY written across it, she said, "Wait." And I did. Then she said, "Can you still read it? Can you still read 'Misty'?"

I didn't know what she wanted me to say, so I told her the truth, "It's real faded. Almost to nothing. You'd have to know what it says to make it out."

She clenched her fists to the sides of her head, and said into the pillow, "Wait."

We sat like that for a long while, her face buried in the pillow and the edge of my hand resting on her shoulder. And it was one of those times, like the time I was fishing off Sykes Creek and came on a golden hawk sitting in a scrub pine not ten feet ahead, and I knew if I moved or looked away, he'd fly off, so we stared at each other until something spooked him and he was gone. It was like that, that if I moved, it'd be over.

Then she said, "Write 'Lonnie.' Write 'Lonnie' in the heart."

I almost asked her if she was sure, but I knew she wasn't. I licked the pad of my thumb and rubbed out the faded letters inside that heart as best I could. Then I started writing. I made the fanciest *L* I could, then wrote out the rest in cursive. After so many MISTYs, it was hard to write another name in her heart.

When I finished, I said, "You want to see it? I can get the hand mirror."

But she just shook her head and said, "No. I felt it."

37

DRUNKS & DUANES

Since Tammy was dead asleep upstairs on a tear-stained pillow, I broke my own rule and decided to have my Chesterfield outside, instead of hunkered down in front of Clyde's Buick. Lonnie was supposed to be tucked in his blue plastic crib on the floor beside her, but I'd snuck him out way past his bedtime so I could work on some rough patches with sand paper. He was standing there right in front of me when I eased down into the comfort of my own trash-picked lawn chair, and even though I knew it couldn't be true, I thought I could still feel the faint warmth of Doris caught in those webs of blue and white.

I took off my shirt. The only upside of cutting down to one cigarette a day is that you still get that first cigarette head rush, and that's not all bad. The coals of the little grill were burnt down to almost nothing, but I could still see cracks of glowing orange through the white ash of each one. I folded my sandpaper in four and blew a thick smoke ring out into the still air before I got to it.

"Nice tiki."

I jerked upright and Duane was standing right there, bleary-eyed and sloppy drunk, swinging a shrink-wrapped coil of clothesline like a police baton.

"Where the fuck did you come from?" I asked.

He waved the clothesline baton in a loose circle around his head, like he meant the whole world, then he burped and said, "Around."

I looked up the street. "Where's the truck?"

He looked up the street too, and closed his eyes in concentration. When he opened them, he said, "What truck?"

The only thing worse than being a drunk is talking to one. "Ole Blue."

He waved the baton around again and said, "Who are you, my wife? How the fuck would I know? He's off doing…something. Prob-ab-ably humping a Ford if I's to hazard a guess." He held the clothesline baton in front of his crotch and made a few clumsy thrusts. "Tearing an F-150 a new one, I 'magine."

"Hope you didn't leave it up at Sassy Merlot's again," I said. "Del Ron's towing everything after closing time. Too many assholes thinking it's long-term parking."

He bared his teeth like a yappy little dog and said, "That nigger."

I stopped sanding the crease behind Lonnie's ear and said, "Yeah, I'm real brave too…when he can't hear me."

He strutted back and forth on the sidewalk and said, "I'm not scared of him. God ain't made the nigger that can take me down." He tapped the side of his nose with one finger. "'Cause God didn't make 'em. You know what I mean?" He stared at me and nodded for a minute but then seemed like he forgot why. He said, "Nice tiki."

"His name's Lonnie."

Duane said, "A boy! Congratulations!" He bent over to look down low between Lonnie's legs and caught himself just before he fell. "So he is, so he is. Lonnie's packing a little tackle. The curse of Lonnie. Pearl wants a baby." He pointed at my Chesterfield and said, "I thought you quit? Lemme bum one."

I sighed. "You know, Duane, the only thing worse than being a drunk is talking to one."

He smiled a sly smile and said, "I got a question for you. And I'm serious." He leaned in close and closed one eye. "You hitting that? The little girl?" He held the baton in front of his crotch again and did a little grind. "Bet that's tight as a tick's ass."

I took a last, deep drag on my Chesterfield and flipped the butt out into the street like a tiny firework, then I snatched the clothesline out of his hand without even getting up. He stared at me with his hand still cupped in front of him. "Give it here. I's just joking."

I said, "I got a joke for you."

I sprang up like a copperhead and hit him across the ear with the clothesline. I shadowed him while he stumbled and caught him with a backhand across the mouth before he went down. That tight coil of woven line hardly made a sound, and if it weren't for the shrink-wrap, I don't think I would have heard it myself even though I was holding it.

I leaned in and said, "What's going to hurt more? When I cram this up your ass or when that pretty little wife of yours has to pull it out?"

I helped him up just enough to bounce him off the fiber-glass panels of his garage door, then I hit him across the face with the baton on the rebound. It was like one of those wooden paddle games you get at the fair, and he was the little red ball at the end of the long rubber-band. But after I caught him square off half a dozen volleys, he slumped down against the door bleeding from his nose with bloody teeth. I knew he was just drunk and stupid, like I used to be more often than not, but sometimes that's no excuse. He tried to say something I couldn't make out and I shouted, "What's that, Mr. Funny Guy? I can't make out a word you're saying. There's too much of Del Ron's sperm gurgling in the back of your throat there." I made a gargling sound before I hefted him up to have another go.

That's when I heard Pearl say, "That's enough, Pere."

She had a small-bore .410 shotgun pointed at me, cocked and ready to rock.

I glared at her, breathing hard, and said, "You sure? I could make this shit go away."

She ran her tongue over her teeth. She motioned me to one side with the barrel and said, "He's a useless, ignorant son of a bitch, but he's all I got."

I thought about that. And I guess I knew exactly what she meant.

I looked at Duane. He'd passed out with the blood still

pouring out of his nose, and was snoring softly. I said, "You could do better, you know."

She looked at him like she was trying to remember something, something so far gone she couldn't recall its face, and said, "Yeah? Look who's talking." She rocked her leg lightly with one bare foot and said, "But not tonight."

I pointed the clothesline at him and said, "You want me to help you get him inside?"

She lowered the shotgun and said, "Screw that. He's not bleeding all over *my* white carpeting. He can come in when he wakes up and hoses off."

I wiped the blood off the shrink-wrap onto my shorts before I handed her the clothesline. When she grabbed it, I held on and said, "If I catch him eyeballing my little girl, you better bring something bigger to the party than that pissant .410."

38

CASTLE KEEP

I reswaddled Lonnie as best I could and snuck him back into his crib, but Tammy woke up just enough to ask, "What's all that noise?"

"Just a raccoon," I lied, "rooting around in Pearl's trash."

She wasn't even really awake, but she said, "That's one big 'coon. Big as Del Ron."

I whispered, "Maybe the chupacabra kitten found its way home."

She smiled and rolled on her side. I stayed until she fell back asleep, curled in the soft light bleeding through that seashell. I tiptoed downstairs and washed Duane's blood off my hands before I fixed myself a big Circle K cup of ice with red Kool-Aid. When I closed the freezer door, I saw the Swampy the World's Largest Alligator postcard had drawing on it. There was a stick woman with curly hair hanging from his jaws screaming, *Help me!* and a little arrow pointing to her said *Reba.* And there was a stick man with a hair helmet smiling and dancing on top of Swampy that I guess was Barry and he was singing, "Cracklin' Rose" with little music notes floating around the words.

I stretched out on the couch to catch the late news. It was just eleven but it felt a lot later. We didn't get much sleep last night. Or maybe it was Duane coming home that made it feel like closing time. "You don't have to go home, but you can't stay here. Last call for alcohol!" I remember that, when you got to serious drinking too early in the day, and you either drank yourself sober or passed out way ahead of schedule. I tried to turn on the TV, but the remote wasn't working. I've kept the two dying AA batteries on life support for the last two months by rolling them and switching them and cleaning the ends with a pencil eraser. The little black plastic lid that covers them has been lost for as long as I can remember, and half the time it doesn't work because one's fallen out and Tammy's put it back wrong way around. But even after I checked that the pluses and minuses were where they were supposed to be and I rolled them and slapped it, it still didn't work. There was another AA in a little flashlight in the junk drawer, but I didn't have the energy to get up and mess around trying to find a combination that might work. I sipped cold Kool-Aid and wiped the cup on my forehead against the heat and the TV suddenly came on.

There was a story on the news about a guy that bought a foreclosed house just a couple of blocks north. It'd been inspected and inventoried and locked up, and after it worked its way through the mountain of foreclosed properties in this part of Florida, a mountain so high it took some seventeen months, this guy just bought it at the sheriff's auction. He got the keys and started cleaning the place out today, going back and forth past the old Dodge K car left in the garage. And it's not till he's gone by it half a dozen times, that he looks in and sees something sticking up that's not quite right. It took him a minute because not too many people would know, in advance, what the mummified leg of an old woman laying across the front seat might look like. You could see the guy was rattled because he was just trying to buy a house on the cheap to flip and this was a hell of a lot more than he'd bargained for. The neighbors were in the background talking to each other and on their cell phones, and the reporter interviewed one of them that said she never came out of the house except to put cinder blocks across the end of her driveway so no one could pull in to turn around. Then another one said she'd sweep up the trash from her sidewalk and throw it over the fence into her neighbor's yard, and another said she let a crazy homeless guy live under her deck, but they were all surprised they hadn't smelled anything. Then the reporter interviewed a deputy that wasn't Officer Orange or the slicked-back one in shades that smacked his head around. This one was nervous about being on TV, but he said that even though it was too early to say for sure, they didn't suspect foul play, and he talked about how hot these little garages get in the summer. But he couldn't say why nobody hadn't noticed her there for seventeen months, when they'd been in and out, inventorying and changing the locks. She had family up north somewhere. I guess they'd been just as happy as not that they hadn't heard from her in so long. The reporter was making it into a joke, which I thought was kind of sorry, because that old woman, even if she was mean and crazy like everybody said, must've meant something to somebody, even if it was a long time ago.

I'd have to try and keep Tammy away from the TV for a few days, because if she knew they'd found a mummy woman a couple of streets away, she might not ever sleep again. And right when I was thinking that, in the middle of a commercial for one of those cash advance places, the one with the cartoon stack of dancing money and the crazy happy Black lady, the TV shut off by itself and I don't know why.

I don't remember exactly when I started sleeping on the couch, or when I started sleeping on the couch with a hickory axe handle in arm's reach. It was when Missy was still here, I know that. Sometimes she wasn't here. Or she'd be on something and thrashing around the bed, calling out and sweat through, or not sleeping at all and scratching her arms. Or other times, if she was on something else, she'd snore like she was in a coma, like my dad did right before he died, and no shifting her around did a bit of good. Dealers and her druggie friends would show up all hours, wanting to sell something or buy something, or beg to see if she might be holding. I ran most of them off, even the ones that showed me pistols tucked in their waistbands like they were tough. You can get a hickory handle around mighty quick without that axe head on there weighing it down. It's shaved and shaped narrow along the front edge like a wing to cut the air and it swings faster than a baseball bat. Strangers that looked dead already would show up at three in the morning to bum cigarettes, mumbling

Missy's name like they were stopping you in an aisle at Publix to ask the time.

And, truth be told, there were times I didn't know who that axe handle was for, like when she came home crazy, looking dead like the others. Or when she finally crashed on the wrong end of a days' long meth run and woke up needing it more than ever, more than blood or breath. Woke up like a fox in a leg-hold trap. I used to think that old expression 'dope fiend' was kind of funny, but I learned the hard way, depending on the dope, that fiend's as funny as death.

Sometimes it was the deputies, looking for Missy or one of her 'known associates' that I didn't even know, and if I saw the shadow of a Smokey the Bear hat on the blinds of the patio door, I'd set that axe handle out of sight in the narrow slot between the refrigerator and the wall. But that last time, they took her away handcuffed in the back of the cruiser, Vera watching it all peeking out from her storm shutter barely cracked open.

I don't know that I'll ever get back to feeling the way I did before, before every phone call was another tragedy and every knock on the door was three steps to a new Hell.

39

FEVERED DREAMS

I don't know when I fell asleep, because one minute I was awake, and the next I was in a dream. I dreamt I was up at Lowell Correctional, looking into Missy's cell and even though I was standing where I should have seen bars, there weren't any bars. Gracita was on the bottom bunk, and Missy was sitting on the floor leaning back against her legs. Gracita was brushing her hair, and Missy was saying, "Oh, Mamita, Mamita. He didn't cuss, or cry, or nothing. And he never even put her on the phone."

And Gracita, like she was singing a lullaby, said, "Ya mi amor, No llores más, Ya mi vida ya."

I don't speak Spanish, but because it was a dream, I knew exactly what she was saying, right as she said it, word for word, "Stop, my love, Don't cry anymore, Hush, my life, hush."

And Missy said, "What did I *do*?"

And even though I could understand Spanish, I couldn't understand what she meant.

"Ya mi vida ya, No llores más," Gracita sang.

Then I saw Missy was sitting in a big puddle of blood, and the smell was so strong I could taste the iron of it in the back of my throat. Missy's prison blues were sticky wet and Gracita's feet were in it, but they didn't even notice.

And in the way of dreams, suddenly it was just the two of us out in the moonlight, out in the moonlight in front of our house. I was on my knees and she was standing before me, naked and looking down at me, cradling her swollen belly. I moved my hands, slowly and more gently than they've ever moved, and they weren't dirty, calloused, cracked or scarred. I placed those hands on her, on that warm, stretched skin. I felt

Lonnie move inside of her and she smiled down at me. And in that moment, everything bad drained out of me in a flood, and all that was left was a transcendent and transforming relief. I knew that's what it was in the same way I understood Spanish, because you know things in dreams, you know things in dreams you never know with your eyes open.

Then I heard Tammy's voice, "Mom? Mom! Where are you?"

Missy's belly started getting smaller, like a leaking balloon, like a tire going flat, slowly shrinking away from my hands. I couldn't move at all. And I knew if I could only keep touching her, it wouldn't happen, but I couldn't reach out even that little bit. She dropped her head down and faded away to nothing, the light going out of her until she just disappeared, and I was left there alone. I was alone with my hands out, like I was holding back some small world.

When I woke up, I was outside on the driveway, and the sand and sawdust were biting into my knees. I must have sleepwalked. Tammy was standing right where Missy had been, shaking my shoulders. She was wild-eyed and glazed with sweat and she said, "We have to put him in the water now." I stared at her, not sure whether I was awake or asleep, whether she was real or another dream. She said, "We have to put Lonnie in the water now."

I blinked and said, "Tammy? Tammy, you must be dreaming, honey. I was dreaming too."

"They're waiting," she said. "They're waiting in the shimmering on the golden sea."

"What?"

"They're waiting. In the shimmering on the golden sea."

I said, "It's late."

She took my face in her small hands and looked deep into my eyes. "Then we have to hurry!"

40

TO THE SEA

Tammy said, "Go get Lonnie. I'll get the boat."

She ran across the street in her sweat-soaked sleep-shirt into Clyde's small yard and started tugging on his old johnboat. I finally woke up enough to stand up and follow her.

I touched her shoulder and said, "Wait." But she shrugged off my hand and kept struggling to lift the boat.

The upstairs storm shutter rattled up a few inches and Clyde yelled, "Who's that? You better leave that goddamn boat alone 'fore I shoot your ass."

I whispered, "Clyde!"

"Sonofabitch," he shouted. "Think I'm playing? I'll shoot your ass twice."

Louder, I said, "Clyde! It's me, Pere. We need to borrow your boat for a little while."

I heard him talking to Vera and then he called, "Hold on."

I watched Tammy struggle against the little aluminum boat. She might as well have been trying to pick up a car. The arclight over the garage flipped on, bathing us in noonday sun. The patio door slid open and Clyde came out in boxers and shower sandals like you get in jail.

"*Now?*" he asked. "You need to borrow my boat *now?* It's close on midnight, Pere."

I said, "It's kind of an emergency." I nodded at Tammy, then I watched him watching her struggle.

She was still wild-eyed and said, "I don't know how long they're going to wait," but not like she was talking to Clyde or me. "We have to put Lonnie in the water now."

Clyde shrugged his big shoulders. "I lent the trailer to my boy down in Pahokee. To clear some cane."

I asked, "Can't I just drag it down to the beach?"

He looked at me with wide eyes. "The *beach*? You can't be thinking about going out on the ocean?"

Without looking at us or slowing her struggle, Tammy said, "Of course, the ocean. The sea. The golden sea."

"It's dead calm," I said. "And we don't have to go far out, I don't suppose."

He frowned. "You got to get out past the sandbar without getting swamped. If I had the trailer, I'd take you over to the river. Then it wouldn't matter. Just a couple of feet deep. No waves."

Tammy shook her head. "They're not in the river. Not now."

Clyde watched her struggle for a moment longer before he said, "Won't wait till the sun's up?" But even as I was shaking my head, I could tell he already knew the answer. He clapped his hands lightly and said, "Let's get her flipped over." It couldn't have been ten feet long, and either one of us could have flipped it by ourselves, but with Tammy fussing around and Clyde not wanting to wake up the whole street, we eased it over like a sheet of glass.

Tammy ran her hand down into the notch in the transom and asked, "What's this for?"

Clyde said, "That's where the little outboard goes."

"The one Pere's helping you fix?"

"Yeah," Clyde said.

And I said, "If the parts ever come in."

"We don't need it, Pere," she said. "Go get Lonnie. Try not to wake him."

Clyde looked at me and said, "Yeah, you go get Lonnie while I find the oars and a *life jacket*."

I ran back across the street and up the carpeted stairs. Lonnie was still in his crib, staring at the ceiling in the dim light of that glowing shell. My crappy swaddling job was loose around him like he'd been tossing in his sleep. I lifted him gently as I could and held him close as we padded back down the stairs. And I knew it couldn't be true, but his face felt warm against my neck.

When we came outside, Clyde's garage door was open and the light was on over the Buick. Clyde had managed to get on a pair of khaki shorts and a wife-beater. Vera was in a floral bath robe and she was lashing Tammy into an orange life jacket so tightly that she could barely turn her head to watch us cross the street.

Clyde motioned to the boat with his head. "The oars are in it. They ain't no-count. Plastic crap, just for emergencies. In case the outboard poops out." Then he laughed. "But it already did, so you don't have to worry about that."

Tammy looked at Lonnie and said, "Why's he so fussy?"

I held him out far enough to look into the shell eyes of the face I made and said, "I don't know."

She motioned with her fingers, her arms poking out from that life jacket like toothpicks stuck in a block of surplus cheddar, and said, "I'll carry him. We have to hurry."

Clyde said, "Why don't we let him ride in the boat? I bet he'd like that."

I said, "It'll be faster."

She looked into the boat and said, "Put him right there, in the center." I stepped in and set him down as gently as I could. When I stepped back out, Tammy bent to stroke his belly and said, "Shhh."

Clyde looked at me and pointed to the transom. "You can have the heavy end."

Tammy shook a finger at us. "You two guys don't get crazy or I'll snatch him right out of there. He's just a baby."

Clyde took a hold of the rolled aluminum along the bow and said, "On three."

But before he could start counting, Vera said, "Clyde." She was standing just inside the garage, at the back of the Buick, holding a flashlight. She walked over and said, "You take this."

He took the flashlight with his free hand and kissed her lightly on the cheek. "What would I do without you?"

Vera watched Tammy worrying over Lonnie. Then she turned Tammy around and fussed some more over her life jacket, tucking her sleep shirt down inside and double-checking the ties.

Vera looked at me and said, "You be careful, now. She's… she's just…" But her words trailed away to nothing as she pulled her robe tight against herself.

Clyde said, "On three. One, two…three."

We started off down the street, the boat sideways between us and Tammy walking along behind, cooing comfort down to Lonnie.

Clyde laughed. "She's making *some* leeway!"

Tammy was lost in her own world and didn't even hear him. Not that she would have known what he meant anyway. I tried to laugh, just to play along, but the sound didn't even make it out.

He asked, "How far did you think you were going to get without oars?"

"Hadn't thought that far, I guess."

Tammy said, "Hush, now. Don't cry. Shhh." But she wasn't talking to us.

Clyde and I stopped talking to save our breath, and the only sound was the soft nonsense Tammy whispered down to Lonnie. When we got to the beach road, we swung the boat around so we could trade arms. If there'd been any cars, I don't know exactly what they would have made of us.

We took a break at the two palms into Cherie Down Park. In the deep shadow of Fleur de Mer, we could hear music close by, soft and beautiful. Up on the balcony of the second floor corner unit, not twenty feet away, Lloyd and that pinched old bitch from the library were slow dancing in their nightclothes, his hair white and wild, her voice clear with pain and regret, singing along to an old song about sending in clowns. We listened as her words came and went as they danced in slow circles. She sang about bad timing and her lost love, and on the next slow turn, he'd "drifted away." When the song was over, they separated, still holding hands, and framed in the light from their condo, you could see her breasts were gone, gone like they'd never been, like she might be Tammy, or a boy. They bowed to each other like it was another time, like they were all dressed up and out on the town, and then they turned and went inside. Tammy was rubbing Lonnie's tummy, and Clyde shook his big head like he had water in his ears, or like maybe he wasn't sure what he'd just seen really happened.

As we crossed through the parking lot, I saw Officer Orange's yellow Jeep glowing green under the one working florescent parking lot light. It was still sitting on four flats, and as we passed close by, the strong smell of piss fogged the air. Tampon John must've got him some payback.

Clyde scrunched his eyes closed like a dog and said, "Whew! Some poor sonofabitch got on the wrong side of somebody. Got his big fancy Jeep tore up and pissed on too. Well, you know what they say, better to be pissed off…"

He waited for me to finish it for him, so I did, "Than pissed on."

"He had it coming," Tammy said. And she'd been quiet for so long, Clyde jerked his head around like he'd forgot she was there.

We stopped in the dark at the crossover stairs to get turned around. Clyde went first, walking backwards while I lifted the stern up almost high enough to clear the hand rails. That little boat made a big noise dragging along the weathered wood, and the cats started yowling up under the far end of the boardwalk.

Tammy said, "Shhh. Shhh, it's okay." But I couldn't tell if she was talking to Lonnie or Flopsy, Mopsy, and Cottontail.

Tammy followed me up the steps with her fingers hooked through a belt loop in the back of my fatigues, and when we stopped for a breather, a voice close by in the bushes hissed, "C'mon down, motherfucker. I'll gut you like a fish."

I kept Tammy behind me and backed against the far rail. Clyde reached over into the boat for an oar.

Tammy said, "It's okay, John. It's me, Tammy. Pere and Clyde are helping me."

The voice said, "Hey, Tammy."

A shadow stood up in the bushes, even closer than he sounded, and all you could make out in the blackness were the tampons woven into his dreads, glowing blue in the starlight like jellyfish. If he'd have made a move on us instead of saying something, a couple of us would be hamstrung and bleeding out.

Tampon John asked, "You need help?"

And before me or Clyde could think of a thing to say, Tammy said, "You bet!"

He climbed up over the rail, saying, "I thought you was somebody else."

Up close he smelled of rank sweat, but something else too. He smelled like rotting teeth. That's not a smell I'd have ever thought would make my heart ache, but it did.

He pushed me gently to the side and said, "I got this end. Watch the girl." Then he turned to Clyde, "Ready when you are, brother."

I held Tammy's padded shoulder, and we followed behind them along the crossover.

Tammy looked down and asked, "How can it be? How can it be that this wood is rough and smooth at the very same time?"

It was just wood, weathered by wind and sand, sun and rain, worn by thousands of folks going for a day at the beach, families with kids, teenagers and newlyweds, fishermen and homeless guys. But I didn't think that's what she was asking, so we just followed Clyde and John down to the water's edge.

When they set the boat down in the damp sand, Tammy climbed in and said, "Where's that flashlight?" After a moment, Clyde turned it on and shone it down into the boat. Tammy was caught in a ring of light, kneeling beside Lonnie and stroking his head. She looked up at Tampon John and said, "His name's Lonnie."

"Lonnie. Lonnie's a good name," John said.

She looked back down at Lonnie and said, "We have to put him in the water now."

John said, "I know."

"They're waiting," Tammy said.

And John nodded. "I know. I saw them."

Clyde shifted the beam of light up to John, who held up a dirty pink palm to shield his face.

Tammy said, "Turn off the light so I can see."

Clyde asked, "What?" but he switched it off anyway.

We all stood there in the dark and the slap of small waves counted away the moments.

Tammy said, "There it is. I see it."

I stared into the darkness. "See what?"

And like I should have known, she said, "The gambling boat. Don't you see it?"

I scanned the horizon, where the black water met the night stars, and saw the distant glitter of those draped curtains of yellow lights, and their shining twins mirrored in the sea.

I said, "I see it."

"Pere, you can't," Clyde said. "You just can't."

I said, "I got this, Clyde."

"Don't worry, Clyde," Tammy said. "It'll be okay."

As John helped me push the boat out into the shallow water, he chanted, "To the sea. To the sea."

He held the boat bow into the small waves so I could climb in over the back. I found my balance on the center bench and fit the oars into their locks. I was facing backwards, looking over the transom at John.

Clyde yelled, "That ain't really a boat for the ocean, but it's glass calm right now. Any waves kick up, any at all, turn tail and get back quick. Watch my flashlight." He flicked the flashlight off and on every few seconds. "I'll keep doing that so you can follow it back in. Keep an eye on the gambling ship 'cause it comes back by one o'clock in the a.m."

I yelled, "Thanks, Clyde."

John's dark shadow bowed its glowing halo of tampons almost to the water before he said, "It's time."

Then he gave us a big push out to sea and I pulled at the oars through the low waves.

Clyde flicked his flashlight on and off and yelled, "Don't let her get that life jacket off!"

Tammy said, "It's okay, Clyde." But not loud enough for anyone but me to hear.

"Tammy?" Clyde yelled. "Can you see me? You watch this light now. Tammy?"

The winking of Clyde's flashlight got smaller and smaller, and he and John were lost against the low shadow that was the land. We heard him call, "Tammy," a couple more times but only when it was carried across the water to us by the shifting breeze.

41

THE TASTE OF SALT

I pulled easy, facing backwards, catching Clyde's flashlight winking in the distance at the top of each gentle swell. Tammy was a shadow at my feet, rubbing Lonnie's swollen belly and humming softly. I turned to line up on the gambling ship.

"Follow the gambling boat," Tammy said. "We have to get closer."

It was heading in, but still a good ways out and moving slow. And in one of those tricks of light, like chasing the fading pink sun down the damp sand along the surf, the golden reflections seemed everywhere but we could never catch them. When the breeze shifted again, we could hear laughter and the murmur of voices across the water. I rested at my oars and tried to stretch out my back.

"Is this it, Pere?" Tammy asked. "Is this where you were?"

I looked around, pretending that I might actually know if this was the spot of ocean Missy and I were looking at, pretending that I was sober enough that first night to even remember which side of the boat we were on.

"Yeah," I said, "this has to be close."

Tammy raised up on her knees and tried to see into my dark face. "It can't be close. You know that, right?"

I knew that. And I knew the impossibility of it didn't make it any less important. I looked over my shoulder again, then pulled twice with my left oar to cut the line to the gambling ship shrouded in its caul of golden lights. Missy said that last night, on the phone, that he was shrouded in a caul. When he came out. She said it meant something, that caul. It meant he would have been special.

Tammy rubbed his belly again and said, "It's okay. It's almost time." She knelt down and sniffed the top of his head, then she looked up and said, "That's the best smell in the world. The top of a baby's head."

I ripped the oars through the water, faster and faster, until sweat ran down my back.

Tammy skimmed her fingertips along the streaming sea and whispered, "Yes. Yes!"

"Keep me straight," I panted. "Tell me if we're going crooked."

The lights of the gambling ship caught in her wide eyes, and she said, "You're good, Pere. You're good at going backwards. Don't forget that."

I pulled for as long and as hard as I could, until I was spent, spent and dripping wet, then I slumped forward, the oars dragging in the water.

"Is this it?" she asked.

I looked around, and lied, "Yes. This is it."

She stroked Lonnie and said quietly, "Here we are." She whispered something in his rough ear, and he looked at me with his white eyes. She touched my shoulder and said, "You have to put him in the water now. They're waiting. Gentle as ever you can."

I knew how heavy he was. I knew what he was made of, but I lifted him up like nothing, lifted him up like an empty burden and held him close. When I turned away, his seashell eyes peered over my shoulder at Tammy. Then I got off balance trying to ease him over the side, and I fell in the bath-warm water still holding him. Tammy shrieked as she rocked away from us in the boat. Lonnie lolled at the surface, and long fingers of fast-moving clouds blacked out the stars like a hand on the night.

I cradled his head and rested my cheek against his. I whispered in his ear and told him not to be afraid, not to forget where he came from, not to forget he was special. When I gave him a little push and let go, he rolled face down. My arms were wasted from rowing, and I could only tread water for a minute, watching the current pull him away.

I swam back and hung onto the low transom, resting my chin in the notch for the outboard, the old Evinrude that's clamped to a sawhorse in Clyde's garage, gutted and bleeding out gear oil on the concrete floor.

She searched the water and said, "Are they here?"

I nodded. "He sees them. They're under the water."

She asked, "Do they have my shoes?"

I thought about that, about those pink Ohio shoes lost to a rogue wave, and nodded again. "Get up in the bow so I can climb back in."

I sat on the back bench and Tammy sat up front, and the strings and strings of yellow lights on the gambling ship glittered on the surface.

I looked at those lights and told her, "He was shrouded in a caul. When he came out. Your mom said that last night, when she called." I tried to see into her shadowed face. "She said it meant something."

"It does," Tammy whispered. "It means he would have been special."

Lonnie rolled face up, his open, infant mouth hungry for his mother.

And then a phone rang, rang so loud we both jumped.

Tammy tried to reach inside her life jacket, and I said, "I thought that didn't work."

She struggled to untie the ties and grunted, "It doesn't."

But it kept ringing, and she tore at those strips of black nylon holding her in. She finally wrestled it off over her head and flung it in the bottom of the boat between us. She watched it through clumps of hair, dark and wet with sweat, and every time it rang, the life jacket glowed orange as a broken egg. The phone was in a little net pocket and she knelt down to get it out.

She opened it and said, "Mom?...Mom? Is that you?" And after a moment, she slumped down and said, "Oh, hi, Vera... Yeah, we're okay." She turned and looked over the water. "Yeah, I can still see him...Uh, huh...We're coming home now... Okay... Bye." She closed the phone and held it between her palms. She said, "It's Clyde's phone." Then she slipped it back into the net pocket. "That was Vera."

I scanned where I knew the beach should be and said, "You can still see Clyde? I can't see anything."

"Me neither," she said.

I thought she was going to say more, but she didn't. I said, "We should get you back in that life jacket. It's not safe."

She shook her head. "No. If anything happens, you'll save me, Pere. I know that."

We sat quiet, and listened to the hollow notes of small waves play on the aluminum hull.

"I just wanted a little brother," she whispered. "Someone to hold."

I said, "We could try again. When your mom comes home." And I don't why.

I can't remember if the tide is making, and I don't know what truth lies between Ocala and this shifting, shallow hole in the ocean that we can't climb out of.

After a moment, she says, "No. No, I don't think you probably should."

She climbs crying into my lap and holds on tight to my neck with her skinny arms, the ribs of her back under my fingers like so many black keys on a toy piano.

Between sobs, she says, "I never got to see her belly."

She pushes her face into my cheek, and her hot tears mix with the sweat and sea water in my stubble, and I wonder if this is the first taste of life, if this was on his tongue waiting for breath that never came.

I say, "I'm sorry."

Turning slowly in the breeze, we rock each other to the lost lullaby playing along the hull.

Tiki Man drifts away from us, just a small darkness. A small darkness in the shimmering on the golden sea.

ACKNOWLEDGEMENTS

I'd like to thank my wife, Tracey (like my father and grand-father before me, I am punching well above my weight in the spouse department). *Tiki Man* could not have happened without her. Period. She was first to read Pere and Tammy's story, first to hear rejections read out loud as performance art, and the alpha and the omega of support. Our boys, Miller and Walker, are men out in the world now, but I would have never understood the awesome and terrible responsibility of Tammy without them.

My late parents, Cliff and Sue, would have been, as they always were, proud and not just a little baffled as to how a machinist from England and a bank clerk from a coal town in West Virginia spawned a writer.

I am lucky to have a friend and mentor in Catherine Ryan Hyde, who is patience personified. She liked a line in my Blue Highway short story about a Neil Diamond impersonator "absently attending to a stray nose hair." Such humble beginnings portended great things. Chris Nickson, a UK writer of fine historical mysteries, has been a friend and sounding board for, I think, forever. They are both so ungodly prolific as to be another species of writer altogether. I will never catch up, and I have made my peace with that.

Dallas Wiebe and Terry Stokes, both incredible writers, both gone, were my fiction and poetry professors at the University of Cincinnati. They recognized something in me that I'd yet to recognize in myself, and encouraged fearlessness in both my writing and alcohol consumption.

The Ohio Arts Council has been generous in their support over the years (five Ohio Arts Council Individual Excellence Awards in fiction and playwriting). They sent me off to the Fine Arts Work Center in Provincetown, Massachusetts in 2013 as Ohio's OAC/FAWC Collaborative Writer-in-Residence. I tried, with some small success, to not shame the great Buckeye State.

And last but not least, a nod to my eighth grade English teacher at Walter Peoples Junior High in Cincinnati, Ohio. She was a dark-visaged ex-nun, and she sealed the deal when she held up my story assignment and told the entire class that I was the best writer…but only on the day I was home sick (did I mention she was an ex-nun?). This only goes to prove that writers, like some rare species of desiccated toad buried deep in the Australian outback, can survive for years and even decades on precious little nourishment.